The Stoker File:

The Lost Diary of Bram Stoker

Tony Noto

With additional material by Bram Stoker

PublishAmerica
Baltimore

First printing

Softcover 1-4241-6652-7
Hardcover 978-1-4489-7724-6
PAperback 978-1-4512-5046-6
PUBLISHED BY PUBLISHAMERICA, LLLP
www.publishamerica.com
Baltimore

Printed in the United States of America

To Bram Stoker whose imagination made it all possible. To my wife Elaine and my two daughters Chloe and Charlotte. Thanks to John Littel, Bruce Hall, Tony Siedl, Neal Laurence, David Salidor, and Vasi Laurence.

Prologue

Journal: L.O. Wynne

If you are reading this now, your life is in great danger.

Walk away while you still can, make the choice that I failed to make. Do not venture any further. If you do so now there still might be hope for you. Time has all but run out for me.

The object of my fear is out there, living, breathing and tormenting me. I can feel it watching me. It stalks me in my daylight dreams and deep into my evening nightmares. I find no rest.

I will find no peace again in this life.

I am the only one left to bear witness to these terrible events. A solitary witness to horrors so unbelievable that even now, as I beseech you to walk away, you will not heed this warning. Trust what I have to say before it is too late.

You must make your own choices. I've already made mine.

What I am experiencing now is what Freud called the "uncanny," the concept in which the imagination accepts horror as a common reality, secure in the knowledge that the horror is not real. It's only when the horror becomes real and is part of that common reality that it turns to real terror and you are trapped within the uncanny and are firmly in its grasp.

I am at that point now. This story is real to me.

Any echo in the wind, any shadow in the darkness, or even the creaking of a solitary sound will fill me with such dread that I begin each new thought with the end as the beginning in mind.

This terror I feel has already manifested itself into real events. Death has stalked those close to me and claimed its victims. Death in its most evil form! Those poor incorruptibility beings were unaware of why they died so horribly. Totally oblivious to the message being sent, they never knew the reason why?

Unfortunately I did.

My fear has already encased me in an aura of desperation. Those worldly things so important to me have manifested into weapons meant to destroy me. In these last few hours all living things seem determined to do me harm. How is it that I can awake from a fitful sleep and find my tiny cat at my throat? Violently tearing at me in a vicious fury? It's once kind eyes wild with anger, her tiny claws now large, sharp and menacing. With this leviathan ripping furiously at my throat, I frantically tried to get my bearings. Finding a strength that only abject fear can facilitate, I was able push this monster away. Rising from my bed, I pounded this viscous animal with my night lamp. Fear pouring through me, I crushed this monster with an unspeakably ugly design.

Only in its aftermath did this creature dissolve into the fragile pet I once loved so much. This lovable little feline was now smashed and broken before me. I had killed the only living thing that had ever given me its unconditional love.

Once again I am alone

The battle has been joined. The battlefield will be unlike any man has faced before. The evil that only a chosen few can understand has somehow survived its supposed eradication. Unlike past battles this evil has taken root and has grown stronger. It rises from the depths of obscurity determined to keep its secrets.

The war has begun.

I look back at all that has happened only a few months ago and I laugh at the excitement we all felt when it began, never thinking that the end was already at hand.

It started off so innocently.

It began with a flood and a wire service story.

Part I

The Discovery

Chapter 1

Reuters News Service

Budapest, Hungary (August 15)

A mysterious diary bearing the signature of Bram Stoker and a box that included additional papers belonging to fabled nineteenth century professor Arminius Vambery was uncovered in a flooded basement of the University of Budapest yesterday. The discovery was made while a cleanup effort was underway after the record flooding that has hit this country over the weekend.

In the Borsod-Abauj-Zemplen area, several settlements were inundated as rains caused local streams in the Cserhat region to burst their banks. Emergency teams worked to channel water away from flooded areas and pumped water out of homes and historic buildings.

In Budapest, the Danube peaked at 610 cm with local authorities closing off several sections of the riverside expressway on the northern Buda side of the city. The prevention work also was applied to protect the scenic town of Szentendre, north of Budapest, which is popular with tourists.

Several historical buildings did sustain damage as the rising water of the Danube overflowed and seeped into basements and street level floors in the Radu district, the location of the university. These damaged structures included the University Library, a handsome renaissance building, which was opened by the University of Budapest in1875, the Town Hall (built 1869-1875) and the National Museum (built 1836-1844).

The calamity, however, brought to light a previously unknown manuscript written in English shorthand by Bram

Stoker, the author of *Dracula*. It was unearthed in the flood-damaged library basement that was once used by Arminius Vambery, a professor of Orientology, in the late nineteenth century.

The leather bound diary was found hidden behind a wall of bricks that were once part of a fireplace in Vambery's office. Additional papers belonging to Vambery were also discovered behind the wall. These included notes and maps and other materials that were later used in his book, *History of Hungary*, published before his death in 1912.

No historical record exists of Bram Stoker ever visiting Transylvania, the setting for his legendary gothic novel, *Dracula* [1897]. It was always believed and later substantiated by his recently found research notes that he used travelogues and historical documents to recreate the Transylvania countryside and culture. It has also been widely speculated that Professor Vambery was one of his sources for the historical Dracula, the possible inspiration for Count Dracula, and the enduring subject of Stoker's novel.

There were two recorded meetings with Arminius Vambery that took place in England in 1892. At the time of those meetings, Stoker was already hard at work on *Dracula*. These two meetings and the speculation concerning the role Vambery may have played in Stoker's research have never really been determined. This has long been a source of debate regarding Vambery's input. Bram Stoker did record those meetings in his book, *Reminisces with Henry Irving*. He never fully divulged what the conversations were about.

At that time, Bram Stoker had been a longtime associate of Irving, the first actor ever to be knighted, and was Irving's manager of the Lyceum Theater in London at the time Irving owned it.

In the novel *Dracula*, the character of Van Helsing attributes his education of vampirism to "my old friend Arminius," which may have been Stoker's way to acknowledge Vambery's contributions to the novel.

The University of Budapest has retained the documents for further evaluation.

From: University of Budapest
To: Dr. Andrew Andersen
English Literature Department
Columbia University
New York, New York
USA
File Copy: L. O. Wynne

Dear Professor Andersen:

The discovery of the alleged lost diary of Bram Stoker and additional papers authored by our legendary Professor Arminius Vambery, has created a set of problems concerning the responsible manner and direction with which we should proceed.

We at the university find ourselves in a dual world of both shock and unbridled excitement. Why were these documents hidden in the first place and what do we do now without embarrassing the university? Assuming, of course, that the diary itself is authentic, what role will it play in the corridors of academic and public opinion?

Regardless of that aspect, the discovery of Vambery's notes is quite an important find for us. He is still a venerated figure among Hungarians and his papers certainly deserve further scrutiny by our scholars.

However, the remarkable discovery of these papers and the problems we face with the Bram Stoker diary, in particular, does raise a wide range of questions. We have already begun to inspire a process of speculative theories on the diary's placement and its possible origins. Still, it begs the question, why was it hidden from view all these long years?

Those of us involved here at the university realize that we need to verify the diary's authenticity before making any announcement. We must translate its contents with the help of noted scholars in this field and then release further details to the public.

While we were able to easily verify that the papers of Professor Vambery were authentic, we found the translation and verification of the Stoker diary to be much more difficult. This is due in part to the English shorthand of Victorian origin that can only be translated by a few scholars worldwide.

We also came to the conclusion that we must tender these documents for corroboration under a strict veil of secrecy. It is our intention to not undermine any individuals involved in this research and to wait until a thorough study of these documents has been completed before issuing any conclusions. We desperately wish to avoid the circus atmosphere associated with such hoaxes as *The Hitler Diaries*.

This caveat precludes us from going to some of the more obvious sources available. That includes the likes of the esteemed Elizabeth Miller or internationally recognized authorities such as professors Raymond T. McNally and Radu Florescu of Boston College. You are no doubt aware of their impressive credentials.

We must be prudent in our approach and keep all the information internally sequestered until we have a clearer understanding of what this is all about. The puzzling thing about this discovery is Vambery's motivations and we find his reasons quite baffling. It appears obvious to us that Professor Vambery never intended that this diary be found. He makes that quite clear in his notes associated with this diary. Still, we are perplexed by the suggestions set forth in his explanations. Why would Professor Vambery do something like that? Why suppress a manuscript of a well-known author? What motivated an educated man like Vambery to censure the diary of Bram Stoker? Until all the details relating to the professor's intentions are clear, we must be sensitive to the possibility of leaks. To insure the confidentiality of this material, we have already decided to have an unbiased third party conduct this inquiry off site and at an undisclosed location.

After a surreptitious search into the backgrounds and capabilities of a variety of candidates, we have arrived at the conclusion that you and your university would be the best choice for this study.

We would like to retain your services and the resources of Columbia University to help in sifting through the materials recently recovered in this "lost manuscript."

While we suspect this to be nothing more than an elaborate hoax or a clever figment of Professor Vambery's prolific imagination, we do feel a responsibility to pursue all avenues available. Conversely, if this manuscript were to be proven the genuine article, it would certainly rank as one of the greatest literary finds in the history of English literature and would require the utmost care in the handling of such a landmark discovery. Your impeccable credentials as a historian of English literature and your papers on the great gothic writers of the nineteenth century are highly regarded. Your reputation for prudence, your passion for all things Stoker, and your access to the resources within your university make you the logical choice.

Enclosed are terms and conditions if you choose to proceed. I will arrange for delivery of the diary upon your acceptance.

We look forward with great anticipation to your findings.

Dr. Yton Oton
Chairman Emeritus
University of Budapest

File copy: L. O. Wynne

URGENT MAIL: Hand delivered
From: Dr. Andrew Andersen
Columbia University, New York, NY

To: Allen Clay Galleries
200 Madison Avenue
New York, NY

Dear Professor Clay:

Although we have never met, we did share a mutual acquaintance: Charles Hamilton.

Shortly before he died, Charles was telling me of his experience in debunking *The Hitler Diaries* and he mentioned that there was no one he trusted more in terms of second opinions than you. I always found Charles to have been a formidable academic and a great friend. So you can understand my delight to discover how much you have in common with him and thus with me. I feel as if I know you already. But to the point…

I've been asked by University of Budapest to evaluate the legitimacy of a diary supposedly written by Bram Stoker. My instructions require absolute secrecy concerning any findings. Total confidentiality must be strictly maintained.

While I'm predisposed to believe that this is a hoax, I do want not this exercise to become a mummery, so I will seek expert guidance from a number of other sources.

I'm aware that these documents, which are written in Victorian era shorthand, will be challenging. I'm confident, however, that there is enough material available for an evaluation of the author's handwriting. I will ask of you only one question: Did Bram Stoker write this diary?

I would like to submit the following documents for your appraisal.

Andrew Andersen
Andrew Andersen PHD

From Andersen file/ L.O. Wynn
Copy Andersen
Internal Memo
MEMO TO Staff/Andersen

The following items will need to be addressed before the team can issue preliminary findings:

Handwriting analysis: Allen Clay

Shorthand translation: Dr. Anthony Sidel / English department

Document and paper investigation: Steve Garrett / FBI

Historical background check: Kevin McManus and staff/ history department

REPORT SAGARRET SERVICES
Forensic analysis: Private Data
Steve Garrett, Special Agent
Re: Bram Stoker Diary

Summary notes of analytical profile and dating of handwritten entries prepared in ink.

Although the author is with the Federal Bureau of Investigation, the methods are not necessarily those of the agency. All opinions expressed are those of the author alone and do not represent the opinion of any other organizations associated with the author.

The results are as follows:

The gallonnatte ink dates back to second half of the nineteenth century. The pages with ink show aging that is consistent with the strong probability they were written upon when the diary was new.

The leather casing of the diary is also of this time period and can be narrowed down to 1875-1880 in age. This is confirmed by the aging of the leather itself.

The diary would have been sold with blank pages and has tax stamps consistent with the purchase of such a book in Austria during the above mentioned time period.

The aging variance of the paper is also consistent with these findings, as it has a cellulose base to the material paper. This texture was a very popular brand for inclusion in diaries of this type.

The glue binding would only have been found in Europe at that time. While there appears to be some minor moisture damage to the casing, the overall condition of the binding is in surprisingly good order.

There is a watermark and a seal that identifies the paper and indicates it was milled no earlier than 1875. The tax seal of Vienna dates to midyear 1880.

Overall, and without prejudice, I am confident to a strong degree that this diary was available and in use during the time period laid out and fits a timeline that lends credence to its authenticity.

STOKER RESEARCH TEAM: code one status
Copy of letter/ L. O. Wynne file copy
Author: Allen Clay
Letter from Philography Department
Clay Galleries

Dear Dr. Andersen:

As per your request, we are able to verify that the handwriting in the diary you send to us is indeed that of Bram Stoker.

We were able to compare samples of Stoker's handwritten documents, currently housed in the Rosenbach Museum in Philadelphia, with the diary. We found an almost perfect match.

In conclusion, we can state with ninety-nine percent certainty that Bram Stoker is the author of this diary.

Sincerely,
Allen Clay

TELEGRAM
To: Dr. Yton Oton
University of Budapest

From: Professor Andersen
Columbia University

I have extraordinary and shocking news. Diary verified! Handwriting definitely Stoker! Will pass on to your research team a full content analysis and historical background verification as soon as available.

Have engaged the resources of the university to assist in converting the shorthand to plain text. I wish to keep this in house until everything is documented. All information must be eyes-only. We must handle this undertaking with extreme care. Additional research and resources must be employed. Until this research is completed and presented to you, our future correspondence be undertaken with the utmost secrecy

INTERNAL MEMO
COLUMBIA UNIVERSITY
PRIVATE DATA

To: Professor Andersen

From: Professor Anthony Sidel
cc: L. O. Wynne
Personal and Confidential

The following document is the complete and literal translation of the so-called Stoker diary.

This was a very challenging undertaking, as at times his shorthand was difficult to read. In some isolated cases, certain words and wording were left to our own intuitive interpretation, a process that we will explain further. For the most part, however, this document was transcribed as written.

Understanding early English shorthand symbols versus later and more modern symbols of the shorthand used today was and is the most problematical aspect of this project. What made this process difficult was that Stoker utilized a hybrid version of Irish shorthand, very popular with the bureaucracy of that time, and incorporated symbols that were clearly of his own invention.

Most helpful to us were Stoker's scripted longhand notes. By using these sections as a guide, we were able to cross-index those against other problematic sentences to identify key words that appear in the text. We would then look for similar words or symbols consistent with his shorthand text and make a match.

Unfortunately, there were some symbols that we could not translate very well at all, despite using the process we've just described.

These few words were difficult to read, but by using and comparing other portions of this diary or just applying common sense, we were able to calculate a symbols match. Following this example, we were able to define possible words that made sense and we were then able to fill in the very few gaps that may have existed.

There are also some references to words applied with foreign language meanings. This required us to cross-reference several different languages to confirm a word's meaning. Thankfully, these words were among those that Stoker wrote in longhand. We speculate that he did not know what type of shorthand symbols to use either, so he wrote them out.

We are submitting to you the entire document in as full a conversion as we could provide. The following is as accurate a translation as possible under the circumstances.

I would like to thank you for this opportunity to allow us to participate in this project. I found this exercise to be quite challenging and especially enjoyable. I must say that this was quite an undertaking and a very exciting project.

Only one other person beside myself was involved and she has also been sworn to secrecy. Her confidentiality document is on file as per your request.

I must say it was quite eerie reading and translating this work. One did get a sense that the author was almost reaching from beyond the grave to have this story told.

Mr. Bram Stoker certainly did have an active imagination. I'm sure readers will enjoy this "lost manuscript."

Try not to read it in the dark!

MEMO
COLUMBIA PRIVATE DATA

To: Andy Anderson

From: Dr. Kevin McManus
Columbia University / Historical research team

Andy,

This diary really does merit further investigation.

While I've not yet had an opportunity to read it in its entirety, I am at once struck by some of the names mentioned by Bram Stoker in his text.

Some of these characters actually did exist. They were, in fact, quite prominent in their day and well thought of in Stoker's time.

We will need to research any information on the names mentioned. There is definitely a fabric in this tapestry. This project's possible authenticity is compelling and we should proceed with an eye toward a true historical perspective.

cc: A. Sidel
L.O. Wynne

Chapter 2

Journal: L.O. Wynne

So it all began, a project so exciting that we foolishly rejoiced in our good fortune. Each and every one of us chosen to work on this project felt blessed beyond all measure. Those were heady times. What a glorious project! Like children on Christmas morning, we exulted in the opening of our presents as each new exploration filled us with joy and happiness. We had begun the journey of discovery and our destiny was full of promise. Little did we realize that our destiny was unraveling, and we were unaware that retribution was to be our terrible reward. Only in the aftermath of these proceedings did we know the depth of the danger we had uncovered, but by then it was too late.

Andersen was as excited as any man I have ever seen—an unusual thing to witness in an academic of his stature. We were all expecting to find this to be nothing more than a hoax. So we were stunned when we found out otherwise.

I must say that the shock of finding this diary to be real blinded us to reality. We dismissed the explanation of the diary's suppression as a mere fantasy by a clever charlatan.

We never truly contemplated the reasons why Vambery chose the road he followed. We never really cared, actually.

We never believed in the adage that truth is stranger than fiction. We accepted the horror as a gift of imagination. Why wouldn't we? Bram Stoker was a very imaginative man. We always believed that this was only a story.

The danger didn't strike me at first glance. I didn't realize the diary's importance when I first began to read it. Anderson was distributing the diary in sections to maintain a firm grip on security. Then, as each additional section arrived, I began to understand. The type of people involved assaulted me with a mounting curiosity.

I grew more concerned with each passing word. This was not a causal encounter of some innocuous personalities. This was a group of men and women who were on a mission.

Unfortunately, the others would never be able to read between those lines when they began to read the diary. Most of them never realized that would be their only mistake.

Chapter 3

INTERNAL MEMO
To: Stoker Research Team
From: Andersen
Re: Introduction of Stoker text

The time has arrived. I will now be releasing the first installment of the Stoker diary. I have also jotted down some thoughts, questions, observations and background information as my way of introduction to this exciting material. I raise some key points that you should consider about key players and what transpires in this diary as a way to help us have a track to go on when we formulate some conclusions at the end.

This project will proceed with full confidentiality and any and all materials generated will only be made available to those with code one access. The following information is only for the participants of this study. The university has authorized this project at the highest level and those who have approved it are sworn to the utmost secrecy.

At first glance, the diary covers a long forgotten and partially substantiated trip the Shakespearean actor Sir Henry Irving and his Lyceum theater general manager Bram Stoker made to Vienna in the spring of 1880 to seek financing for the theater.

This includes a continuation of a documented trip to Vienna that would have the duo traveling farther east to meet a mysterious Count Lonvay, who appears to have domiciled in Budapest. While this trip to Vienna is a fact, the events recorded by Stoker cannot be verified. We can only determine that Henry Irving arrived back in England without Bram Stoker. We also have evidence that Stoker was available for the Lyceum's winter season.

Needless to say, this document of his travels is extraordinary in nature and appears to be a very creative work of fiction. If, however, this diary were somehow the truth, this finding would be most difficult to contemplate.

No researchable document exists that shows any historical record of Bram Stoker ever having been to Transylvania, or even Hungary for that matter. It has also been well documented that he has never traveled farther east than Austria, yet he describes the landscapes of the east in great detail.

Despite this, records that may have once existed, transportation files for instance, could have easily been destroyed or discarded over time. All the papers, records, and transactions of both Bram Stoker and Henry Irving are limited, so this means we will not be able to dismiss such a trip out of hand.

The story Bram Stoker tells is one of a horrific struggle for survival against powerful and unknown forces. Together with the help of some remarkable men and women, who united to meet and destroy those forces, they were able to defeat this evil, but at a great cost to all of them.

This is by far the scariest story I have ever read and quite possibly Bram Stoker's best. But this horrific tale raises a plethora of questions about its origin:

What is the source for this grim adventure and who were the people he traveled with?

Did this come from his imagination? Were any of these journal entries based on fact?

Because history states Stoker didn't start writing *Dracula* until 1890, ten years after the events recorded here, why was this work never mentioned when the rest of his diaries were rediscovered in 1994?

How was it lost?

Why was it hidden in the walls of a fireplace of Professor Vambery's office?

While Stoker alludes to working on his first fiction work, *Under the Sunset*, which he published in 1882, why has no record ever been uncovered that mentions or even alludes to this work?

The diary seems to have been a publishable document with proper editing. Was it possible that this diary was lost to him without his knowledge? In light of the discovery, this is both an odd and baffling question.

Why didn't he ever publish this work?

Can we even speculate that this work was an early form or the genesis of a *Dracula* metaphor of some type?

When we inspect the entire dossier, we are presented with some clues within the diary itself. Additionally, some explanation does exist within Professor Vambery's papers as well.

If we assume that it was not true, why didn't Stoker reconstruct his notes and publish a novel or some short stories based on these very notes?

What barriers really existed to prevent such a scenario?

Was he ever aware that his diary ended up in the hands of Professor Vambery?

We have no record of Sir Henry Irving traveling farther east than Vienna, although he was known to make sojourns throughout Europe. We cannot verify his trip beyond Vienna, but does that mean he didn't go?

Ironically, this diary does cover several unaccounted months that do coincide with Sir Henry's and Stoker's trip to Vienna shortly before the events in the Diary. There is no proof that this has any bearing on what is before us, but it does add an element of intrigue to the equation. They were close enough to the area and within a timeline that makes it impossible to rule out that the events that transpired were false. This raises a number of perplexing questions that will need to be addressed.

Did they move eastward after visiting Vienna? There is also no verifiable proof that they did and no real proof that they did not!

Did Irving end up in Budapest to meet with his hoped for benefactor, Count Karel Lonvay, who appears to have been associated with the Hapsburg dynasty and a cousin of Count Menyhert Lonvay, a prominent Hungarian politician whose own chronicle is lost to history save for notations of some obscure financial nature.

Would the nature of their relationship and the purpose of this trip lend any credence to Irving rendering Bram Stoker insignificant in dealing with this Count Lonvay?

Did Henry Irving end up seeing this count at all? The money apparently was forthcoming and the winter season did commence on time. No record exists of them ever having met, but this in itself would be insignificant to a recording of the public record. Investments in theatrical ventures were of a clandestine nature at that time. Bookkeeping was lost to the ages. If records were keep at all. Box office receipts and other financial information would not necessarily stand the test of time. Only sporadic information still exists. Benefactors are not named. Creditors yield little information to our study.

Lonvay was known to have been a major investor in the Paris Circus, yet there is no longer any documentation to prove that it was so. So this scenario remains plausible, however remote.

What was the state of mind of Stoker and Henry Irving in regards to this journey?

It's apparent that neither man was happy about this short and rather impromptu trip to Eastern Europe. With that in mind, it's understandable that they would be on edge. While not much is actually revealed in terms of their relationship with each other, some of the aspects of their complex relationship are revealed in the diary.

Much has been made of Irving's influence over Stoker and his robust personality. That sense about this interaction is somewhat captured here.

We should then also look at the historical Henry Irving and what we know about him.

Irving was spontaneous. Irving was profligate. Irving was prone to spending money thoughtlessly. With this in mind, we could actually support the hypothesis that a search for an investor to finance the Lyceums upcoming season had merit.

The Historical Stoker: background notes

Bram Stoker's contribution to London theater history and the Lyceum would have been overlooked if *Dracula* had not been published. His subsequent fame as an author of a classic novel like *Dracula* created Stoker's legacy. It also cemented Irving's fame as well, a thought that would have seemed impossible at the time.

If it weren't for his novel, *Dracula*, Stoker's theater career would also be nothing more than a footnote in the illustrious career of Sir Henry Irving, the first actor ever to be knighted.

Stoker's experiences with Sir Henry Irving, while interesting from a theatrical historical perspective, are only remembered because of *Dracula.* The same holds true for most of Stoker's other literary works up to and including *Lair of the White Worm*, which was Stoker's final book. While an interesting horror story in its own right, Lair has been given only passing notice in comparison to *Dracula.*

Ultimately, Stoker surpassed Irving in notoriety only when *Dracula* first entered in the realm of twentieth century popular culture. Interestingly enough, almost all of Bram Stoker's fame came years after his death in 1912 and only after the F. W. Murneau's classic silent film, *Nosferatu* brought new attention and renewed interest in his gothic horror masterpiece.

Finally, we must ponder the ramifications of what could be true and what might not be true. The possibility exists that this story is an evolving matrix for a historically based docu-fiction, that is, fact and fiction cleverly merged together to give an appearance of authenticity. This is in fact how Bram Stoker wrote *Dracula.* Historical facts merged with imagination. This may be all that the following really is.

Or is a major cover up at work here? I leave that conclusion to the team, but this should not be the domain of academics like us who cannot stretch our credibility beyond an accepted boundary. We would be called lunatics. An Interesting dilemma, don't you think?

While its truth would be to frightening to contemplate, its fiction does fit perfectly within the recognized realm of Bram Stoker's imagination.

The historical figures represented in this story beg many of the same questions first raised by scholars about Stokers actual sources for *Dracula*.

For instance, was Dr. Von Hanes a model for the future Van Helsing? It is also curious that the American cowboy, Quincy Morris, a character in *Dracula*, and William Mathewson, who is mentioned in this diary, were both adept at the use of a Bowie knife? Similarities like this abound within the text and certainly make intriguing reading for those of us who respect the essence of *Dracula*, the novel. These questions and others like it will need to be evaluated further.

The historical research team will be required to obtain as much information as possible regarding the individuals named in this document.

Speculation and myths aside, this diary changes all dynamics in regards to the writing of *Dracula*, yet answers none of the questions. Additionally, it raises many other questions that can never be answered. We will, however, try to answer what we can.

These questions can only be answered with speculation. For example, the role of Professor Arminius Vambery is a curious one since he was most responsible for this diary being "lost." While he explains his reasons carefully, it is predicated on his belief that this was not a work of fiction, but of fact.

I will not question his rationale at this time because I do not wish to prejudice your views. My interpretation will be forthcoming upon the completion of this study.

His cause and effect may have an ominous consequence and must be evaluated closely. His act of suppression is based on an assumption of an extraordinary nature or a tongue-in-cheek manner that may have been lost in the translation.

This, then, leaves us with the diary itself and the events recorded in it. The participants, whether real or imagined, came face to face with an evil force far greater than anything Victorian gothic horror could ever have conceived of at the time. These pages describe an occurrence that, taken as a whole, had no equal in popular imagination.

The writing is not in the classic gothic horror style, or even Victorian era science fiction. Bram Stoker and the resources available to him would never have been able to create this calendar of events, which in it self begs the question: Could this have been possible?

I can only explain my concerns, but I'm leaving it to you to judge the contents and draw your own conclusions.

We shall proceed cautiously, but with great excitement I am sure.

I present *The Lost Diary of Bram Stoker* for your evaluation.

Andy

Journal: L. O. Wynne

Dr. Andersen in his endearing, but long-winded way had set the stage for us. He did not give us the entire diary all at once, but issued it to us in sections because he did not want to taint our observations or lose control of the project. He already had lost control but he never knew it.

I believe he already knew what we would find there would be difficult to believe?

We never did challenge his reasoning. He was very sincere in his attempts not to influence our evaluation of the material. That was the assumption of most of us. Even with all the mounting evidence this whole bizarre story was difficult to believe. And In most cases we probably kept waiting for the other shoe to drop. My co-worker Jonathan actually believed that Andersen had forged the evidence entirely, but, of course, he never lived long enough to know that was not true. The other shoe never did drop, but death did step on them with a stride of appalling force.

The beginning of this adventure would be so different from the end. I know I must leave some legacy, some explanation of what transpired, as I fear I will not live long enough to tell this story.

So I will assemble this journal in a way that you can understand it. I feel I need to show you how this project unfolded. I have laid out the dairy for you as I received it.

I failed to see the clues at first, I'm hope you already have. That would mean this journal is now in the right hands. I do pray that is so. If you do understand the paradox, I do not need to explain my flight to you, my reasons are now obvious. For any others who may read this journal and do not yet grasp its meanings I say to you carefully, Ignorance is bliss but it may not save you.

All I know is that I must contact those who may be able to help me. Until then, I am forced to hide myself as thoroughly as I hide my fears. I can only hope that I have not been forsaken and that somehow I will not been forced to face these fears alone. "While a hero may find the answer, it was a brave man who first asked the question."

L.O Wynne

Chapter 4

I'm looking for Laura Olsen Wynne, he thought.

While others may have wanted to be at one with the universe, Detective Arnold Walters only wanted to become one with his subject. In this case, a missing person named Laura Olsen Wynne. No matter how long it might take, Walters would never give up searching for her. It helped that he preferred missing person cases because they always came down to good old-fashioned detective work and offered him the opportunity to help reunite a family. He liked that. Even better, he liked working alone.

As usual, he would immerse himself in as many details of the case as humanly possible. That was his method, his madness, and his special way to motivate himself for the chase. He would work the case with such a single-mindedness of purpose that his fellow cops only half jokingly referred to the fifty-two-old detective as "Mounty."

If it were only true, he thought. That would be a terrific compliment if he were actually worthy of such a comparison to the Canadian Mounted Police. How he wished he always got his man. In real police work, however, he knew you hardly ever get your man at all. In those quiet places of his mind, in those deep recesses of his lonely solitude, he always wondered what had really happened to the ones he could never find. Unfortunately, too many of the missing remained that way despite his dogged pursuit.

The one thing he did know was that he would never abandon the lost. That was why Arnold Walters wore the badge. If he didn't care about the missing, who else would?

He knew all too well that there always came a day when the others stopped looking for missing persons, and it was usually the police that stopped looking first. He would never allow himself to become that type of policeman—the type who stopped caring, the type who went to his job every day, but never did his work.

He knew he had paid a heavy price for his tenacity. He had forsaken the conventional goals of friends and family for a cop's life. Arnold Walters had sacrificed it all for the job. Now, his loneliness had been ripping away at him and his satisfaction was starting to fray. Looking back on twenty-five years of police work, he had begun to confront the question: Was it all worth it?

Then along came Laura Olsen Wynne.

Laura Olsen was different, he thought. Looking at her picture, looking at her mystifying smile and beautiful almond-shaped eyes, he sensed a kindred spirit—a person who lived her work more than she lived her life. Like himself, she had armored her emotions behind a shield to protect her vulnerability. When he studied her face, he felt he was almost looking at himself. She seemed to him a person who had spent most of her life trying to make a special connection with someone, only to be disappointed. For some reason, he just knew that was true. He also knew what it was like to be that way. L.O. Wynne made him want to care again.

Stuffing a half-eaten bagel back into its brown bag, Walters slipped it into the side pocket of his soiled raincoat. Once again his mind began racing. He needed to think about what he planed to accomplish on this next call. He was on his way to meet Carl Lawson, a vice president of Columbia University. Stepping up from the subway station, he was hit by a cold rainy wind. He walked north on Broadway until he reached the gated entrance of the university. *How strange*, he thought, *why isn't there much ivy on the walls of this Ivy League campus?*

Columbia University was a different world. This was not a school that Walters could have attended. He had never had the grades. That didn't stop him from being a very good detective, though, and his years on the force had confirmed that fact. Maybe that was why he was so focused on his work—to make up for the lack of commitment he had exhibited before becoming a cop.

Reaching the executive offices at the Low Library, he groaned when he saw that he had to walk up an additional flight of stairs. Entering the gray columned archway, he trudged up a long marble staircase leading to the offices. Just his luck, he thought, the elevator was not working. With each heavy step, Walters could sense that he was looking for more than just the whereabouts of a beautiful thirty-two-year-old woman with impressive academic credentials. In some strange way, he felt he was looking for his own destiny as well.

Why was she missing? he wondered.

There was an aura about this woman that was palpable. Over the years, he had learned to trust his inner voice and it was practically shouting at him now. Something was just not right about the case.

Finally, after so many exhausting steps, Walters reached his destination. He took a minute to catch his breath and curse his poor conditioning. He needed to start working out or he would probably die sooner than he had planned. Buttoning his sports coat to hide the ten pounds he kept promising himself to lose, he flashed his shield to a secretary. He was always interested in the reaction of people when they saw his badge and he was not disappointed by her response. She looked him over intently before alerting Dr. Lawson of his arrival.

While he waited patiently, one recurring thought kept jumping out at him. Why would this woman, this L.O. Wynne, just disappear without something being terribly wrong? It didn't make any sense for her to just to pack up and leave. *She was running from something*, he thought, *something that had overwhelmed her*. But he felt he was missing something. He hoped her work would provide a clue.

In most missing person cases, Walters would look for the usual suspects—the jilted lover, a large debt, some evidence of enemies or bad blood. Nothing like that appeared to be amiss in Laura's personal life. She seemed pretty normal for a high-powered academic. But all she left behind was a lawyer who barely knew her, a large trust fund she rarely used, and a resume of scholarly achievements that obviously made her smart.

If this woman had a love life, she had somehow managed to keep it a secret. She had no significant other, no real friends, and very few visitors to her apartment. Not a lot of activity appeared on any of her phone records. There were also no phone calls since her lawyer reported her missing. Other than normal business calls, she hardly used her home phone at all.

Her job as a researcher for Columbia University was everything to her. She was well on her way to receiving a PhD. *The answers must be here*, he thought.

His experience has told him that people who disappear without any reason are the ones who usually turned up dead. The file cabinet of missing persons was filled with the names of people whose final destination was the morgue or an unmarked grave.

Looking out the windows of the outer office, he marveled at the view overlooking the impressive campus and wondered what it must be like to be a part of this strange world he had entered. This was a long way from the endless hours of night school at John Jay College he had attended. Overwhelmed by the stress of working toward a degree in criminology, he had slowly begun to retreat into himself. Over those years, he had lost contact with just about anyone who might have been close to him. He realized now that the degree took far more from him than the many years it took for him to complete it.

It never came easy, he thought. *None of it.*

Looking at the students rushing from class to class, he realized he was now in the company of what his father once called the "higher profits," a term he used to describe the denizens of the educated upper class. Succeed at the world of academics, his father had said, and one day you will sit atop a pedestal of privilege. All Arnold Walters did was put the cuffs on them when they stepped over the line.

He was surprised at how intimidated he felt when Dr. Lawson came cautiously to the door. While Lawson gracefully ushered him into the office, Walters could tell by the man's body language that the slim and graying administrator did not consider him to be a peer on any level. That made him mad. But he also knew from long experience that his anger and anxiety were only temporary and would fade once he took control of the situation. Although he didn't know it, Carl Lawson was about to enter Walters's world. Usually one hard look and a skeptical and humorless demeanor unnerved even the most guiltless person. There was something about the badge, the power of authority that quickly evened the playing field.

Taking Walters's raincoat and hanging it on a hanger, Lawson smiled slightly. "Interesting outfit. Do you have affinity for Colombo?' Lawson said, as he effortlessly slid behind his polished oak desk

"Why would you say that, Dr. Lawson?"

"The raincoat…isn't it a part of your costume? You know, like Colombo?"

Walters stared intently at Lawson, who shuffled uncomfortably in his leather chair. It had become clear to the administrator that this conversation with Walters would not be a humorous one. The plump and balding policeman in the rumbled brown sports jacket and bulging jeans was making a point at his expense.

Looking intensely at Lawson, Walters said sarcastically: "If you look out the window, you can see that it's raining."

With a condescending eye, Lawson decided that this was not the approach he wanted to take. "I can see you are a not a trivial man. What brings you to my office?"

Walters smiled. He knew he had marked his territory. "I'm looking for Laura Olsen Wynne," he said.

Lawson grimaced; it was obvious to Walters that he had raised a painful subject.

"So you have come here to look for her? We have been trying to reach her for several weeks and we have become very concerned about her," Lawson said. "When we tried to reach Ms. Wynne ourselves, we found that she didn't have many contacts in her file."

"I know. We are having the same problem," Walters said. "That's why I am hoping you can help me here."

Walters shifted in his seat and moved closer to Lawson's desk "I was hoping to find some information about her professional life…people she might have been close to at her job."

"We are all very concerned about her," Lawson said. "Have you called the human resources department?"

"Funny you should mention that," Walters said. "When I called them, I was told that anything pertaining to Ms. Wynne needed to be discussed directly with you? Odd, isn't it?"

"How so?" Lawson asked answers calmly, totally unaware that Walters had noticed Lawson's eyes were darting back and forth—a sign that the vice president was desperately trying to think how he was going to answer the question.

"Because I'm sitting here talking to a vice president of a major university about a mid-level researcher. She must be more important than her title. Surely you can see my confusion, Dr. Lawson?"

"Confusion comes easily to you, doesn't it?" Lawson said, and sniffed proudly as he relished his little joke. He gained some confidence with this remark "She's a highly educated and valued employee. With the murder of Professor Andersen and the subsequent investigation, I thought it prudent that anything related to Andersen and his work should be cleared through me. I suppose HR felt the same way and referred you to me. We are not hiding anything and I will cooperate with you in any way I can." Lawson pulled a file folder from his desk and handed it to Walters.

"Do you think there is some kind of connection between Andersen's murder and Ms. Wynne's disappearance?" Walters asked.

"None whatsoever," Lawson said, his eyes starting to dart again.

"I'm sorry. I can't buy that. She worked very closely with Andersen and she went missing shortly after his death. You will have a hard time convincing me that there is not something connected to these two events."

"Really?"

"Yeah, really. You are not telling me everything about their relationship. You are lying to me," Walters said firmly, watching for a reaction to the accusation.

Lawson paused for a long moment before answering: "Well, there have been some rumors that she may have been more than just an assistant to Dr. Andersen. You know, office gossip, but I really don't want to go down that road. I have no proof. Far be it for me to venture an opinion about two unmarried individuals. Even if it were true, it was strictly their own business."

"Are you trying to tell me that she's running away from her grief over Andersen's death?" Walters asked skeptically.

"Why not? It's plausible."

"Well, I don't think it's true. If you look at her phone records, you will see that Andersen rarely called her at home," Walters's said, combing through the file.

An important looking document with a large red stamp caught his eye. "What is this project they were working on, this code one status?"

"I can't divulge any information concerning Dr. Andersen's file."

"Why not?"

"Because Dr. Andersen had the authority to implement such a confidential study without full disclosure—approved by the president of the university himself."

"Do you even know where the file is now?"

"Unfortunately, the file was stolen when they ransacked poor Dr. Andersen's office." Lawson shivered "What a horrible tragedy! Do you know if they have any leads concerning his death?"

"I'm sorry, Dr. Lawson. I'm not handling the case, so I can't tell you anything. And even if I could, I wouldn't. You understand, code one status and all." Walters relished Lawson's grimace and he placed Laura's photograph on the desk.

"What can you tell me about her?"

Lawson picked up the photograph and sighed deeply. His sadness was apparent now. "She is even more beautiful in person than this picture shows. But there is not much more I can tell you about her that you don't already know."

"Assume I know nothing, Dr. Lawson," Walters said, knowing that Lawson would attempt to be witty.

"I made that assumption a while back, Detective Walters." Lawson said, smiling happily. "She went to Yale University, graduating with a major in English literature and a minor in Latin."

"So she speaks Latin?"

"Not only Latin, she's fluent in at least ten languages, including French, Russian, Greek and Romanian."

"Impressive," Walters said. "Didn't she stay at Yale after she graduated?"

"Yes, she did…to do graduate work. She earned two master's degrees, one in medieval studies and the other in religious studies. After Yale, she came to work with us as a researcher and to complete her PhD.

"She was highly sought after for research assignments by both Dr. Andersen and Dr. Kevin McManus, who headed up the history department. They utilized her skills because of her background in historical studies and her fluency in various languages. Her background is quite extensive, frankly, and she is exactly the type of accomplished individual we employ here at the university. Only the best."

"How about her co-workers? Was she close to anyone?"

"I'm too far removed from the day-to-day activities of the departments to know. I can only mention the names of the people she was most in contact with, like Andersen and McManus," Lawson said testily. He was anticipating Walters's follow-up question and he was trying to get his guard up. Walters noticed.

"Can you give me some other names?' Walters asked, thinking this was the right way to proceed.

"She may have been friends with John Spellman, a fellow researcher, but he passed away recently. Drowned, I'm sorry to say," Lawson said.

"Where can I find Dr. McManus?"

Lawson looked back at Walters blankly before answering. He was in the midst of an inner turmoil. "Dr. McManus was killed in a car accident. Is there anything else I can help you with?"

"Yeah, I do have another question. Has anyone else been looking for Laura Wynne?"

"A man by the name of Rufus Arsine," Lawson said in a strained voice. "He came to my office about a week ago asking about Laura and the Andersen file. I gave him the same answer I gave you. We can't find either one."

"Rufus Arsine?" Walters asked.

"Yes, have you heard of him?"

"I've never met him, but I am aware of his reputation. He deals with missing and stolen artwork, if memory serves," Walters said.

"Rufus Arsine is one of the most respected experts of paleography in the world," Lawson said. "That's the study of ancient inscriptions and the deciphering of ancient writings. Mr. Arsine also has a very impressive track record for finding rare books and lost manuscripts. Some of the most important finds of the twentieth century would have never been recovered without his assistance."

"Still, Dr. Lawson, why would he be looking for the Andersen file?"

"I just assumed that he was hired by an insurance company. Dr. Andersen had a number of rare books and ancient texts in his collection. They were all stolen during the robbery. Arsine most likely was trying to find them."

"Okay, I'll buy that. But why did Arsine ask about Ms. Wynne and what did he ask about her?"

"He asked me where I thought Laura could be. Although we had not seen her for a few days, it still hadn't crossed our minds that there was something terribly wrong. She was working on a project with code one status, so we wouldn't necessarily be keeping track of her. That job fell to Andersen and McManus, but both of them were dead by the time Arsine came to see me. In retrospect, I suppose I should have been aware that she did not attend any of their funerals."

"Did he ask about the others—Andersen, McManus or this John Spellman?"

"He asked very little about them. Mostly just about Laura. In fact, he asked a great deal about her. Strange, isn't it? I was under the impression that he suspected Laura of something. Could it be that she may have taken Andersen's collection and this is why I'm talking with you?"

"I only said that she was missing."

"She knew the value. You can't discount that possibility, can you?" Lawson said smugly.

Walters took a long look at Laura's photograph before he put it back in his pocket. "My instinct tells me Ms. Wynne did not steal anything, and I'm willing to stake my life on that."

Walters got up stiffly, indicating the interview was over. He felt he was no closer to finding L.O. Wynne, but there was something about Lawson's guarded attitude that made him wonder more than ever what all these ill-fated researchers and professors were working on. It had to be a book, a document or a piece of art of some kind. A man like Arsine wouldn't be interested otherwise. There had to be a link.

Part II

The Lost Diary of Bram Stoker

Act 1

Chapter 5

I had another nightmare last night. I dreamt that some anomalous creature of the earth had risen in anger and tried to attack me. This snarling beast was then joined in his pursuit of me by a herd of other unworldly animals, equally possessed with a terrifyingly angry continence. I just knew they were intent upon feasting on my soul. The voices in my dream kept telling me so. I frantically tried to run away from them, my essence the only prize they would accept. I could not seem to escape them. They kept getting larger as they came closer to me, scorching putrid breath hot upon my neck, an acid like saliva melting painfully upon my back. I ran down the narrowing corridor of my imagination and could find nowhere to hide. In unison they beset upon me, their large carnivore teeth cracking deeply into my skull. My head cracked open like fragile shell. They feverishly began sucking out the marrow of my brain. Sharp anteater like tongues piercing through the gapping wound in my head, they kept inhaling deeply, reaching all the way to my dimming eyeballs. I was now blind and could not see. I had lost my mind so I could not think. They devoured my tongue so I could speak. In doing so did they take my soul?

Suddenly I awoke from that nightmare.

I find myself ready now to tend to matters at hand. I realize how much I need to chronicle my thoughts and dreams in some organized fashion. Is it possible that these horrible night sweats will become the fuel for my imagination? As it is now the engine of my writing skills has stalled upon a track of indecision. While I so painfully endure these horrid dreams, it may yet lead me to conclude my vacillation. I must finally decide on how to finish my latest works,

So I have purchased this journal in a shop and will attempt to record all happenings whenever possible.

Musings

Almost completed the short stories for *Under the Sunset.* I wonder how well it will be received. This certainly was a book to remember as I had a chance to share many of those Celtic fairytales my mother Charlotte used to tell me as a child. With this book I will explore the perplexities of both good and evil. These are lessons to be learned by the harsh reality of evil's pursuit of our most benevolent soul. Only through the righteous power of benign understanding can trust save our mortal souls. Still, evil in all its disguises presents its enticing challenges cloaked in many forms. The seduction is the lure of its own rewards. The choices we make are still our own.

Working on this project has brought back many fond memories. Surprising, I think, because my mother's choice of content was always on the dark side.

I remember so many nights when we would sit together as I listened spellbound and on the edge of my seat. I was totally captivated, a prisoner of a delightful cerebral darkness. I became a spectator to a world of wonder and delight. My imagination was joined under the covers by a blanket of moonlight.

I was mesmerized by her sweet voice when she told me those fanciful folktales. Some of them made me laugh and some made me cry, but I rejoiced in the rich text filled with limericks and colorful characters bent on mischief. I ran the gamut of emotions; all to the better I must say. Thus, I began the formation of my heart's desire to explore beyond the normal boundaries. I looked beyond the door and toward the reflection in a mirror to search for the soul. The face that I see is my own.

Through this experience, I have also learned to trust in the beauty of an imperfect soul. It is that very struggle between good and evil that is the basis of a delightful character study.

This is the gift that my mother gave to me. She nurtured in me a genuine love of story and a love for storytelling. I am forever grateful to her and all those memorable characters that populated my imagination.

Memorable characters, indeed, in this netherworld that she created for me. A universe with a passion, stroked charmingly with a love that only my mother could provide for me. With my night's dreams swirling with the macabre tales of ghosts and goblins, I learned to feel safe in the darkness. It is easy to forget that good and evil have an equal partnership in the realm of fantasy. Sometimes, it is hard to remember that either can be entertaining if the story is told well.

Seems so strange to have such memories comfort me. My frozen days of invalidism warmed by her attention. I think back to how helpless I was at Clontarf, all those dark and frustrating years bound to my bed like a prisoner.

I still wonder how eight years of misery could so suddenly and miraculous disappear. The doctors certainly couldn't explain the cure. The ReverendWoods always said it was my father's strong belief in the Church of Ireland that was responsible for the miracle. I suppose it had to be his faith because my dear father Abraham could never have afforded the cost of a donation sizable enough to accommodate a miracle like that.

The power of mind over matter is an intriguing question, much as the relationship to good and evil is a universal one. Was my affliction a covenant with the devil rendering me helpless to a heretofore-unknown contract? What prayers then did I elicit on my behalf to expunge my relationship with this malady? No doctor could ever explain this to me and they could not even give my affliction a name.

I've never even been given a diagnosis. No doctor has ever been able to explain why this infirmity came or why it left me. I presume only providence had my best interest at heart. Providence cured my malady despite the intervention of medical science and not because of it. I certainly accede to a belief that all this has prepared me for important things.

Munich

I have ideas for the last thirty pages or so of my manuscript. I hope this travel will inspire me to another project, but I feel confident that *Under the Sunset* will finally reach my expectations.

Still, Irving has his doubts that it will do well. He questions why I should expect tales that frighten small children to sleep should be considered children's fairytales at all. I must say he has a point, but I also believe that the eternal child in all of us responds to that little tuck of fright. We mark our merry way through the perils of our imagination waiting for story's end. We are then to be comforted by the warmth of goodness that follows us in our love of make-believe.

Glorious heroes emerge to transport us back to the safety of our own humanity. This is the essence of fantasy and the reward for our belief. I look forward to publishing when we get back.

Misgivings

Posted a letter to Florence and hoped young Noel is well.

This is the most difficult aspect of this chase…leaving my newborn son. Of course, when I brought this up to Irving he was quite put off.

Considering he had to leave his wife Ellen, who wasn't that much less of a newlywed than my Florence, I should not have expected anything less.

The need for investment is too strong. Money will be extremely tight.

We both feel that the Lyceum is about to take off and will eventually become a nest egg for us all. We must continue to mount shows and build a following.

Florence did not speak to me when I left. This is not new, but I fear she will be overwhelmed with the responsibility of our young son. The pressure will only make her tighter and more terribly wound up when I get back.

Time is pressing as I correspond with London. I fear as we move farther east it will be more difficult to post letters, so I race to finish the long list of tasks I've accumulated.

The new diary will be kept in shorthand as much as possible to facilitate time. I hope I can remember all the symbols because I've rarely used shorthand since my Dublin days. I do need the practice, so I will use it now.

My time is consumed by managing the finances related to winter season. Cash is low and we'll need to have large advance sales to insure a sense of financial security.

Letter writing slow and laborious on the road…so many to send when I get back. Many people to contact.

Notes: Lonvay

I look forward to meeting Count Karel Lonvay, a man that I've heard of about even in England. In fact, this supposedly anonymous backer is better known to me than members of my family.

Even with this knowledge of background, his name is not recognized outside of our small theater circle. When money is on the table, you quickly discover that you must burrow through the earth of confidentiality to uncover the gold lying in the ground. We in the theater are always in search of that mother lode, and no stone will be left unturned. I always believed that Shakespeare meant to say the play's the thing—if the money's there.

Lonvay's cousin is well known in Hungary. As for Count Karel, I already know that he backed museums like Barnum's in New York and, from what I hear, is one of the financial engines for the Paris circus.

This trip has both Irving and I thinking that we should take one of our productions to America. What a challenge for me! Many logistical problems to solve, but would be an historic event if such a tour were accomplished. To our knowledge, no theater company has ever brought to America an entire production, complete with scenery and equipment.

I think we would also be profitable there as this chasing Eastern European royalty around the world is quite exhausting and I miss my family dearly.

Update for Diary

Still at the hotel. The count should be meeting us as expected, I will be looking for a telegraph to confirm our arrival in Vienna. We must now move to meet him; he's leaving Budapest. Should arrive around same time.

Irving is disappointed that Count Lonvay would not come to England, but present turmoil in Budapest makes it difficult for the count to be out of pocket for so long. He reiterated in his message that funding will be forthcoming. We have been assured of investment and this coming season we will be able to mount the boards.

We will discuss road company travel show concept on the way, I imagine. I'll use the time to convince Henry.

All New Ground

I've telegraphed Budapest. The count is delayed, and so we will stay in Munich one more day before leaving for Hungary.

Irving willing, we will spend one month with the count. And then home to prepare for the winter season at the Lyceum.

Nurnberg

We are making the short trip to Nurnberg to see the legendary and sinister terror towers in the morning. We will then catch the train tomorrow night.

I look forward to seeing Nurnberg's towers at this time. I wonder if they are as exploited as the Tower of London. The morbid crowds in England are so fascinated by the gloomy history of the tower there. I'm sure to expect much the same in Nurnberg. The Bavarian monster is no less real in its illusions.

I wonder how different the Germans will be as they fill this city with a perverse curiosity, crowds assembling to view the sinister towers. What trepidations await those who dare to visit the infamous Iron Virgin?

Irving

As we travel along, so many matters to take up with Irving. He has been somewhat difficult lately, but these things do pass and there is much to go over. I believe the strain is weighting on us both. We pass the time planning which plays to produce next season. Irving is a man in search of a rehearsal.

Henry Irving has not been playing Faust, but will soon. He longs to play that role on stage, and we look forward to accomplishing that with the upcoming winter season. That is, of course, if we can fund a winter season. All hopes rest with Count Lonvay. Isn't it ironic that we must make a Faust-like bargain with the devil just to breathe life into our dreams of success. I expect that we would indeed take that bargain. Like Faust, we would contract for such success if twenty years were in the bargain. Twenty is an impressive run.

Mephistopheles will be Henry Irving's greatest role and he will finally be universally recognized. With proper rehearsals happening as soon as we get back, the play will be ready for the public. This knowledge puts him in a better mood.

However, one maddening facet of his preparation is driving me crazy. He is trying to become one with the character by becoming the character. I hope he can finally leave that role on stage and not live it off stage. For my sake and for all around me I hope he loses this annoying habit.

Irving has been experimenting with the concept of staying in a character before and after a performance. By living inside the skin of his character, he hopes to define a role to a more personal level. I found him most disagreeable when he performed this way. Everyone seems to. I found him intolerable when he played Hamlet this way. He could never make a decision.

I know his wife was on edge throughout the *Othello* run.

Wait until the other actors look to be paid. Negotiation will be fun when he plays Shylock.

Irving now believes there's a method to this madness and is planning on having others in the group emulate this practice as part of a rehearsal regimen. I, for one, fear the impact on the others.

I also fear his methods of teaching others to act in character while not on stage will only work for a chosen few. Besides, I thought the skill of acting is to convince the audience that you can become that character for those few hours on the stage. They should then become themselves at curtain call.

To me, that's the genius of Henry Irving, a brilliant actor, playing a cosmic character on stage brilliantly. Offstage, he should just remain the brilliant Henry Irving, not the Merchant of Venice or Shylock.

I, for one, do not want to be held responsible for the ramifications of an actor assuming a villainous character and playing it so well that he is killed in some hateful retribution because he played that offstage character even better.

This only makes us argue.

We still do not agree about America. He is backing off the full-company concept to America because he fears the costs and the daunting logistics.

If he gives me enough time, I can solve these problems.

We cannot even agree on which play to perform at all.

Selections of Shakespeare in a one-man show would be easier to mount, but how will such a cavalcade be accepted in America?

Irving worries about this.

As for his other scenes, they can hardly be known by the majority of the public. But perhaps New York, with it sophistication, would be suitable.

I believe that Irving's building reputation will insure us success, but Henry is not so sure.

The rewards would be enormous. Imagine the glory of a full English company touring America. With the proper vision and planning, all things are possible.

The Burg: A strange and wonderful encounter

We spent most of the morning at the local attraction referred to as the "Burg." It is a bleak and forbidding part of this city, though rich in history.

The Burg is seated on a rock dominating the town with an immensely deep fosse that guards on its sheer rock northern side.

To the right, the towers of the Burg rise ominously. It was late morning when we started climbing up toward the towers. That's when Irving ran into an old acquaintance. He is a gentleman that Irving had met in London during his Bateman days. He turned out to be no ordinary man. Just by the very mention of his name, Dr. Von Hanes, you will elicit a wide variety of opinions. Especially if you are an esteemed member of the scientific community here in Germany or an illustrious but disapproving member of the London Medical College. All told they will differ in their feeling about this great man.

In scientific circles throughout Europe, the name Dr. Von Hanes is one to be reckoned with. Ask any number of doctors, scientists and members of the judiciary throughout Europe and you will likely be able to find an opinion on Dr. Von Hanes—one ranging from genius to crank.

Dr. Von Hanes is a renowned philosopher and a metaphysician and one of the most advanced scientists of our time.

I also remember that my brother Timothy, the rich doctor in our family, had once attended a lecture of his. While my brother was impressed with Hanes' theory, he had said that he did not plan to utilize such methods in his own practice. Then again, the need to perform an autopsy on his patients cannot be very good reference for his business. Now would it?

To our surprise, Dr. Hanes happens to be here in Nurnberg on a very short stay to see the towers. He is on his way east to join a hunting party arranged by the Archduke Alexis of Russia. The young and famous archduke is known worldwide for staging colorful hunting adventures. This latest excursion seems like a dandy. The archduke has arranged an excursion to hunt the indigenous wildlife of Ukrainian Russia and the Carpathian Mountain ranges.

While Hanes was taken by surprise that he would meet an Englishman of Irving's stature at such a place as Nurnberg, he was more than humorously inclined that it would be at the torture towers no less. This amazing man was genuinely glad to see Irving. They exchanged hellos like very old friends. I find it odd, however, because Irving never mentioned this relationship to me.

Naturally, Dr. Hanes is quite excited about his trip. Archduke Alexis has toured the world on hunting expeditions while using his diplomatic cache to promote Mother Russia. I must say that I'm quite envious.

How did Dr. Hanes manage an invitation?

The archduke has recently completed arrangements to bring some of his favorite guides—a very talented and colorful bunch of characters, indeed—to accompany him on this grand adventure. They will be joined by some of the best-known personalities in the world, men like G. P. Sanderson and Paul Stanley.

This troupe will include an American Indian medicine man by the name of Gray Shadow and a legendary tracker and one of America's greatest buffalo hunters, William Mathewson.

The legendary elephant hunter Phillip Possely and India's renowned Singh Laden will join them. Laden, who has killed more tigers than any man alive, is a legend to the white hunters of English aristocracy. They will also be joined by several of the esteemed members of the European nobility who are no slouches when it comes to a foxhunt.

Irving chides Hanes that he should have had actors with him as well, especially if he wanted to include any really interesting people. Actors are hunters in the search of an identity, he says, and laughs.

Hanes also mentioned that the two Americans, Mathewson and his Indian companion Gray Shadow, are now en route from America. It was through them that he was invited and he has offered to travel a part of the way with them.

He plans on meeting with them in Culjia as they travel through Romania. They will rendezvous with the archduke's party in Bukovina.

Hanes explains that he's using the time to see Nurnberg. As a criminologist, the Burg's history of crime and punishment certainly should interest him greatly.

I have to admit that I am very happy to meet the legendary Dr. Hanes.

I have heard about him over the years, a result I'm sure of my own fascination with the search for cures of rare diseases. When you investigate the medical debate on rare disease and their causes, one cannot easily avoid coming across his views.

Dr. Hanes always seems to be on the forefront of new ideas—ideas that can be controversial, yet truly provocative in nature. I, for one, have found them to be intriguing.

In my research at Trinity, his name came up repeatedly, especially in my last year when I was finishing my thesis on rare diseases. I completed my science curriculum, and in many ways I have Dr. Von Hanes to thank for that. His theories are definitely well thought out, but probably a little too far advanced to ever really be considered practical to an uncompromising mind.

I find that his hypothesis that insects might be the cause of the spread of contagious diseases makes a great deal of sense to me. I've always had the view that the exchange of blood can have a disastrous effect on a human being. Of course, I've always been a little skittish when the possibility exists that my blood might be sucked from my body by a foreign lifeform.

I also remember reading about his lectures about the science of criminology. His theory had the upper classes howling mad when he suggested that they could possibly become deviant criminals if they were not brought up properly. "Social Victimology," he called his idea.

The three of us are keen to see the torture tower. Hanes, like so many before him, expresses an almost morbid curiosity about the history of the towers—a history so sinister that only in fiction can one find relief from sadistic reality. Sadly, the towers' story is true. Humanity is not immune to the demonic expression of a cruel and human soul.

No history of the towers would be complete without a visit to the Iron Virgin, the main attraction here. The Iron Virgin is the lure and its role as the gruesome avenger and demonic source of painful pleasure. This instrument of evil is housed in the deep recesses of the torture tower.

For centuries, the tradition of the Iron Virgin of Nurnberg has been handed down as an example of the horrors and cruelty of which mankind is capable. The fact that a woman to enhance her own sick desire for sadistic pleasure invented it makes it even more horrible.

While I find this perspective enlightening, we grow weary from the long walk. We are energized and awestruck at the same time when we finally enter the towers. They beckon entry to us in a cold stone awakening to its unrelenting pain, a pain housed for the ages as the towers engulf us in their shadow of human misery.

Unimpressed, Irving wants to go to lunch. I, for one, am captivated, as I can feel centuries of somber images engulf me in a cold shiver, leaving my soul chilled and numb. My mind replays the tortures of lost souls enraptured by the towers' cruel ironies. I proceed haltingly down the corridors of blood, all of it etched painfully in my mind.

The torture tower is truly a grim place. Even now, when many visitors have infused a stream of life into this place, all joy evaporates, and only the gruesome aspects remain. The dust of ages has settled here, the darkness and the horror of its memories become the sediment of its very spirit.

The lower chamber is filled with incarnate darkness, and the sunlight streaming in through the door is lost in the vast thickness of the walls. The beating light of sunshine cannot penetrate the wall's coldhearted darkness.

If walls could speak, what tales of fear and terror would purse their ugly lips? What frantic cry for help would escape from these painful indignities? People died horrible deaths here as the walls bore witness to their final moments.

Behold the pain these walls have seen so clearly in the light of contemplation.

The central object of this chamber of horrors is a torture engine known as the Iron Virgin. It is a rudely shaped figure of a woman, something of a bell, yet lacking that sliminess of waist and perfect roundness of hip that marks the aesthetic purity of a feminine figure.

One would hardly have recognized it as intended for a human figure at all had not the founder shaped on the forehead a rude semblance of woman's face.

Its deadly purpose, inflicting pain seduced by this feline wile, came by way of a rope fastened to a ring in the front of the figure and then drawn through a pulley fastened on a wooden pillar. The pace of this pull dictates the harmony of the pain inflicted, piercing, on demand, vital organs. The measurements of pain rest solely at the pleasure of the cruel hands at the end of the rope—the hands of Countess Elizabeth Bathory.

She would close the shapely wooden door upon her victim. The evil fingernails of destruction, spikes positioned to pierce the eyes and limbs, would elicit screams of agony, while Elizabeth watched with sickening glee.

Of course, Sir Henry is not moved. Too much like his wife Francis Terry taunting him when she's angry, and just like the Countess they both have a point he sniffs.

Von Hanes relates some interesting details related to the inventor of the Iron Virgin, the infamous Blood Countess Elizabeth Bathory.

"The Iron Virgin was used by the Transylvanian countess to torture her female servants. She bathed in their blood, believing it to be an elixir of eternal youth. She would later progress to the bathing in the blood of innocent children and was deluded that by soaking in their youthful blood, she could reverse her own aging.

"This blood lust also titillated a sexual proclivity in her," Hanes says. "She reveled in the inflicting of pain. She quivered with delight while drawing a sadistic sexual pleasure by watching her victims struggle in agony. She devised various forms of torture to satiate a cruel blood lust.

"She is a perfect example of my Social Victomology concept. So-called superior social breeding does do not insure normal behavior.

"The rich and powerful are not immune to violent and sadistic tendencies that can lead to murder, violence and savage crimes of passion. The exact opposite. The aristocracy is just as likely, if not more so, to breed violent sons and daughters capable of horrific deeds.

"Deviant crimes are not about the size of a nose or the color of skin. The road to barbarous behavior comes from the subjection of the person to abnormal learning brought on by an environment seeped in cruelty.

"These monsters become so because they are inadvertently exposed to abnormal life circumstances that can lead to violent and unacceptable behavior.

"Countess Elizabeth Bathory was just one of many that occupy a long list of murderers and sadists who have been labeled vampires or Devil's disciples by Transylvanian and Germanic folklore.

"In reality, she was nothing more than a sexual deviant, a robustly evil personality driven by a sadistic cruelty. She would reach a heightened sexual ecstasy at the sight of blood and pain. While only pain and death sated her unnatural lust, she was not alone in rolls of European nobility in her excesses. Such was her inventiveness that she was held in such terrifying awe.

"The sheer volume of macabre and frightening endeavors that made her contemporaries gasp is what transcribes her evil genius. Even those of her bloodline, who also valued life so cheaply, were shocked by her excesses.

"An historical family portrait of violent and antisocial behavior was influenced by her cruel upbringing and decadent way of life. Abject cruelty and entitlement ran rampant in her family lineage. While this was also true of many of the European nobility, her upbringing alone did not create an unstable mind, but it certainly encouraged it.

"An arousal of sexual appetites, aided by this sense of privilege, helped her to accept the rational that she could do these unnatural and evil acts unencumbered and without retribution.

She felt that her rank and privilege allowed her to sexually assault victims she thought to be beneath her. She toyed with those poor children as she stoked their hair and drove objects of pain and humiliation deep into their bodies. She rejoiced in a sickening display of lust and unnatural sexual gratification as she shuttered with orgasmic joy. Those around her remained silent. They had been conditioned to turn the other way because they feared her rank, and even more so, her possible retribution.

"Finally, when the overwhelming evidence was too much to deny, these transgressions were used by her rivals to take away her fortune and the mayhem finally stopped. Not because they condemned her acts. The servant class had long been a cruel sexual playground for those who shared her linage. They brought her down because of their own greed. They wanted her wealth, not justice. She spent her last days walled inside her room with only a small opening allowed for food to be administered.

"The Iron Virgin is only one of the charming contraptions housed in these towers. There are also devices that were used by the old Nurnberg police.

"There are other torture tools housed here and they were a staple of psychological criminal investigation during medieval times. Confess or make your way down to the bowels of this living hell. The mere thought of what lay in wait produced a confession as readily as the use of any device.

"The police introduced a psychological torture that was almost as cruel as the breaking of skin and bone. They utilized a practice of humiliation and depravation to break down the will of suspect. How many innocent men and women entered these towers guiltless and then left guilty? Probably not as many as you might think, but one at all is one too many.

"We are magnificent in our ability to be crueler in seeking justice than we are inflicting cruelty caused by crime."

Later, we sat down with Von Hanes at a café in the village.

Of course, I indulged my passion for strudel. It was an almond variety. The crust was just magnificent!

Irving jealously inquired of Von Hanes how he was able to wiggle an invitation to the archduke's hunting party.

Hanes explained that it had happened during a serendipitous meeting with the Archduke Alexis in New York, where Hanes was completing a short lecture tour on his theory of Social Victomolgy.

They had met years before when Dr. Hanes had traveled east to assist in an outbreak of cholera near Kiev and had developed a lasting friendship. After having dinner together, the archduke, who was still marveling at his grand time with the cowboys and Indians, took Hanes to see a Wild West show authored by Ned Buntline, a dime novel writer. The show itself was quite entertaining and they enjoyed watching and then meeting William Cody, also known as Buffalo Bill.

Cody, ever the showman, proposed that he would one day like to come to Russia to stage a Wild West show. Alexis offered to invite Cody to hunt Siberian bears with him, but Cody declined. The archduke then mentioned that he was planning to reunite with members of his various hunting parties to go on a master hunt in Russia and other parts of Eastern Europe. The archduke plans to spare no expense and make arrangements for all those invited.

While backstage at the show, they had happened to meet Mathewson and Gray Shadow, who were both in New York to visit Cody. They also knew the archduke well, both having participated in some of his hunting parties. Of course, when Alexis tendered an invitation they both readily accepted.

At Cody's introduction, Hanes had an opportunity to meet William Mathewson and he took an immediate liking to him. A friendship was born that day.

Cody graciously announced that Mathewson was the best buffalo hunter and Indian scout he had ever known. Mathewson was so named "Buffalo Bill" for his prowess at killing buffalo. Legend has it that Mathewson could track and kill an entire buffalo herd in a single day. Cody joked that Mathewson could do it with a single shot. Regardless, William Mathewson was renowned for this skill throughout the West and to his fellow hunters he was and would always be the "Real Buffalo Bill." Even to Cody.

According to Hanes, Ned Buntline transferred the nickname to William Cody when he began to write Cody's biography. Mathewson didn't seem to mind, especially because he already had a slew of nicknames. He was quite attached to his Ghost Hunter name, apparently.

William Cody, who was fulfilling his contract with Ned Buntline at that time and was planning on staring in his own production, was trying to get Mathewson and Gray Shadow to join his Wild West show.

Mathewson and Cody, along with Wild Bill Hitchcock, had all sojourned with the Archduke Alexis on his much-publicized hunting party.

Matheson was also his guide on another excursion far from the eyes of a prying international press. This one was shorter and much quieter. The archduke wished to do some additional hunting. Mathewson and Gray Shadow had also arranged for Alexis to meet several Indian chiefs. The archduke was apparently very impressed with the two and had been thrilled to meet Chief Oruay. Mathewson is very well known and respected by the Indians, it seems.

Gray Shadow is what is known as a shaman or medicine man of the Ute tribe. Shamans are religious practitioners who can diagnose and cure illness. Sometimes they cause illness and are men to be feared. Most of all they drive away evil sprits. They are said to have a special relationship with the supernatural and are capable of controlling spirits. Much like the witch doctors of Africa and the wizards of Asia, the American Indian shaman enjoys prestige and power among the tribe. This ability would certainly be of enormous interest to someone like Hanes.

It is clearly evident that Hanes has developed a great respect and affection for Gray Shadow and Mathewson. Most apparent in the way he speaks about them.

According to Hanes, they are of that breed, brave and honest in character that separates them from but a select few. They are true knights of their domain.

To his great excitement, Hanes was invited to join them as well. Now, after almost two years of planning, Hanes was on his way to meet with his American friends and travel with them to the agreed destination.

We inquired of Hanes if he had ever met our Count Lonvay. Unfortunately, he knew only the more well known cousin and that was but a one-time introduction.

That having been said, he did verify that in most circles the Lonvay fortune was considered genuine, so we certainly appear to be on the right track.

After a delightful conversation, we wished Hanes well and will look for him in the future.

An interesting man.

Update: Change in plans

The count has requested we come to Vienna and has arranged passage and accommodations.

Irving seems weary. He's looking forward to meeting the count and he has high hopes that the British royal family will be a major source of investment for the Lyceum.

But Irving has burned too many bridges in London to safely count on support from other venues to relieve the financial stress, so we are eager to find new wells. If we succeed, that will make this godforsaken trip worthwhile.

Posted a letter to my wife and I hope she has forgiven me this trip.

After two years of marriage, this is our first separation. She has not acknowledged me once in post and I fear a cold reaction upon coming home. I do miss her beauty. To think that she chose to marry me over Oscar Wilde. My reliability can't be the only reason, can it?

I wonder if anyone even knows I'm gone.

How I miss Noel. He is only a year old and I fear he may not even know me when I return.

Irving slipped out of England in the dead of night to avoid his creditors and has kept our escape a secret.

Left Munich at eight thirty five p.m., arriving at Vienna early next morning. Should have arrived at six forty six, but train an hour late. This was a good thing, as Irving had a dalliance with a young actress and we barely had time to pack our bags.

When we started our journey, the sun was shining brightly in Munich. The weather in Vienna is dark and cold.

A curious thing: just as we were about to depart, Ludwig Delbruck, the maitre d'hotel of the Quatre Saisons where we had just stayed, came down to the carriage and after wishing us a pleasant journey said, "The sky looks bright, but there is a shiver in the north wind. I feel a cold wind come over you, so beware of what you do. Be not late at night this week, for there are strange goings on in this darkness. I can only warn you of danger and only you will know what it is. It will come from blackest night, so be not late this night."

"Tell us what is this night we must not be late for, Ludwig," scoffed Irving.

Delbruck crossed himself and answered: "Walpurgis Nacht."

With this, Irving took out his watch, a great old-fashioned German silver thing as big as a turnip, and while his eyebrows gathered, he shrugged and said, "I'm sure, Stoker, we will be late. Walpurgis Nacht to you, Ludwig, and to all a good night."

Chapter 6

We have arrived in this most glorious of cities, the beautiful and historic Vienna.

While everyone always marvels at the pastries of Paris, I, for one, cannot wait to indulge my passion for the strudel. German baked, indeed, but with that Hapsburg twist. I find the rich flavored layers of fruit are what separate these Teutonic desserts from the soft and powdery Parisian pastries. Of course, I would never turn down a Napoleon, especially whenever his namesake is sitting on the French powder keg.

The count telegraphed that we must continue to his home in Budapest. We are very disappointed in this news; we debate whether we should go on. But we need the money, so we will go on. Short additional journey, but assured again by the count that money would be at hand. We are hopeful and expectant. Irving is making noises like he wants to see the count alone. I did not come all this way for absolutely nothing.

Leaving tonight, as Irving is quite optimistic that this journey will bear fruit.

As we sit on the train and I watch this world change before me, I think back to the days four years ago when Henry and I became friends. I never thought that my review would touch him so deeply.

The rhythmic sounds of the wheeling motion of steel moving powerfully forward on these tracks of such mysterious and historic design is having a hypnotizing effect on me. Spellbound to the thumping music of the rails, I transfix my ears to the sounds of the Orient Express. We move swiftly and in sequence, mesmerized by the dancing majesty parading before our windows.

I see a reflection of days past in the mirrored glass of my subconscious. The image in my mind's eye is one of gratification. I feel content at last.

As I think through this all, I realize that Henry Irving is the most important person in my life, more important to me, literally, than Florence and Noel.

Our two souls have looked beyond each other and through that looking glass we have connected full measure in what we both seek—a rapt affinity for that lightning in a bottle we call theater.

The play's the thing, and Irving and I believe in that, too. For Henry Irving and Bram Stoker, the theater is indeed our lifeblood.

Spellbound in my railroad trance, I can hear his voice delicious in its tone. I'll always cherish the memory of the night he read Hood's *The Dream of Eugene Arum.*

It's an experience I'll never forget, such was Irving's commanding force.

So great the magnetism of his genius, his dominance so profound, I was at once captivated and rendered speechless.

Outwardly, I was of stone, frozen by the sheer will of his incarnate power, incarnate passion. I remember my stone countenance crumbling to hysterics upon his finish.

Bewildered by my lack of strength, I found myself yielding to a superior force and bending emotionally to his will. I've never seen such warmth in a man's face as the affection shown by Irving toward me that night.

The sense of gratitude of our connection forever bound that night by the photograph he gave me. His words scrawled joyfully upon its bottom: *God bless you, Stoker. Bless you.*

Budapest

Have arrived in Budapest after crossing the Danube. The beginning of two great worlds in conflict as the old city Buda sits on one side of the Danube and the new city of Pest sits on the other bank. So much is mirrored in the storied conflicts of two great cultures that represent such different values, the Muslims from the east and the Christians from the west. I see the traditions emerging of Turkish rule clashing with Western sensibilities.

This dichotomy of the East and the West are views widely shared and widely rejected. The changing patterns of Western civilization and Eastern mysticism are still interlocking. Distrust reigns in their interpretive cultures—cultures that are at once suspect to each other's motives. The fusion of the fertile mind can still cling to an individual adherence to past teachings. The reliance of one truth being the only truth is based solely on their own traditional values. They mistrust the future because it always seems to resemble the past.

This is a gateway to divergent thoughts and beliefs geared more to a sense of dominance of one culture over another, but justly influenced by a world that always changes its position. Somehow, these changes are prone to the weakness of an unseen power that ebbs and flows with the holy might of each new conquest.

This is the challenge facing the region now—the challenge of a growing sense of nationalism. Of a young and complex nation that is frantically searching for a collective personality.

To the east is Romania, the land of lost dreams. Old at heart, yet newly birthed as a national entity, this fledgling nation is even more diverse. A complex mixture of Germans, Hungarians and Muslims, they are forged by the eternal fire of the Roman Empire.

Roman by name and by early design, Romania will not easily extinguish the tribal differences forged by many lifetimes. A cultural melting pot of ethnicity and conflicting religions all served by the spoon of a nationality rising to the top.

I remember reading with interest about the formation of Romania. All of Europe watched with rapt attention. The product of European skullduggery, the principalities of Moldavia, Bukovina and Walllacia were merged. Only promise remains.

What then of Hungary and its German influence? Did they just fade away with time? What is to become of the Slovak adherence?

I inspect this congregation of national personalities with great interest. How will this confluence of regions honor thy neighbors?

Then again, as I study Budapest I see the outcome of just such unions as cultures brace themselves to such inspection.

As I travel through the streets of these wonderful sister cities, I am quite taken with the mosques that coexist within these narrow avenues. An ultimate melting pot of diversity, how much blood and tears have been spilled to make it so?

Budapest is a wonderful place.

The largest town in the kingdom of Hungary, it is one hundred sixty-three miles from Vienna. The two towns of Buda and Pest sit on either side of the Danube and were incorporated into one municipality in 1872. The city lies at the point where the Danube takes a decidedly southward course. To the north are the imposing Bakony Alps as they converge with the Carpathian Mountains. We crossed the Ketten-Brucke Bridge and reached the ancient town of Buda. The town rests among a series of small, steep hills, commanded by the fortress Blocksberg. The hills are filled with luscious vineyards, which I hear produced a full bodied and rich red wine.

Yet when I look east towards the mountain ranges I can sense something different, an ominous sense of superstition and fear. A fear fueled by an unwavering acceptance of something evil. The winds blow so much colder in those mountains. The people living there have lived in the misery of hateful days and nights. They were victims of cruel hands and even crueler spirits. Ghosts of haunting visions, werewolf's and monsters lingering dangerously outside their doors just waiting for the opportunity to spirit some lonely child or unprotected villager away to face a horrific death. A sense of foreboding overcomes me now. I somehow feel I will be in those mountains soon. I feel dread and I feel lost. I cannot explain these feelings.

Irving

Another exchange with Henry. He feels I should wait at the hotel while he visits the count's country estate. He's convinced that it will be the romance of the theater and not the appearance of a business arrangement that will entice an investment from the count. I am to be sent home or I must await his return. As usual, Irving wants to do this himself.

Why did he even bother to bring me then? To carry his bags!

In these types of financial matters he is ignorant of the details, but is robust in the asking. The great gift of communication is the key to our support. Image will out. Irving will command the investment through the sheer will of his presentation.

In substance, he alone will not be refused. Such is the persuasiveness of a genius unleashed upon an unsuspecting quarry.

If the general manager of the Lyceum theater is along with him, it's a transaction. A visit by the great Henry Irving is a coronation.

At least that is how he looks at it.

We are at it again, for Irving refuses to acknowledge my disappointment. But he did call me a genius again. A genius for failure.

The American tour idea is wonderful, yet I have my doubts that people who read little English literature will gain much from Shakespeare. That having been said, an American road company still seems a credible venture.

Look to try in a season or two despite travel logistics of up to one hundred in company,

I lean toward assembling casts as we go. Irving wants his players.

We agree on not shipping the scenery.

We will commission props and scenery wherever we go.

The one-man show idea will not happen again for us on tour. We will need the tapestry of a full production to entertain the learning masses. They will embrace the pageantry of the plays. The colors of costumes and staging rich in voice and texture should soothe even the most savage beasts.

We have spent a great deal of time considering a tour of the colonies and how to do it. Because this has never been done before, the task at this time seems both formidable yet highly feasible.

Irving grows tired of basking in his glory without the minions paraded before him.

He seeks the challenge of a full play, yet all by himself he is brilliant. It is the cadence of his words—richly stated in deep hypnotic tones.

While the Americans won't understand the words of Shakespeare, they will still devour the trappings of the language. I'm always amazed that the audience sits transfixed by the overwhelming spectacle of Sir Henry's performances. He is vested royal in his presence and his presentation. What is that makes Irving such a great actor?

They fear the sacred monster of his ego. Such is his command, the dual creatures of good and evil can be manipulated to his will. Deep pain resonates from the depths of his character's dying soul, leaving his audience awash in fear and pity. They are never quite sure when the character finally achieves redemption, but ultimately they delight in the puppet master's skill as he manipulates their emotions.

As the Irving character fights the turbulence of its dueling will, Henry Irving is bending word sonnets so grandly that those spoken words are swirling fluently into an eager acceptance. Arrows of his heart are pitched forward in the search of the listener's soul. Once captured, the audience vainly searches for the good and the evil within their own personal existence. They are his obedient slaves now. His genius has gained control of them.

Then he is gone, leaving an empty stage upon which their cheers roar like thunder. All at once, he materializes again in the full flower of the great actor taking his final bow.

There is no doubt that he is a star beyond all measure.

It is only on a scale of his personality that one feels his overweight.

We have been traveling at a slow pace as the weather has been more fall-like and rainy than we had anticipated. The trip from Vienna was laborious.

We packed up and went to the hotel to check in after the last train. They tell us that trains to the east are not very reliable. We have planned our itinerary and now we must await the information about the meeting.

I am already homesick and my mind races with possibilities. I can imagine a day when even the Italians will run their trains on time. Irving jokes that Nostradamus predicted such a momentous occurrence.

We'll be soon heading back to England. How much I long for it. To see my family and to bask in the sun—every third day or so. Ah, England.

Irving

Irving is still insisting that he should meet with the count alone. He can be so boorish. He recommends that I see the city or plan the season. Either way, it's going to be an Irving production for now. He says I should be thinking about the problems we face.

We have two months before the upcoming Lyceum season and we have a lot to do—scenery to order and costumes to be fitted. I think having a cast in place will help, too.

We cast next month for new blood. Irving wants to keep the current troupe in place, but is reluctant to cover such a cost. An increase in their wages will drip him dry, he rants.

He expects me to negotiate down the wages and regroup old cast members as quickly as possible. This is always a nasty business.

If they have no other options, I will be fine. If not, woe is the wrath of Henry Irving. We must do his bidding.

Diary notes

I have been perusing historical material in the English embassy. From the train I had gotten the sense that we were leaving the West and entering the East. Now, as I visit this ancient world of Budapest, I can see it all so clearly. History here is rich like a fine wine. I am drinking in the aroma of centuries of fruition.

The most western of splendid bridges over the Danube, which is here of noble width and depth, took us among traditions of Turkish rule. This historic city speaks volumes of the continuing struggle of man against mankind. The steps stand before me as a ladder climbing from an uncertain past. This is a land of confused values and this is a city that reflects the influences of each of the cultures that have arisen from it.

In this world of righteous conquest, the emperor of Rome once ruled this subservient city. Until the Goths and other peoples swept away the empire in a desperate flight from the Huns, the city was referred to as AK Ink, meaning spring rich water. The Hungarians appeared around the end of the ninth century and, recognizing the strategic location, established their prince here and called the place Pest.

The second city of Obuda was the seat of royalty in the thirteenth century.

The Western civilization of Pest also began at that time as the bourgeois of the German-Hungarian population expanded.

After the Tartar invasion, a walled city was built on Castle Hill situated on the other side of the Danube, a site that could be easily defended. This third city was called Buda and drew its growing population from the Hungarian towns.

The Turks occupied the Buda and Pest for one hundred fifty years until the end of the seventeenth century when the population was liberated. Never truly overcoming that domination, the two cities look eastward with a trepidation that remains to this day.

The cities were united to form Budapest in 1867, and with it a Hungarian struggle for independence and modernization. The national insurrection against the Hapsburgs began in the Hungarian capital, although it was quickly defeated. In 1867, the Hapsburgs reached a compromise with the nobility, and Hungary was named an equal to Austria within the empire. This made a city of Buda and Pest, the twin capital of a dual monarchy. There still exists a double identity within this city and within this land, so many different cultures amalgamated together in their common histories.

This land has always been much sought after prize by the Turks. The inhabitants have been branded by that knowledge from generation to generation. Even as East and West have been assimilated into this unique culture, the continuing threat of the infidel or the crushing saga of a Jihad remains the city's most basic fear.

This country is at once a mosaic of beliefs rich in convergence of ideals. The tide of its history cascades back and forth like waves of fury, ebbing and flowing with the sea of time. The shores of destiny are navigated by the might of a sacred sword. Each blow is struck for the glory of a different god.

This is the prize for an endowment of diverse ideals.

Such is the confusion of this land to the east.

Irving

Irving jokes that if he gave up ego for Lent, he'd go to Hell.

I've started drinking again to calm my nerves, a practice that is frowned upon by Irving and upsets him. But I cannot seem to find any other way to help me sleep. The loneliness is always there for both of us and it makes this a difficult journey. I keep having these terrible dreams. They seem to be getting worst as we move further east. I also cannot escape this gnawing fear. I become overcome with anxiety and become paralyzed of all thought by some deep seated trepidation.

Irving is not as amusing as usual and can be quite moody when we are together. Sometimes, he does not speak to me for hours; other times he is Irving in all his grandeur. Something is happening to him as well. He has not been happy here in this city. He has been acting strangely to some correspondence he has been receiving, but he will not share them with me. I'll be drinking more I suppose.

Dinner with Irving

The atmosphere is loud and smoky as dialogue swirls over and around us. The clicking of glasses, the murmurs of conversation and the pungent smells of tobacco fill the dining room of the tavern with a geniality of human life. I manage to get quick glimpse of the native dishes, all blessed with colorful spices that are aromatically wonderful in an unfamiliar way.

I've tuned out Irving as he bombards me again about his life lessons. At times he can be overbearing. His acceptance of his own importance defines him. The towering citadel of his ego is such that he dominates even his own conversation. Other times he can be quite insightful and funny, but his own contempt of any perceived weakness of character clouds his judgment of his fellow men.

The lessons he wishes to impart are lessons learned by one who was born with great gifts and does not struggle with a lack of talent. He equates this talent solely to his own hard work, which has always been impressive. He does not fathom that such a talent is not universal and he cannot seem to bring himself to forgive the weakness of those who were not born with it. The rationale that skill is only a barometer of the effort holds little meaning to most of us. It is wasted on those pedestrian actors who work just as hard at it, but lack the grace of Irving's talent.

On the other hand, Irving pretends ignorance or lack of interest in the more mundane aspects of theatrical production and treats such things as prosaic and thus beneath him. However, this does not preclude him from voicing opinions on such matters. He is all too willing to dismiss inertia as mere incompetence. Of course, he would have done it the right way if he only had the time!

Of course, Henry, of course, if you only had the time. And one day you'll even learn to lick your own stamp!

When one becomes great at something, why do they insist they are great at all? I must say that life seems easy for those few blessed with it. Unfortunately, most of us are just blessed with the mediocrity of our existence. Rejoice in the common man, I say. We are the miracles of God's green earth. We are in our numbers the worker ants, who by the will of our own determination make it possible for the hill to be built. The gifted would not be celebrated if it were not for us and our labor and our toil. Better still, we have the perseverance to accomplish those important details every bit as daunting as remembering the cadence of a Shakespearean sonnet. Most of the time, it is only by the flicker of candlelight that we are allowed to bow in our own spotlight. One man may draw a pyramid, but a thousand men must lay down the stone.

Despite this occasionally and annoying forbiddance, Henry Irving can also be a wonderfully giving and compassionate man. Still, he is frugal with his praise and as his custom he only grudgingly compliments my work during our most recent season. However, he is now calling it our theater, so that brings me great joy.

All of the stress seems to melt away upon his approval. The rewards seem so much sweeter. Four long years together and now he finally says "our theater."

Henry Irving has gone as far as his ego will allow him to acknowledge my contribution.

As we were just about to finish dinner, we recognize Von Hanes entering the dinning room. His dignified manner simply cannot hide a sense of fear that seems to swirl about him. He has a look of uncertainty, weathered by a forlorn expression.

He appears so different from the last time we saw him. The coolness has melted away to reveal a layer of ambiguity. The thoughts of a thousand worries seem to be lining his face.

He is a paradox, both preoccupied yet alert, with a world-weariness that belies his fit disposition. He is not the energetic icon we had met in Nurnberg. He joined us almost as surprised to see us as we were to see him.

Something of great importance had dissipated the abject joy he had when last we met. Always a gentleman, he greeted us warmly, but with a distance not related to any dislike of our company, just a burden of an unspoken gesture or frustration.

He inquired of our journey and we asked about the strange turn of events that had brought him to Budapest. Before Hanes could even answer, Irving began by continuing his conversation about himself.

I felt a bit sorry for Hanes as he appears a little glazed over by Irving's domination of the conversation. Still, he sat quietly and gracefully listened to our talk. Whatever had preoccupied his thoughts before had been washed away by Henry Irving's monologue.

While clearly relieved to be among friends, Hanes at times feigned interest in what Irving was saying about life. When Irving finally talked about the upcoming season and why we are here in Budapest, Hanes perked up with keen interest. Everyone in Europe knew that we at the Lyceum Theater were on the verge of a major success. Such was the growing respect for Henry's immense talent.

Irving was quite confident of the future and of the inevitable triumph of the Lyceum. In both word and deed he was excitingly looking forward to the coming seasons. He waxed poetically as he prepared the world for his Hamlets to come. He also mentioned the possibility of new works being staged. He was quite taken by a young writer called George Bernard Shaw. We recently put Shaw under contract to write a play for us. Irving does warn that Shaw's humor might be a little sarcastic for the stage, but we anxiously awaiting the results of his first work.

Hanes finally made an attempt to bring me into the conversation by inquiring about my writing. He did this while Irving took a breath. Irving was not quite stage left yet, however, and before I could respond, he began to speak for me.

He takes great pleasure in both praising and slyly deriding my attempts at writing. He is both proud and a little fearful of my possible talent. Such is his love for me that he does not want to lose me.

Irving recounted articles written by me going back to *Shamrock* magazine. Writing them was a labor of love. It had to be for love, for they never paid me. He also mentioned my book, *The Duties of Clerks of Petty Sessions*.

Politely, Dr. Hanes feigned some recognition. Then he confessed that he has not read my nonfiction book.

Dr. Hanes did allow that he had read a few of my London articles about Shakespeare. I couldn't tell by his expression whether he liked them or not.

I'm really not surprised that Dr. Hanes had not read the book. I'm not even surprised that he had never even heard of it. No one has heard of *The Duties of Clerks of Petty Sessions* outside of Ireland. Then again, based on the book sales, most petty clerks in Ireland didn't read the book, either.

Hanes, while pretending to be impressed, had no clue about my subject matter. At one point, he assumed the book was about manners and he joked that he didn't always use the proper fork. Sensing an opening, Irving jumped in and relayed some the plots of my other writing. Crowing like a proud father, he exalted my short stories and other articles with his usual embellishments—meant to be entertaining. Unfortunately, the theatricality made us humorously uncomfortable.

"Bizarre short stories and failed attempts at comedy. That is the literary world of my dear friend Stoker. He has, however, been the author of many marvelous short stories. Whoever can forget that searing melodrama 'The Crystal Cups?'" Irving said, his eyes twinkling with delight.

"As a theater critic, Bram Stoker has few equals. I must say that his glowing review of my performance was one of the most insightful reviews about me that I have ever read. With a talent like that, can anyone doubt that he will indeed be a serious writer?"

With comic effect, he said with an almost sardonic wink, "And as for his comedy, Hanes, it is more frightening than his horror stories. One day, one hundred years in the future, when they mention his name they will say, Bram Stoker! Now, he was not a humorous man."

Hanes seemed to enjoy this little show on my behalf.

As is his way, Irving next warmly praised my almost completed new work, *Under the Sunset*, even though he thinks it won't sell. Then he touchingly praised my credentials for serious writing and offered up some of the better newspaper articles that I've written over the years.

Hanes asked of my newspaper days and other experiences not related to the theater and I gave a quick overview of my background as a publisher in Ireland. He seemed impressed by my intention is to publish *Under the Sunset* and was most interested when I termed the exercise a collection of allegorical fairy tales.

He was especially intrigued when I told him I was incorporating the literary motifs of good over evil, of morality's victories over sin, as the recurring thread. This remark elicited a great deal of conversation and I discovered that the good doctor was much interested in the continuing search for those very answers.

I listened intently as he spoke, all the while drawing these impressions of him.

I could sense immediately that the fascination with the forces of good and evil ran deep within him. I've seen it in only a few others and they were very much like Dr. Hanes. He is, I think, a man who is at his best in the worst of times.

Although he is deep-rooted in the sterile environment of a clear science, he still maintains an almost reverent approach to the occult. The alluring possibility of the unknown is what draws him to the flame of continuing knowledge. Only ignorance is the bane of an enlightened mankind. I could learn a lot from this man.

Hanes has made it his life's work to go beyond the constricting borders of exact science and to reach past prejudices born of myopic fear. It is in the mystical world of folklore that rests the future of modern science. There is a true reality to its purpose, a purpose only lacking an explanation.

These are the views I'm most familiar within recollection of his teachings. They fit so perfectly within my own beliefs, however humble, on the future of science and mankind.

One day there will be a scientific and rational explanation for the potions and medicines that seemed to work for those ancient occult cultures. Just by saying that, Hanes has been labeled a charlatan by the uninspired doctrines of his so-called colleagues. How shortsighted.

Dr. Hanes fascinates us with folk tales related to this region, a world rooted deeply in the fabric of the unexplained.

"This is a land of werewolves and vampires," he says. "Legends are born by a distrust of the night by those uneducated to the reality of human behavior. It is in this way that these people substitute a myth or a legend for a rational response to the unknown.

"Human predators cannot assimilate the truth of human cruelty beyond the intended purpose of their own design. They leave it to others to deal with the aftermath and to judge it as historical poetry. These human predators have only their own ends in mind. Cruelty has severed their beliefs in an uncompromising evil purpose as they logically accept the mandate of such behavior. By such a birthright, they believe that all they do is justified by destiny's rationale.

"The victims may have another view entirely. They identify such cruelty as an act of an unnatural demonology—the Devil's work. No one is right to think this way, but they do. Truth is truly stranger than fiction in this dark world."

The conversation took a different tone when Irving brought up London and gently prodded Hanes about his "voodoo arts"' and how it was the talk of the town.

Hanes' views raised havoc when presented to the British Medical Society and was scoffed at by Scotland Yard. Regardless of the skepticism he received, Hanes believes his vision will become a staple of modern crime solving. Despite all these doubts, Dr. Hanes claims that the layers of skepticism are peeling away.

He even believes his embracing of the black arts, the occult factor as one skeptic dubbed it, will become accepted. I challenged that I sensed his view on the validity of the occult was going to be a much longer process than he imagined. This, he admitted, was an explosive issue, but he still had faith in the chemistry of these mythical potions. With proper study, they will be revealed to be just that—simple chemistry, he said.

In regards to the study of the human mind, he felt that he was no longer alone in his beliefs of legitimacy of the science of the mind. More and more of today's scientists are beginning to understand his concept of victim sociology, he said, meaning that the forces of environment create a canvas for abnormal behaviors.

Throughout Germany and France, there are like-minded scientists who believe in similar ideals. They are the enlightened scientists whom Hanes says have ventured even further than he and would surely surpass him in stature. These are dedicated men committed to mapping the power of the mind. They will clearly be the wave of the future, he says.

He talked at length about his recent visit with Ernst Brucke, the head of the Psychological Institute at the University of Vienna. While Brucke favors a concept, he calls "mechanism," the theory that physics and chemistry can explain all vital processes—not biology or religion. His is a well-thought out archetype that parallels many of Hanes' own theories. Hanes also raved about a cadre of young doctors who were highly intelligent and inquisitive. Unlike the dusty environment of most medical training schools, the school of medicine at Vienna is highly charged. Greatness and great things will be achieved there and Brucke is to be commended, Hanes said.

Hanes was especially impressed with Josef Breurer, a young Austrian doctor working there with Brucke. He is a man whose views are similar to Hanes'. In fact, Breurer's theories have moved past Hanes' and that has encouraged Hanes to continue to monitor his own less scientific studies. Hanes believes this young doctor will be responsible for breathtaking research into the discipline of the human mind. Breurer, like Dr. Hanes, believes that the mind plays a much greater role in the theater of life than is now currently understood.

Studying the concept of hypnosis with Brucke, Breurer is developing a theory that he refers to as psychoanalysis. While Hanes is interested in the mean causes of abnormal behavior, Breurer's studies attempt to chart an even more complex course: Precise and intricate mapping of human behavior as a clinical scientific guide and referenced as a purely medical practice.

Breurer contends that neuroses arise from an unconscious process and cause neurotic symptoms. These symptoms can be made to disappear when the underlying causes become a part of the conscious mind. This is very much in line with Hanes' theory of Social Victomolgy, but it relates to a more detailed form of behavior. Breurer proposes that ordinary people, not just violent individuals, have quirks associated with root causes, influencing the status of their mental health.

I joke that in essence Breurer has found the cure for Hanes' cause.

Luckily, Hanes found the humor in this and laughed heartily. He joked that God was still the highest authority on who was right.

After dinner, Dr. Hanes mentioned that he had just come from a visit with the legendary Arminius Vambery. Irving almost dropped his glass; I lost my breath for an instant. Hearing that name definitely got our attention.

Arminius Vambery is a world-renowned Orientalist who is also a professor at the University of Budapest. Professor Vambery is spoken of with reverence. His tales of intrigue and his breathtaking journeys into Asia Minor have held us spellbound. But no one has seen or heard from Vambery for about five years now and there are rumors that he had been killed in an adventure. So it was breathtaking news indeed to hear that he was still alive. Oddly, Vambery is one the most famous men in the world, yet he is one of the least well known.

Dr. Hanes told us he had come to Budapest at this time to see his old friend on a matter of utmost importance.

Arminius Vambery! I still can't believe it. He is a mystery inside the paradox of an enigma. The usual gossip of his whereabouts has thrived all these years, as have the rumors of his death. One report claimed that Vambery had been blinded by the Turks and was now living as a hermit in Palestine.

So now the Scorpion's Cross is finally making an appearance. The great Professor Arminius Vambery.

Just the mention of his name conjures up an image of a magical and mystical man—a gifted wanderer cloistered in some remote location and, clothed in native garb, gazing upon the magical world of the exotic and shadowy Asia Minor.

He is famous for his chronicling of the ways of the East, so that we in the West can understand it. He is also rumored to have been some sort of a spy, having supposedly warned the British of Russia's upcoming war plans. That allowed England to prepare a stern warning to avoid war.

Vambery is quite popular in England, the darling of the aristocratic society. Europeans have also been charmed and universally fascinated by this brave and daring adventurer. It was certainly Vambery's chameleon-like qualities that made his books so interesting. Disdaining all danger, he secretly joined Asian caravans in the guise of some local dervish and recorded the many interesting sights and sounds of the Muslim and Turkish cultures.

Arminius Vambery has taken us to places one can only imagine, worlds of mystery and passion. Unfurling the veil of secrecy for all of us to see, Vambery has brought the exotic to the reader.

Nestled warmly at home, we cozily enjoy his adventures from the safety of a comfortable couch. Together, we join Vambery as he takes us to another place far removed from the cobbled streets of urban life.

While Vambery is an expert in all things Turk, it's the mystery of those far off lands that most holds our attention. The intriguing question of how someone like Vambery could assimilate himself secretly into the Asian culture and not be detected adds a texture of color and danger to his stories. No one before him had ever been able to accomplish this, certainly no one heralding from Europe. His chameleon-like features and his ability to speak so many languages, while mimicking the movements and expressions of the natives, obviously helped. So, too, did his own courage, as he must have been in danger many times—danger that required him to use his wits. All of this makes for interesting storytelling.

So we embrace his journeys as our own. Protected by the immunity of adventure as we read his fascinating pages unfolding from the safe distance of our imagination. With Arminius Vambery as our guide, we seek those strange and provocative worlds. Joyously we celebrate his success and revel in his exciting dissertations of life among the Turks and other strange peoples.

Only my dear friend Richard Burton sparks such a brave and romantic aura of invincibility.

After a delicious cup of thick Turkish coffee, Dr. Hanes became comfortable enough with us to share some startling news. He is moving on to Bistria in the morning. The source of his concern is an urgent message he had just received from an old friend, a man named Brother Jacob.

Hanes then announced that he was no longer able to go on the planned hunting trip with Archduke Alexis. He had also been forced to abandon his rendezvous with his American friends because his summons had forced him to push eastward with the utmost urgency.

Something terrible had happened in Transylvania, something that required his immediate attention. He had hoped that Professor Vambery would join him on what he alluded to be a very dangerous mission. He was somewhat dismayed that Vambery stated he would not go, but he had also communicated the details to his American friends in the hope that they might accompany him. Hanes expressed the thought that they might heed his call instead of going on the hunting trip, but he was not at all certain of success. He stated he could use their skills.

I must say this sounded fascinating and stimulating. I pressed for more details.

Hanes was very secretive about what was occurring in Transylvania, but whatever it was, it must be something extraordinary, something of great importance that is forcing him to change his itinerary. No matter how hard I urged him, he would not divulge any details. He cautioned that this was the type of situation in which Vambery would be of great benefit and he was mystified by the professor's lack of commitment.

He mimicked Vambery: "When it is time, I'll be there. Look for me in the clouds." That is a quote from one of Vambery's books.

Hanes described Vambery as a great friend and a fellow scholar who happened to have mutual interests that lent credence to the issue at hand at the Borgo Pass. He would be one of only a few men in the world who would understand what had happened and know what needed to be done about it. They both had an abiding interest in the occult and shared a curiosity about its workings. The Hungarian professor also shared Hanes' fascination with Oriental folklore and the love of adventure. I tried vainly to understand what type of situation could possibly require Vambery's utmost attention.

I mentioned that I found it odd that an Orientalogist would be so necessary at the Borgo Pass in Transylvania. Hanes was silent. I pressed him, but he simply danced around my questioning.

So it is with a great deal of interest that I seek to know more about the relationship of these two remarkable men. I wish to join their club. I wish to seek out and share the danger with them. I can sense within myself a yearning to be part of such a journey. To spend time with Von Hanes and possibly someone like Vambery would open great new avenues for my future writings. I do envy their knowledge.

Their vast experiences seem so exotic and one can only imagine Vambery dressed in a sorcerer's coat, coaxing the moon and the stars to do his bidding. According to Hanes, that was why Vambery was so important to the journey. He would understand the spiritual significance of what was happening and then relate to those issues at hand with a human touch, He had the experience in providing rational explanation to what will be perceived as some dark force. Hanes already expected that they will instinctively brand whatever occurred as an occult episode and he needed Vambery's skill at communicating why it was not.

It had also been long rumored that Vambery was a knight of great importance to the world of secret societies. In this there must be some link to Hanes I suspect.

Vambery is more esoteric and far more ethereal in his approach to the question of human understanding. He holds the view of the enlightened. He is a believer in those dark corners of man's understanding that can never be explained and should only be accepted. This is not the view of a scientist. It's the wizard's way, no doubt. That is why he may be needed when chasing the ghosts of a not-so-subtle imagination—ghosts of imagination bringing havoc to the mountain villages of the Borgo Pass.

The reality of a mind blinded by an adherence to a mythical mathematical certainty is doomed to the fate of repetition. In this, it all adds up. With Vambery along, the angles would be covered. These issues seemed to be conflicting in Hanes and the conversation was most peculiar.

I asked one more time for details.

I said to Hanes that something did seem to be amiss and he took a long time to answer. It was if he were debating how much he should tell us. Clearly, something important was unfolding and I sensed that his anxiety was related to the situation. He seemed to want to tell us, to alleviate some heavy burden. He kept looking at Irving for some acknowledgment. Irving seemed conflicted as well. I could sense that I was the interloper in what both men had wanted to say to each other.

Very carefully, Hanes conceded that he was guarded about sharing information with us. He also expressed disappointment again for missing his American companions who had traveled great distances to join him. He wished he had more time.

Irving and Hanes then shared a look that I found very strange. With a simple nod of their heads I could tell that some form of communication had been exchanged.

"Its best if you tell us, Von" Irving offered gently

Finally, after much thought, he gave us a further inkling of what had caused this disruption. In the towns near the Carpathian Mountains and the Borgo Pass in eastern Romania, several baffling murders had taken place and he had received a request to investigate these strange occurrences. All the evidence pointed to demonic behavior, far removed from usual criminal conventions. Hanes had been asked to debunk the supernatural before it took root as an accepted fact among the villagers. His task was to help track down the villains who were skillfully using fear as a weapon to discourage capture. He did not feel he could do it alone. He will be leaving tomorrow with the utmost urgency and embark on this very dangerous mission.

Irving immediately jumped in. "If it's that dangerous, why don't you take Stoker here? You did say you could use some help. He would be more of a help then I could ever be"

I was immediately hopeful because I really had nothing to do for the next month—except wait for Irving. But I sensed right away that Von Hanes was not enthusiastic about me joining him.

He thanked us both for the offer, but implied that it was far too serious a situation to involve me in. Politely, Dr. Hanes bade us a warm goodbye. He had much to do before leaving at dawn.

Irving and I discussed once more his meeting with Count Lonvay. It was decided that he will make the journey alone. No amount of pleading could deter Henry once he gets a thought in his mind.

I expressed my disappointment at having traveled so far for nothing, but Irving as usual seemed to bend me to his will. I will remain in the Budapest area for a few weeks and then head back to England to set up the winter season. Irving expects to see me in London in about four weeks. He had granted me a vacation as a consolation.

Henry then began to flirt with our fetching waitress, who apparently aware of his stature, reciprocated. He got up to leave with her and counseled, "Our work is done here and I'm leaving for the count's estate in the morning. Of course, Stoker, I'll give the count your best. Go back to England, my old friend, and I'll be along shortly with the money and the Lyceum will live for another season. Enjoy the sights and stay out of trouble."

With that, he disappeared arm-in-arm with the young and seemingly eager young lady.

I have just finished my last entry in the diary. With my tremendous ability for recall, I must say that I should have been an actor. When I was a child and was once in a coma, I still managed to recall many things that I was not supposed to remember. This amazing capacity to grab pieces of life and record them in my conscious record is a gift that I gratefully accept from the Almighty.

As I write this all down, I once again yearn to be part of this adventure that Hanes is going on. I cannot sleep. I sit restlessly on my bed.

I realize suddenly that I *must* go with Hanes. How I might regret not making this journey. I can see many benefits, including the luxury of absorbing the color of this strange country.

Also, the chance to investigate such bizarre events with a world-renowned criminologist may be the very thing I've been looking for as a writer. I know that there are many great stories in me. But I've never grasped until now what I've been missing is the element of danger—a comb of fear electric coursing through my hair. I need to experience first hand what I have only read about.

It is adventure that is lacking in my life. My curiosity at the dark nature of mankind beckons me on. I thirst for a knowledge of human understanding as a canvas for a picture I know one day I will paint.

I resolve to try. I'm going to see Dr. Hanes.

Success!

It took much more doing than I expected, but Hanes will allow me to go with him. I'm surprised at how dangerous he felt this trip will be and I could sense an acute concern for my safety. It wasn't until he shook the sleep from his eyes that I was able to make headway. He genuinely respected my earnest desire to be part of the journey.

I presented myself as an interested journalist. While I impressed with the names of the newspapers I had written for, I didn't have the heart to tell them him that the only pieces they ever published were unpaid theater reviews. I also told him I was physically fit, determined and would be a great asset to him as a scribe, recording the events as they unfolded. He agreed with this assessment, believing there would be one less burden for him.

Part III

Under the Sunset

Chapter 7

Journal: L.O. Wynne

So we have our first glimpse of the travels of Bram Stoker. So far, a mere historical travelogue enhanced with a bit of spice and the promise of a slight twist. The veil of mystery is still apparent, but the terrible trail of what awaits us is yet to be revealed.

All this information is fascinating for a theater buff, but already anticlimactic to those of us who are waiting in anticipation for what will come next and wondering where this was all going.

Unknown to us at the time, however, the elements of our danger were being introduced to us under the simple guise of meeting participants like Vambery and Hanes. They hold the keys to the future, not only our story, but also to our lives. Still, we did not take notice. I knew, however, that there was more to Vambery then what the others would have seen. This was the point that I began to become concerned; there was something not right about what was happening. The answer lay in the journey I was sure. Unbeknownst to Stoker, these players knew each other before and had shared secrets he would never have imagined. The coming together of these individuals was more then just an accident. Yet, I could not speak because I would compromise my own position and how I had this knowledge.

Something terrible is in the offing. We will no longer be following the mundane adventures of Bram Stoker, but will embark on what will be a terrible trip to our own personal hell.

We primed for the events to come by setting up our action items while we awaited the introduction of the next group of pages. As per our assignments, we would begin our research.

We immediately went to work trying to verify the authenticity of the time lines that would have coincided with such a trip. That fell into Andersen's bailiwick. We certainly found no evidence of time lines being out of synch with the events described. We were able to verify some of the movements related to Stoker and Irving going as far as Vienna, but no explanation was evident concerning their motives. We lose proof of their movements at this point. No record concerning Budapest was available.

Lonvey would prove to be an elusive reification. He did actually exist and was involved a variety of financial investments. That was all we knew. Anything was possible.

The members of my team set about researching the other characters in this drama—names that were faintly known to us, if obscure. We knew from the beginning that a great deal of information would not be available about the persons named by Stoker—all except Vambery.

I was assigned to research the Americans, William Mathewson and Gray Shadow. What I found would be in retrospect a clear signal that all was not right with the adventure of Bram Stoker. The clues were there, but we never saw that a myth is so much more in its reality than mere legend.

> INTERNAL MEMO
> From: L. O. Wynne
> Re: The Americans
>
> I am submitting the following information about William Mathewson found in the files of the University of Kansas Historical Society. Additionally, I have uncovered an excerpt from an unpublished document written by him, which was found in the Kansas Historical society. I've included that as well.
>
> This excerpt is relevant because it refers to another individual noted in the diary, Gray Shadow. I believe this is the very same Gray Shadow mentioned by Stoker.
>
> While I can attest that these two were real individuals, I cannot commit that they ever knew Stoker. I imagine, though, based on time lines, it could be possible.
>
> William Mathewson, like another now obscure Wild West legend, "Texas Jack Omohundro," was a real person, yet today he is largely unknown. He fell victim to the passage of time and his own shyness and distrust of the press. He remains hidden by history due to his own humble opinions and his desire to play down the notoriety he most

richly deserved. Few men of the plains were equal to William Mathewson.

Comparatively little is known about him, although he was an associate of Kit Carson and did perform many highly important scouting services for the U.S. Army. He was a contemporary of William Cody and William Hitchcock, among others, and with them served as a scout with the 7Th Cavalry on several occasions. He was much sought after as a guide for European nobility looking to hunt buffalo in the American West. He was also highly respected by the Indians and was involved in resolving disputes between tribes and as a peacemaker for the American government.

William Mathewson was born 1830 in the Dakota Territories. He was an orphan of Scottish descent who apparently was raised by Indians from an early age. Very little about his early years can be accounted for, and nothing remains about his parents.

As an adult, Mathewson trapped all over the Rockies in the days before there was any thought of settlement. He later traded among the Indians in western Kansas for many years. In 1853, he established a trading post known as the Cow Creek Ranch on the Great Bend of the Arkansas.

It was here that Mathewson earned his Kiowa name Sillipah Sinpah, meaning "Long Bearded Dangerous Man." This resulted from his treatment of the celebrated chief, Santana, who was attempting to help himself to a part of Mathewson's stock without paying for it. Mathewson gave the chief a terrific beating with his fists and ended up defeating several braves as well before throwing the lot of them from his storeroom. Ironically, his fierce demeanor and powerful skill as a fighter endeared him to the Kiowas and he became Santana's lifelong friend, which would later save his life when the Kiowas went on the warpath.

On June 20-22, 1864, Mathewson, along with five of his ranch hands, fought a pitched battle with the Kiowa. Such was the respect the Kiowas had for William Mathewson that they did not sneak attack the great Sillipah Sinpah when they had the chance. They gave him a warning of their intentions to go to war with the white man and advised him that his settlement would be under attack. The great chief Santana himself rode out to tell Mathewson what the Kiowas intended to do. This was done so that Mathewson would be prepared and able to defend himself with the honor. The Kiowas would not ambush a man of his stature. The warning once given, they would hold no further quarter with him and Mathewson and his famous scalp became fair game.

Mathewson was to become a national hero during this Indian war when he later rode through the lines of a hostile band of Kiowa Indians who had surrounded a wagon train of one hundred fifty men, women and children to direct a spirited defense and preventing a massacre.

Mathewson was aware that the wagon train was secretly carrying a load of munitions, which had been destined for the Cow Creek post, a fact that neither the Kiowas nor the frightened travelers were aware of at the time. Fearing such firepower would fuel an Indian uprising, he directed the wagon train defenders to the ammunition and, once armed with the additional munitions, they were able to fend off the Indian attack.

In 1864, Mathewson rode as a scout for General Blunt's expedition. Later, he did much to bring the Indians together for the Little Arkansas treaty, which preceded the great medicine lodge peace council.

When the government wished to treat with the Indians, move them out of Kansas, and into the Indian territory, it was Mathewson who went out at the risk of his own life and visited tribe after tribe. With his reputation as a great warrior and one who spoke his truth, he was able to induce them to attend the council.

It was in approaching Indian villages, where he feared being killed before he could identify himself, that he developed the ability to move so silently that when he revealed himself he would appear almost as an apparition. Luckily, his reputation for honesty and bravery preceded him, so when he did appear he was instantly recognized as the "Ghost Warrior."

His reputation as a buffalo hunter and scout made him a much sought out guide for the European hunting parties that were in vogue at the time. Mathewson signed on as a scout with one of General Custer's most famous sojourns, the hunting party of Archduke Alexis of Russia. He was joined on this expedition by two other famous Bills, Cody and Hitchcock.

Mathewson's name is mentioned in several articles about William Cody. Cody acknowledged William Mathewson as one of the best trackers of his day and the premier buffalo hunter of his time.

Mathewson was once a lawman and is listed as having been a police commissioner in Wichita, Kansas, in the early 1870s.

In his later years, Mathewson toured with smaller Wild West shows and frequently traveled to remote places to hunt. But his last years are lost to history, except for a passage to England in 1895. Very little of what his purpose was or who he saw during this trip can be verified.

I had success substantiating Mathewson's relationships with the Indians and was able to acquire some information about Gray Shadow and his connection with Mathewson.

It was as a "Ghost Warrior" that Mathewson achieved his greatest reputation among the Indians and was one of the few white men universally respected by the many different tribes.

Based on archival records, Mathewson was engaged on several different occasions to investigate what we might now call paranormal activities. These encounters appear to have been of a mystical nature and revolved around spiritual matters. On two separate occasions, local tribes asked him to investigate the unexplained desecration of their burial grounds.

This in itself would be unusual because it would be unlikely that the Native Americans would turn to a white man. But this verifies Mathewson's overwhelming presence and reputation.

Not much information exists about Gray Shadow,

although archives do mention a Ute Indian medicine man who was with Mathewson on one of his "ghostings."

This then is what we can ascertain in regards to William Mathewson and Gray Shadow.

Mathewson was a celebrated tracker and buffalo hunter who was a legendary Western character of his day. His fame, however, did not endure, perhaps as mentioned, due to his self-imposed low profile. He was, however, a part of Indian folklore and was spoken of with reverence. As the famous "Ghost Warrior," Mathewson was the subject of a number of Indian songs.

In several Native American stories passed down by from generation to generation, Mathewson may have also appeared under his other Indian names (assuming they are all one in the same person). This being the case, he did have several additional experiences with unfriendly Indian spirits.

Gray Shadow was a Ute medicine man who was respected by his people and accepted by other tribes as a holy man. His reputation was such that he was able to mingle with other tribes at no apparent risk of being considered an enemy to them. He, like Mathewson, may have been referred to by other names in Indian tribal stories.

Gray Shadow was acquainted with European royalty and was much sought after as a guide. We lose track of him in the late 1870s and nothing about his death could be found. William Mathewson is believed to have died in 1912.

Finally, after exhaustive research, we were able to uncover a short excerpt that Mathewson had written for a possible autobiography and I've enclosed those pages that may be of keen interest to this investigation. Only about twenty pages exist, mostly handwritten notes about his buffalo hunting days and his meeting with Santana. But the following excerpt should be of great interest to you.

University of Wichita
The following photocopy contains handwritten notes of William Mathewson, 1878
Excerpt:
Autobiography of William Mathewson

The trails of the plains are the roads that lead to the sweet tears of the mountains. The object of our journey is to drink in the rain of life. The life we lead is the endless search to quench the thirst of understanding. This is an old Indian saying that pretty much explains it all…

With the long and endless prairies stretched out before us, we travel through mile after mile of rolling hills and greasy grass. God's country is nestled all around as we take in the beauty and look out for the danger. What you do with it is up to you…

Sometimes, when you ride alone with the wind and the sun as you're only companions, you long for some company. Anyone to talk to. That is if you discount your own memories as interesting company. I've been blessed with many memories and observations.

The solitude of the lonesome plains plays strongly upon a person's imagination. That must be true for everyone, but I suppose that what makes us human. So, while I rest a bit, I write these thoughts to anyone who cares to hear them. I reckon that folks living in the East have their own myths and legends, but for sheer serious contemplation, never discount the Indians. They've got a history that defines them as a people just as great as any civilization you learn about in books.

And if you were to examine the makeup of these noble people, you would find that they take a backseat to no man as far as courage is concerned.

I've never seen anything as beautiful or as frightening as an Indian warrior prepared for battle. An Indian warrior fears no man or beast. Yet when you watch them with their children, all warm attention and filled with spirit, how can anyone call them savages? They are as graceful and imposing in their demeanor as any royalty I've come across, and I've met plenty.

Still, when you look at the hierarchy of these tribes there is a pecking order unto itself—a pecking order based on domination of territory and won through battles with other tribes. There are no maps or boundaries, however, and you can never parcel or corral the Indian spirit. Like the white man, they do have their own societies, but their societies are based on the understandings of the Great Spirit. Their rules and politics are different from ours. To the Indians, the strongest man in any situation tends to decide the issues in his own best interest. Most Indians respect courage more any other quality and that can be the difference in any circumstance.

If you look at these grand tribes, you can see how they stand out in the order of all things. While size does matter, and the Sioux do have size and great skill, there is a special place for those blessed with the gifts of determination and courage.

While the Sioux and the Apaches are remarkable people, the Ute are something very special. They are the one of the most revered tribe of warriors on the planet, in my opinion, and certainly few Indians would dispute that.

They have powerful medicine, these people, deeply mystic and foreboding. Just the mention of their name or the sight of their warriors upon the horizon will fill any other Indian warrior with a certain dread. And that is not an easy thing to do.

The Ute

The Ute are graced with a reputation that sets them apart from all the other Indians. I've heard that they could scatter the buffalo soldiers just by the sound of their horses. The mere approach of the Ute puts fear in the eyes of their enemies. Provided you can see them. They can appear and disappear better than any Indians I've ever seen. Having a fierce history that stops the heart in its telling doesn't hurt matters either.

Long before the white man came, the stories spoke of the early Ute. According to legend, they were the last American tribe to be cannibals: They'd beat you, then they'd eat you, or so the Indian song went. While I do not necessarily believe it's true, just having cultivated a reputation for something like that can sure put a fright in an opponent.

The Ute would prey on unsuspecting villages and carry off the enemies to be eaten. Over time, their hunger for human flesh decreased, but not their fighting skills and their renowned fierceness. When the great Sioux migration came and it was time to settle down, the tribe bypassed the Ute. While the Sioux conquered the other peoples of the Ute mountains, they could never control the Ute.

Such was the legend of their fighting skills, they existed peacefully with their neighbors; no one wanted to get them angry, except the Apaches, which is another story for another time. Now the Ute seek peace with the white man.

Ironically, their great Chief Ouray was one of the first to advocate peace with the white man and has acquitted himself well with the terms he has negotiated for them…

It was a great surprise when I was asked to visit the Ute Mountains to help deal with a troublesome problem these great warriors could not seem to solve. The Shoshones were a cousin tribe to the great Ute nation. These Shoshone were as capable as any tribe that ever lived or hunted in those magnificent mountains, but they were unsure of what they were up against.

My Indian compadre, Gray Shadow, and I were traveling through the Bruneau River in the Owyhee country, home to the Nez Perce and the ferocious Shoshone. With its hot springtail tributary and granite side walls, it is more awesome than even the Grand Canyon.

A particular section of the Bruneau River runs through a narrow canyon that cuts like a snake through antediluvian lava flows. That transverse leads to the sacred burial grounds of the Shoshone, high upon the ridge. It is here also that the ancients told tales of a terrible creature, a beast called Tsaw-haw-bitts. White men refer to this brute as Ja-ha-bich.

According to the legend, this giant creature would prey on the Indians who ventured in the mountains. Ja-ha-bich would strike suddenly, cart his victims off in a basket and eat them later. Whenever there is a rash of disappearances in these mountains, either white men or Indians, the curse of Ja-ha-bich is always mentioned.

Interestingly, some Indian folklore states that Tsaw-haw-bitts cooked his victims before eating them. I wonder how he learned to make a fire? Maybe this Ja-ha-bich spent some time in the East.

Gray Shadow and I arrived at the camp of Chief Morning Dove late one night. I remember that the full moon hung brightly over the western sky and the glow from the fire danced seductively about us. We sat at ease with the chief and several of his warriors. Then he told us an extraordinary story. Their sacred burial grounds had been desecrated and the corpses dragged away. The warriors sent to investigate all disappeared, presumably victims of the ancient spirit that resided in a cave.

Chief Morning Dove spoke with clarity: "In the beginning of all things, wisdom and knowledge were with the animals, for Tirawa, the one above, does not speak directly to man. He sends certain animals to tell men that he shows himself through the beast, and that from them and the stars and the sun and the moon shall man learn. This is the way of Tirawa.

"All things in the world are two. We are good and we are evil. We have the right hand to strike for evil as the left hand strikes for good—a good that is filled with kindness, an evil that is ripe with hate.

"Everything on Earth has a purpose and every person has a mission. We have as our mission to meet this evil and destroy it.

"We will learn from its purpose that Tirawa has spoken and has warned us of the new ways. I need the strong medicine of Gray Shadow and the spiritual strength of the Shadow Warrior to make this place safe for the Lenni Lenape [genuine men] that we are.

"You will defeat Tsaw-haw-bitts. It is your destiny as you are the man of two minds and of two bodies. Your skin is white, but your soul is with the *Wakan-Tanka*, the great mystery, and with that comes your power.

"One day, a great fire from the sky danced into the mountain. A strange glow flickered high above the hills and lasted for many moons. Then the *machapunga* of death swirled across our land."

I have to admit that what he was saying was strange to me. I never knew an Indian who feared death in any form.

The chief continued to speak in a wise and eloquent manner, but a strange fear cut behind his every word. He spoke sadly of the young warriors who had lost their lives searching for the monster.

"Only one with courage equal to that of the Great Spirit can you defeat the monster in the cave. Tsaw-haw-bitts has been found and his lair is behind us," the chief whispered.

At that very moment, a growl as deep and as primal as any I had ever heard pierced the stillness. I must say it gave me pause.

Then the chief turned to Gray Shadow and, with a look of stern veneer, asked him solemnly: "Who among us can defeat Tsaw-haw-bitts?"

All eyes turned to Gray Shadow. The ceremony had reached the point where a warrior must be named. Only by his blessing, the centrifuge of his reputation, could these great people allow a white man to accomplish this dangerous task. The honor of their bravery required that I was named in this ancient way or they would be deemed cowards to their duty. Upon his request, I became one with them. I became the spectral Indian warrior, the blood of their blood.

Gray Shadow said, "Mathewson."

Almost on command, the terrible beast in the cave let out a piercing screech so unnerving that even Gray Shadow, the bravest man I ever met, fixed me with a look of fearful concern, a look I had never seen before. We had faced death many times together, but we had never been so apprehensive. Such was the hate coming from that cave, we were uncommonly filled with doubt. I mustered my wits and pulled in a deep breath.

I rose from my crouch. "I will kill Ja-ha-bich and avenge the desecration of this holy place. I shall fulfil my destiny.'"

Of course, I pronounced this more boldly than I actually felt.

Gray Shadow and the chief nodded their heads approvingly.

I leapt up and grasped my Winchester. Then the howl came again, more frightening than before. I thought to myself, *I'm going to need a bigger gun!*

I decided to pick up my Rolling Block Remington, a single-shot hunting rifle. That fierce howl made me think I might need a cannon, but at short range, one shot of Remington would hit whatever was in there like a freight train.

Gray Shadow, as was his way in times of danger, smiled and said, "Mathewson, you may also need a knife." He tossed me a penknife, the smallest damn thing I'd ever seen.

I smiled back at my good friend as I unsheathed my large Bowie knife and with bravado answered, "Already got one."

I entered the cave and immediately noticed a strange smell—a humid, putrid smell like that of a dirty swamp. All around me I saw the rotting carcasses of many types of animals. I found several human skeletons as well. I pulled my sidearm and unlocked the safety. I was going to need everything I had, so I readied the Remington, too. I just knew I was not going to have a lot of time.

Moving cautiously through the dark, I sensed something sleek and powerful trying to outflank me. I could hear it, but I couldn't see it.

I slid along the wall of the cave so the creature couldn't get behind me. Through the darkness I saw red eyes staring right at me—eyes that were cruel and definitely not human. The beast gave me a look that I had never seen before or since. There was intelligence behind those red eyes. This creature had yet to know fear.

Then, out of the darkness leapt the great beast with such fury that he knocked my rifle from my hand. I was overwhelmed by the speed with which it came at me. Powerful hand-like claws and long sharp teeth started slashed at my throat. I frantically pulled my Bowie and ripped hard into the belly of the beast. At that moment my knife plunged into hard firm muscle like no other I had ever felt.

There was no blood except my own. I grabbed at its body and tried to fling it down so I could draw my pistol. The Remington was out of reach. I struggled with the creature, so much stronger than I expected, as he stubbornly held onto me.

A shot rang out and burst the beast's head wide open; a mass of matter splattered on me and the monster slipped from my grasp.

Gray Shadow had come in the cave behind me, retrieved the Remington, and had expertly blown the creature's head off with a single shot.

Lying before us was the likes of nothing I had never seen before. It was a creature much like an oversized black panther, but with strange human-like claws. I could have sworn that it had moved on its two hind legs, but it all happened so fast, I am still not sure.

This beast had a grace and a swiftness that was frightening. It seemed to have an evil purpose, a devil of life, as much as an angel of death. The dying animal began to melt away in front of us—that was the only way to describe it. We covered it with gunpowder, burned out the cave, and sealed it up. The Shoshone burial ground was moved away. No one will ever go there again.

The legend of Ja-ha-bich is no longer a legend.

Chapter 8

Journal: L. O. Wynne

There was less material about Dr. Von Hanes than we expected. Up until he became more vocal with his theories, he seemed to have been a respected scientist. Then he became a victim of his fleeting fame and an object of some ridicule because of his defense of the occult and its medical remedies. All we found was a passing mention of him in an obscure medical periodical and very little mention of him by his contemporaries after his death. The few newspaper articles that we did find concerning his presentation of his theory in London where unflattering. Why was Dr. Hanes forgotten? How could this impressive man have been rendered an obscure reference to the history he helped to write?

Whatever information remains only serves to give us a faint glimpse into a provocative mind. But the light of his legacy was dimmed greatly upon his death. Very few of his credited initiatives were acknowledged, even as his theories were proven true.

Dr. Hanes paid a terrible price for his convictions. He was sentenced to historical anonymity unworthy of the accomplishments he had achieved in life.

Columbia University Private Data
INTERNAL MEMO
To: Professor Andersen/Dr. Mc Manus
From: Adele Simmons, research coordinator, L. O. Wynne Team

As per the request of Dr. Kevin Mc Manus, I have researched the life of Dr. Von Hanes.

Von Hanes was once a highly regarded criminologist who ultimately was considered an unorthodox scientist.

This was because of his pioneering views on forensic medicine and his disputed views on the use of psychoanalysis, scientific autopsies, and criminal profiling. He developed far-reaching theories that were many years ahead of their time. A medical doctor affiliated with Dr. Ernst Brucke, Hanes' work in establishing a behavioral science philosophy was prescient.

It was his advanced views that caused a great deal of criticism when he presented them to the London medical community and to Scotland Yard. He became embroiled in a heated debate that did much to tarnish his reputation at the time. Interestingly enough, only a few short years later, his methods were embraced by the Metropolitan Police in the famous Jack the Ripper case.

Hanes was also an early advocate in the use of behavioral science as a way to ascertaining the makeup of potential suspects in violent crimes. Dr. Hanes believed that studying a suspect's background could lead to finding motivations for abnormal antisocial behavior. He refereed to this theory as "Social Victomolgy"and it was based on the concept that personality is the product of environment and that abnormal behavior was learned, not ingrained. This form of educational and emotional stereotyping, which is now the basis of modern profiling, can be traced in specifics types of people who later will become criminals or sexual deviants.

He also believed in the prevalent Victorian view of good versus evil, but with the caveat that exposure to evil influences could help evil to flourish in human beings.

His early form of profiling was not well received, and it was almost a century before profiling became a respected vehicle for serial killer investigations. Hanes' positions must be viewed against the formulaic racism of his era. Much of the content was based upon ethnicity more than any influences related to background. Also, his theory that privileged breeding could not assure decent behavior was very explosive for its time.

The concept of behavioral idiosyncrasies associated with childhood experiences and emotionally unhealthy encounters causing deep psychological damage ran counter to the prevailing views of the day. Early profiling, if used at all, was limited to identifying physical features and stereotyping based on race, lack of intelligence, and poor sociological backgrounds.

Hanes' theories were a forerunner to the methods incorporated a few years later by pioneering psychoanalysts such as Josef Breurer and Sigmund Freud, both of whom studied with Ernst Brucke.

Dr. Von Hanes' belief that life experiences were a cause of criminal behavior was extremely controversial. If adopted, his views would have undermined the racist theories prevalent in Victorian times.

Hanes also specialized in investigating the cause of rare diseases. He was a proponent of the study of heredity, believing that inbreeding had a great deal to do with the continuation of certain family medical traits passed down from generation to generation. Indirectly, that made him an enemy of some powerful royal families in Europe, who, through scandalous inbreeding, had spread hereditary diseases such as hemophilia and pollex throughout their bloodlines.

Hanes was also a very vocal advocate about the role insects and rodents played in the spread of diseases and clashed many times with the medical community over this.

Some of his early papers had an indirect linkage to the work done by American doctors who discovered that mosquitoes were the vectors for yellow fever.

Hanes was also known as an alchemist who believed in the validity of folk medicine as a viable cure for disease. This, more than any other views he held, labeled him as a quack in some quarters, even as he was considered a genius in others.

Dr. Von Hanes was an early advocate of using the potency of organic potions and natural remedies as prescriptions for illness. He viewed the possibilities of homeopathic medicines to be a legitimate avenue of study. Such studies, he believed, would lead to finding cures for a variety of illnesses.

Although world renowned as a chemist, Hanes was an also a leading figure in the shadowy world of alchemy. While nothing exists to dispute it, it was possible that Dr. Hanes may have studied in the so-called mystery schools, which have their roots in biblical times.

Dr. Von Hanes was also an author of an almanac that charted the cycles of the seasons and advocated herbal remedies to promote health. Many of his remedies are almost verbatim prescriptions endorsed by occult sources and this caused a firestorm of controversy. Society looked upon these homeopathic remedies as the hocus-pocus of gypsies, wizards and medicine men. He was viewed by many in the medical community of endorsing the occult.

All of these controversial views did not endear him to the plodding European medical community of the nineteenth century and certainly contributed to his relative anonymity today.

Hanes was also an avid scholar of European and Oriental mythology and was a contemporary and a possible mentor to Arminius Vambery

Vambery is credited by some to be the person who introduced Vlad Dracula and the vampires legends of Transylvania to Bram Stoker.

It is possible that Hanes may have met Sir Henry Irving during his extended London stay. It is a known fact that Stoker did meet Arminius Vambery at least twice. There is very little material about Dr. Von Hanes and he is only mentioned in passing in Vambery's writings, but clearly they were friends. Bram Stoker does not acknowledge Dr. Von Hanes in any way, except in this diary. That is, unless the character of Van Helsing is really based on Dr. Von Hanes in some form or fashion.

Interestingly enough, Vambery is not mentioned or credited in any research notes for *Dracula* either. So all theories are pure conjecture. However, the name "Arminius" is used in the novel *Dracula* when Dr. Van Helsing credits his "good friend Arminius" for his teachings on vampires and the occult.

> Hanes died on October 17,1880 due to injuries sustained while on a hunting expedition in Bistria, Transylvania. He expired from his wounds shortly before medical help arrived. Hanes was fifty-seven years old, never married, and left no children.

Journal: L. O. Wynne

Arminius Vambery was the most recognizable name in the diary and thus the most easily researched participant. At least the others thought so. Unfortunately, they quickly got the sense that Professor Vambery was far more complex than the plain vanilla information we found out about him. I knew that the real history of Professor Vambery was sitting in the halls of a different library.

What we do know as historical fact is that Bram Stoker and Professor Vambery did meet on several occasions long before *Dracula* was finished. No proof of any earlier meetings exists. The only link between Vambery and Stoker concerning *Dracula* was the previously mentioned reference to "my old friend Arminius."

We also know that despite having spent a great deal of time together in 1892, and several times over the next few years, very little documentation exists on what they talked about, save for some innocuous dialogue from *Reminiscences of Henry Irving*. We can only imagine what the gist of these conversations entailed, but the historical trail and direction of the novel as documented in Stoker's notes related to *Dracula*, took a much different turn after these early meetings. Substantial changes to the *Dracula* text were apparent from that time on. The most obvious was that Stoker changed the name of his title character from Count Wampry to Count Dracula after these recorded meetings. In retrospect, Professor Vambery's influence seemed perceptible.

We have always found it uncharacteristic that neither Vambery nor Stoker ever mentioned having any discussion about the novel. Yet, such a discussion would appear to be obvious, given Vambery's background and Stoker's search for information about the region. We have always found this to be odd.

Still by applying the degrees of separation I could see the possibilities of linkage between all the participants in this diary. More importantly I knew more about Professor Vambery then I let on and in many ways he was the most important unifying link.

Then again, in hindsight, there is so much about Professor Arminius Vambery that we just did not know. Myself included. There was something deep and forbidding about Professor Vambery, something not readily placed in the documented history available. The most important role Arminius Vambery played in history will always be left in the shadows.

I know now that is where he wanted it be.

INTERNAL MEMO
Re: Arminius Vambery
From: Wynne Research Team

Arminius Vambery was a Hungarian philologist, Orientalist and explorer. He was a full Professor of Oriental Languages at the University of Budapest in 1865. In the early 1860s, he traveled through Armenia, Persia, and Turkestan and, thanks to his unusual proficiency in languages; he was able to gain a deeper insight into local customs than any European had before.

In Constantinople, he learned several languages and dialects of Asia Minor and then traveled through Armenia and Persia in the dress of a native. He published the recollections of his travels in *Central Asian Journey* in 1863 and *Journey in Persia* in 1867. In 1886, he wrote and published *Arminius Vambery: His Life and Adventures*. His linguistics works are mainly in Turkish. He was known to have spoken at least seven different languages

In the 1860s and 1870s, Vambery was famous all over the world. Today, of course, his name is forgotten and there are few who have heard the dying echoes of his fairytale adventures and bold works. The books he wrote about his adventures disguised as a dervish or a religious beggar, while wandering through the countries of Asia, are little known now.

Back in Victorian times, however, the countries of Asia Minor were remote, mysterious and exotic, not the well-studied lands they are today. Vambery opened the veil of secrecy to the West and created an international sensation.

Vambery was born in 1832 to a poor Jewish family in Hungary. His real name was Hermann Bamberger, which he changed much later in life. While in school in Pressburg, and later while traveling through cities like Prague and Vienna, he would board with priests and Benedictine monks. It's quite possible that he would have come across both Brother Jacob and Dr. Von Hanes in any of these cities as the time lines would certainly match.

He traveled incessantly throughout his life, frequently in the company of pilgrims and wizards. This certainly helped to encourage a passion for the occult—a passion no doubt fueled by his relationship with Von Hanes.

In 1864, he was invited by the Royal Geographical Society to lecture on his travels and he was celebrated by the Society's president, Sir Roderick Murchison.

Murchison was a great friend of the explorer and newspaperman H. M. Stanley and he probably knew Henry Irving. Years later, Murchison may have had a possible association with Bram Stoker when they were both members of the Golden Dawn Society, a more literary version of the Masonic movement.

Additionally, in another possible connection, Murchison hosted several of Dr. Von Hanes' controversial lectures when the German scientist came to England to present his views on science and criminology. So, if Hanes was a member of any number of these societies, a possible connection could exist between them. Although Professor Vambery remained rather reclusive through most of the 1870s until his death, his fame and his fortune were at an apex in the 1860s.

At around that same time, while Vambery was in England, he warned Lord Palmerston of Russia's war aims and gained a reputation as a spy. This made him a hero to the English.

For all his nineteenth-century fame, very little about the real Arminius Vambery is known. Such was the fact then, and even more so today.

Professor Vambery was a very complex and shadowy man who hid behind a veil of secrecy that was his trademark. Sadly, we may never really know who this remarkable man really was.

He died the fifteenth of September 1913 at the age of eighty-one.

Journal: L. O. Wynne

We were unable to find any information about Brother Jacob related to this time period. The Catholic Church, stonewalling us at every turn, refused to even acknowledge his existence.

What we did find was information about another Brother Jacob who lived during the reign of Vlad Dracula. This Brother Jacob was witness to the execution of his fellow monks by the Impaler, which was the basis of the first Dracula horror story included in the poems of Michael Beheim. There was no another information concerning either Brother Jacob, save for the tales about this bloody event.

Although we were disappointed in our quest for Brother Jacob, we were fascinated that Bram Stoker was actually in Transylvania. While the prevailing view is that Stoker used secondary sources to depict the countryside in *Dracula*, what he describes in his diary is so telling that he had to have been an eyewitness. This probably explains why Stoker was so successful in capturing the wild landscape of Transylvania in his novel.

Chapter 9

Sitting behind his desk at the Midtown South precinct, Walters pondered the consequences of his meeting with Dr. Lawson. The Rufus Arsine wrinkle was a very confusing one to him. Could it be possible that Laura Olsen Wynne spirited away something of great importance? Was Rufus Arsine engaged to find whatever it was? Laura had enough money to live comfortably for years, so he couldn't think of her as a thief. Something just didn't make sense.

The case must be about information, he concluded—some type of information that Laura knew about or was holding. That was what Arsine wanted to find. If he could uncover the information, he thought he could find the key to unlock this perplexing case.

Walters realized that there must be some connection to Andersen. Whether it was the Andersen file or something else—that was the question. He made the assumption that if the file was not taken during the Andersen robbery, it was plausible that Laura or someone else might have already taken it. That was what Walters imagined Arsine was also trying to find out. Regardless of the reason, he was no longer just trying to find Laura, he was also chasing her. Unfortunately for Laura Olsen Wynne, Rufus Arsine was chasing her, too.

When Walters called his contacts at the FBI about Arsine, he was not surprised to find that little information actually existed about the man. In the dark whispers of law enforcement, however, Rufus Arsine had been linked to several murders, though it was never proved. No charges had ever been filed in any investigation he may have been a suspect. While he had been linked indirectly with a number of cases of stolen artwork and missing documents, the file on Arsine contained only limited proof of his involvement. The files listed a few instances where he was engaged by insurance companies to investigate stolen property, but there were few details. One case that Walters did remember was the one in which Arsine had arranged for the recovery of documents taken from the J.P. Morgan Library in New York.

A very professional crew had stolen some rare manuscripts and other valuables from the library's vault. In the hope of keeping the robbery secret, the library brought in Rufus Arsine to help recover the items. They asked that the police not go any further, but allowed Walters's friend Bill Johnson to follow the developments.

Rufus Arsine had obviously awed Walters's friend when he had arrived at the scene. Johnson described him as brilliant man and marveled at his cool and calculating manner. He seemed to know exactly what he was looking for, so much so that Johnson became suspicious. Arsine seemed to have a great deal of inside information on how the break-in occurred and who was involved. Although he could never prove anything, Johnson started to think that Arsine himself had something to do with it.

Arsine negotiated the return of the documents to the library. Then he collected a large fee. The Morgan Library wished to keep the whole affair secret and asked Arsine to arrange for the entire case to be sealed by the courts. No charges were ever filed against anyone. No news reports ever surfaced about the episode. Rufus Arsine must have had some very powerful friends to accomplish something like that, Walters thought. It was clear to him that he was dealing with very serious man who was not to be taken lightly.

It was the Gardner Museum heist that brought Rufus Arsine's name to the attention of the law enforcement authorities. The official file stated that Arsine was listed as a suspect in the case. The theory in Boston was that Arsine had masterminded the theft. They believed he planned it himself and then arranged delivery of the stolen artworks to his network of unscrupulous dealers. There was no real proof that the theory was correct—only that Arsine happed to be in Boston at the time of the robbery. Such was his reputation; he was thought to be guilty by reason of proximity. Despite the rumors, Arsine continued to find missing and stolen artwork for his underground clientele and redirected them to the secret galleries of the rich and powerful.

There were also the rumors of Arsine having used violent methods to unlock the lips of those who would not share their information with him. While these people may have been of bad character unto themselves, the stories of his cruelty were the stuff of criminal urban legend. Walters shivered at the thought of what might happen to Laura if Arsine got a hold of her. This was a very sadistic man if the stories are true. So strange this Rufus Arsine, a man of his background having such a frightening reputation.

Walters had pieced together some facts about this mysterious man. Arsine was a graduate of Harvard and had earned a doctorate in papyrology, the study of ancient papyrus manuscripts. He also held a degree in art. Arsine was a highly educated and very accomplished man, who had started at an early age as a collector of rare works, which he bought and sold to make his fortune. It was at this time that his legend took root. He had unveiled many ancient works that had been presumed to be lost to history.

For the past two years, the trail ran cold on Rufus Arsine as he slipped into the mist of his own legend. Likened to a phantom, Arsine's name was whispered through the corridors of the art world's dark underbelly. His ethereal presence hovered like a predator from behind secret places. They said that the walls of his wealthy clientele were lined with pilfered masterpieces and that Arsine was their curator.

Although he had substantial holdings in New York, Arsine had suddenly disappeared. Even his lawyers didn't know where he was. He could be anywhere in the world right now and Walters would not be able to find him. While he was not surprised that the man had not returned any of his phone calls, Walters knew that it was very important that they talk. But he also realized that he would only find Arsine if Arsine wanted to be found.

When Walters called Laura's lawyer, the man stated categorically that he had never hired Rufus Arsine, although he did say that it would have been a very good idea.

It had been seven days since the filing of the missing person report and now Walters could obtain a search warrant and enter into Laura's apartment. He was anxious to see what he would find there.

Larry Dasagmon, the building manager at Laura Wynne's upper eastside apartment building, was waiting anxiously for Walters in the lobby. Decked out in a garish wide blue tie that covered his starched white shirt like an apron, Larry wanted to usher Walters up to the apartment as quickly as possible. He was concerned that the tenants might get upset about a police investigation.

The short and fat middle-aged super led Walters directly to the service elevator. While waiting for the elevator to arrive, Larry said something about Laura that resonated with Walters.

"I'm never sure if I make any impression on her, but there is something about the way she smiles that always keeps you interested."

Larry seemed to have a thing about Laura because all through the ride up to the fourteenth floor, he went on and on about how much he liked Ms. Wynne, how he just loved her smile, and how he wished that she would smile more often. He was quite taken with her, Walters knew. Larry's infatuation made Walters a bit uncomfortable considering his own fascination with Laura's photograph.

At Walters's request, Larry had checked the visitors' log for the building and found that no one had been to Laura's apartment since the day she was reported missing. That included Laura's own lawyer and, most important, Rufus Arsine. Shortly after Laura's disappearance, Walters had made a trip to the building to talk with the staff about her. On that occasion, the doorman had confirmed to Walters that Laura rarely had any visitors. He also recalled that, except for going to and coming from work, Laura didn't go out that much either. The concierge confirmed that. So all he had to go on was what he found in her apartment.

Walters handed the search warrant to Larry and the super opened the door. Despite Larry's protests, Walter asked him to leave the floor. With great anticipation, Walters entered Laura's apartment. He was not surprised to find it as he had expected. The apartment was spacious and airy. He had thought it would have been decorated more luxuriously, but the furnishings reflected the sensibilities of a very sophisticated woman.

Laura's home was also meticulously kept, with everything stacked neatly and in its own designated place. He walked around the apartment thinking that her memories were displayed openly in a playfully romantic way. Artifacts from different cultures, some quite provocative in their design, some just pornographic enough to make him blush, were displayed in glass-fronted cases.

Along the hallway that led to her bedroom were swords and armor leaning in odd positions. Did they represent her wish that only a knight in shining armor would be allowed into her chamber he wondered? On one polished table, idols from some ancient civilization were grouped together like a little family. Emotions frozen in stone, they seemed to say that life was meant to last forever.

Taking stock, Walters could see that her secret soul was the spirit of this place. There were no flashy or expensive furniture or paintings. Except for the artifacts of a distant past, there no modern artifacts he expected a wealthy young woman to possess. There were no expensive stereos or TVs, just a simple CD player with modest speakers.

Laura did have a humorous side, he noted. On display there were masks of some type, ones that bore a striking resemblance to her in a comical way. She reinforced this paradox by having her caricature presented next to them as if to highlight her awareness of the similarities.

The paintings on the wall give Walters more clues about her. Deep dark colors spaced in symmetrical patterns made Walters think that it was meant to be Laura's way of communicating her complex personality—a structured order that was both chaotic and controlled at the same time. *Maybe those psyche classes did help*, Walters thought, laughing to himself.

He saw only two framed photos in the apartment and they were both of an older couple he took to be her parents. She seemed to have made a conscious decision not to display any other photographs. Was that her way of saying that no one else had reached that special place in her life Walters wondered?

He knew he was the same way. He didn't display any pictures in his Brooklyn apartment either. No on in his life had been important enough to celebrate. He carried no photos in his wallet, either, except for Laura's. She was now a very special person in his life. She had become his obsession.

Looking at the overall layout of the apartment, he perceived that something was just not right. He sensed that fear had taken root here, that this woman has been spooked in some way. It was evident that she had packed very quickly and left. Drawers and closet doors were open and the bathroom was devoid the necessities like a toothbrush. *She must have thrown some things in a bag and left*, he thought.

Once again, Walters's inner voice was speaking to him. He was rarely wrong about these feelings. There is something amiss. This is all too pat. He got the sense that someone else had been there. Looking closer, he could see signs that someone has already searched the apartment. Items were placed in a too perfect way, even for Laura. And if she had not been home for the past two weeks, why was her apartment so clean? He had already verified that she did not employ a cleaning service, yet the furniture had no dust. Someone had wiped away his or her fingerprints. *What could they have possibly been looking for?* he wondered. *The Andersen file?*

Walters walked into her study. He saw no computer, a necessary tool for her research. Did she take it with her or had someone taken it? Her desk was bare and a small file cabinet was empty. *Who took it all? Laura? Or did someone beat her to it?*

On the bookshelves were numerous volumes about the occult and secret societies. They dominated her study. He figured that in her line of work that might be normal. *A few romance novels would have nice,* he thought, *but that wouldn't have been Laura.* She was obviously consumed by philosophy, the occult and languages.

He looked for clues about the possible connection between the Andersen file and Laura's disappearance. *Maybe that's what she had taken with her*, he thought as he flipped through the pages of a biography of Bram Stoker that had been left open on the bookshelf. Caressing the book in his hand, he tried to figure out who Bram Stoker was and what in the world Andersen's project might have been about. What caused this chain of events?

Then a thought hit him like a freight train. Bram Stoker wrote that Bela Lugosi movie. Taking a step back into the middle of the room, Walters stared intensely at the bookcase. There was something about this bookcase that didn't seem right. He pulled books from the shelves and tapped the inner walls. *Why do several short books seem to be perfectly in line with the longer ones?* he thought. *Was there a false wall built in the back of it?*

Walters emptied the bookcase and threw the books on the bed. Then he popped the wall behind the second wood panel of the third shelf and revealed an opening. Reaching into the small space, he pulled out a brown steel container. Forcing the lock, he found himself looking at Laura's personal papers, including her passport. There was also a blue cloth bag with some expensive looking jewelry in it and neatly stacked and wrapped in rubber bands were large denominations of both foreign and domestic currency. *If she had come back to the apartment to get some things, why would she leave all of this money behind? She's not that rich,* he thought.

Sitting at the bottom of the container was a business card for the Allen Clay Galleries and a sheet of paper with a name written on it: *Sunimod.* It is quite apparent to him now that Laura never returned to the apartment to collect anything. She was so afraid that she went into hiding almost immediately. Her life was in too much danger to take a chance.

Someone else had been there, someone who had snuck into her apartment undetected and had taken her computer and whatever else they could find. Then, whoever it was, made it seem as if she had packed her bags and fled. Laura had been set up and made to look as if she was on the run, possibly with something belonging to Andersen.

Walters was both relieved and worried. He knew he could eliminate Rufus Arsine as a suspect. Arsine would have found this hiding place in minutes. *But if not Arsine, who else was looking for Laura Olsen Wynne?*

This case was getting stranger by the minute. Now he suspected there were more then one entity looking for Laura Olsen Wynne. While Arsine may be a dangerous man, was it possible that whoever else was looking for her might be even more dangerous?

Walters shook his head. He had no flash of inspiration to guide him to the answer, only diligent police work to fall back on. He picked up the business card from the Allen Clay Galleries and the sheet of paper with *Sunimod* written on it.

He was going to follow up on both, but he was most interested in who—or what—Sunimod was.

Chapter 10

There was a chill in the air and the sky was turning as dark as Walters's mood. What had been a simple missing persons case was now so much more intricate, confusing and possibly dangerous than he had ever imagined.

The December rain was finally letting up as he stepped off the M31 bus. The wet pavement was glazed with ice and the hard wind sounded even louder when it whipped against the windows of the shops along Madison Avenue. *Not exactly a winter wonderland*, Walters thought, shoving his hands deep into the pockets of his dirty raincoat. *But at least there was no snow.* He had never liked winter.

He trudged the two blocks to the Allen Clay Gallery, but when he got there it appeared to be closed. He checked the business card again. *It should be open,* he thought, but all he could see was a lonely storefront devoid of activity. The large gallery windows were draped with brown paper. The store lights shining behind the paper, however, indicated that someone might be inside.

In the amber glow of the lights illuminating the brown paper, he could see the flickers of movement. Knocking on the door, he saw a shadow rise and move ominously toward him. The lumbering silhouette opened the front door slowly.

Instead of an imposing shadow, he found himself face to face with a smallish security guard. Walters flashed his shield, which immediately drew the guard's full attention. Then Walters handed him his card, but before he could even speak, the guard ran to the back of the store and disappeared through a door.

Awaiting developments, Walters gazed around the largely empty wood-paneled gallery. What he saw was the last vestige of a once-proud institution in the final stages of its own demise. All of the glass cases were empty. The picture hooks were empty of frames. The final remnant of the Allen Clay Gallery was packed away in brown boxes.

His curiosity roused, Walters nosed around, examining the contents of various boxes. There, lying before him, was an amazing collection of letters, books and speeches by people whose names were not just historic, they were history itself. *The hands of greatness had scripted these pages*, he thought, *documenting hopes and dreams and wishes*. The chronicle of their ideas sat in these boxes, waiting to be encased in bubble wrap.

Still deep in thought, Walters was slow to pick up the click of high heels behind him. He was caught off guard when a pleasant voice said, "Robert Louis Stevenson once said that all speech, written or spoken, is a dead language until it finds a willing and prepared hearer. What voices do hear, Detective Walters?"

Walters turned to see a handsomely attired woman of about sixty. Her dignified smile and dark brown eyes were comforting and helpful. Her silver hair was brushed straight back and tied in a ponytail. Despite her silver hair, she was youthful looking and attractive. She has a way of smiling as she spoke.

Walters returned her smile. "In my job, I need to be selective about which voices I actually listen to."

"How may I help you, then? I'm Claire Wilson, the gallery curator," she said.

"I'd like to talk with Allen Clay. Is he available?"

"Oh, I'm sorry. Allen Clay is no longer with us. Please step into my office," she said, pointing to the balcony level overlooking the gallery.

On the way upstairs, she told Walters that Allen Clay has passed away only a week ago from food poisoning and that the gallery was in the process of being sold. That didn't surprise Walters. It was just one more screwy turn in this case. Everyone involved seemed to have met a terrible end. He hoped Laura herself was the exception.

"Did Allen Clay ever have any dealings with a Dr. Andrew Andersen?"

"Sorry, but I've never heard of a Dr. Andersen."

Walters could sense immediately that she was telling the truth.

"Is it possible that he may have been involved in a project with Allen Clay, one that you might not have known about?" Walters asked.

"Yes, that's possible," she said. "Allen was often asked to review materials that were for his eyes only."

Walters pulled Laura's picture from his pocket. "Have you ever seen this woman before?" he asked.

Claire's facial expression showed immediate recognition and surprise. "Why, yes I have," she said "I don't remember her name, but I do remember her face. She came in about a week ago, saying that she needed the Stoker file. She said that Allen Clay had been contracted by Columbia University to do work on it and she had come to pick it up. I had no idea what she was talking about, but I went into his office to look for it. Unfortunately, I could not find anything related to Bram Stoker."

"How did she react when you told her that?" Walters asked.

"Not very well, as I recall. She insisted that there was such a file and demanded that I look again for it. I did, but I still couldn't find anything."

"What happened next?" Walters asked.

"When I returned empty handed from the second search, it seemed to have a strange effect on her," Claire said. "She turned white. With fear, I thought at the time. Then she rushed out of the gallery without saying goodbye."

Curious, Walters thought, *but at least that proved Laura was still alive the day after her lawyer filed the missing persons report.*

"Did you have any idea what she was looking for? Any idea of what she meant by the Stoker file?" Walters asked.

"I'm sorry, I don't," Claire said. "But there is something interesting about all this."

"What?"

"The day before his death, Allen Clay had a phone conversation with someone about Bram Stoker, but I do not know who it was. In retrospect, I can see there is more to this now than just coincidence."

"Could it have been Rufus Arsine on the phone?"

"Mr. Clay knew him very well," Claire said. "They had worked together for many years, but I don't think it was him on the phone, but then again, those two had their secrets."

"Has Arsine been in contact with you since Mr. Clay's death?" Walters asked.

"No, not since last week. He would normally call Mr. Clay directly on his private line. The last time I remember Mr. Arsine calling was the day before Allen Clay's death. They spoke for quite a while and afterwards Mr. Clay appeared to be very upset."

Walters asked her if she had a phone number for Arsine, and she reached for a black leather phone book on the desk. She wrote a number down and handed it to Walters. He saw that the number was different from the one he had been calling.

"One last question," Walters said. "Do you know who Sunimod is?"

Claire Wilson's entire demeanor changed. Her smiling face froze in astonishment. Just by her reaction, Walters could tell that the name meant something more than he had realized. It now occurred to him that it may not be a name at all, something else entirely.

"No, I do not recall such a name," she said. "I just don't have an answer for you."

Sunimod sure had put the fear of God into her, Walters thought. But he decided not to press her any further. He sensed the timing was not right. It was better to keep her on his side. He might need her later.

"Thank you for all your help," Walters said. "I'll be in touch."

Clair Wilson was visibly relieved. "I hope Rufus Arsine will be of more help to you."

"Yeah, I hope so, too," Walters said confidently.

One way or the other, Rufus Arsine would give him the answers he was looking for, he thought. *That was a guarantee.*

Chapter 11

After leaving the Clay Gallery, Walters decided not to go home, but return to the precinct house. He immediately placed a call to Rufus Arsine at the number Claire Wilson had given him and left a message on Arsine's voice mail. Then he sat back to wait for the return call. He was sure that it would be coming shortly because Arsine would want to find out how Walters had gotten the new number.

He was relaxed now. He always felt most comfortable sitting at his desk at this time of night. He preferred the night, its solitude. He hated the day. All around him, detectives pounding on key boards, talking on the phone, bullshitting with each other, and arguing heatedly. It was a circus—one he had lost interest in long ago.

When he had been in uniform, he had never gotten the rush the others felt when chasing down the dregs of society who were trying to survive in their cruel world by executing lawless acts. He had had his fill of those predators. He much preferred finding the missing now. It was a mission that still had hope. He had stopped caring about the rest of the malevolent world.

He only wanted to operate in his own private world. That way he didn't have to engage in the locker room banter that was going on all around him. A cop's life was too fragile, he thought, always one step away from retirement or a bullet. He was long past those interactions of false camaraderie and hurting sarcasm. He didn't need to be part of the sacred bonds of partnership that were so unwieldy and way too permanent. It was a ritual that drained him. He had grown tired of all that years ago.

As he had done for almost a week now, Walters placed Laura's picture on his desk, propping it up against a pile of papers on his left. *Was it possible that her picture would one day end up in his file cabinet with the other still missing persons?* he wondered. *Would he ever find her? Would she realize the commitment he had made to her? Would she be grateful?*

"Who's the broad?" Detective Gene Ieirney asked, hovering over Walters's desk.

"Case," Walters said.

"Oh," Ieirney said. "Fucking good-looking bitch. She run off with the fucking butcher or something?"

"Mmmm," Walters murmured, hoping Ieirney would go away and leave him alone. He felt that Laura had somehow been violated by the foul language. In his heart, he knew she would never stand to be treated that way in person.

"See ya around, Mounty," Ieirney said, losing interest in both Walters and Laura. "Good luck."

Thankfully, Walters leaned back in his chair and put his tired feet on the scarred and scratched metal desk. He wanted to spend the next few minutes to thinking about his quarry.

Funny, he thought, *my mother was the same age as Laura when she died.* That was a loss that had changed his life and ruined his father's. Although he always tried to forget, he still could not get the memory of that horrible day out of his mind. Just like Laura, his mother had been a well-educated and inquisitive woman. A top investigative reporter when she had married his much older policeman father, she was well known in journalistic circles for her amazing undercover work. It was while she was investigating the disappearance of a young New Jersey woman that everything changed. This beautiful young woman had last been seen in the company of a young man whispered to be a member of a satanic cult. They never did find her, but the story of a satanic sacrificial murder would not go away. In investigating this story, his mother had somehow managed to infiltrate that dark mysterious world and whatever she was learning seemed to unnerve her. She became more and more depressed. Something was changing in her as she immersed herself deeper and deeper into this weird world of satanic sagacity. It seemed that in the end she discovered something she did not want to find. A light had gone out of her and she suddenly had lost touch with reality. In doing so she quickly became unhinged and within hours spiraled into a madness that manifested itself into increasingly odd and violent behavior. It had all come so quickly that fateful day.

In her madness, she suddenly turned on them, desperately trying to kill them both. Screaming that her son must die, she tried to grab his father's hunting rifle, forcing his father to restrain her while he called for help. Somehow releasing herself from her bounds, she smashed a mirror and attacked his father. She stabbed him with a jagged piece of glass, the blow piercing his lung and rendering him prostrate on the floor. She then turned on her son and in his terror he watched this once loving woman charge at him in a frightening and contorted rage. Only the shot fired by his father into her head stopped her. She died almost instantly. Strange that in the thirty-five years he was a cop the only person his father had ever killed was his own wife.

After her death, his father was lost, his mind wandered, and his world was totally shattered. The two of them had faced their brave new world as bravely as they could, but they had failed and became strangers to each other. The only bond they shared was the love that had been taken from them so suddenly. Over the years, they had moved so far apart emotionally that Walters had never even cried when his father died seven years later. *He had been like Laura in that regard*, he thought, *just old enough to face the world, but too young to face it alone.*

Walters had already learned to shut down his emotions by then, especially during the holidays. He would spend those days on the job. Only the job had mattered to him, even as it had slowly drained the life out of him, leaving him worn out and weary.

He knew what it is like to not have any family. *Laura did, too,* he thought.

Walters put his feet back on the floor and glanced at the Andersen case file. He was waiting to see the reports on Clay and the others, hoping he could find a connection between the victims of sudden death and the connection between Laura and Arsine. He also had to find the Stoker file and figure out what Sunimod meant.

The phone rang. The voice on the other end was quick and to the point: "Meet me at the bar on the west balcony of Grand Central Station in fifteen minutes."

Walters didn't even bother tracing the call. He knew who it was and the caller was too smart to leave a trail. Rufus Arsine wanted to talk.

Chapter 12

Journal: L. O. Wynne

Rest is that luxury beyond my comprehension. I look behind me in my desperate attempts to feel safe. Just as my demons stalk upon my reverse imagination, the winds of uncertainty give rise to the sails of my existence. We are about to unfurl the mast on a journey of no return.

Cold winds of doubt sear this frigid heart. No daylight comes to me in the sunlight now, but darkness preys eternal. The shadows are not friendly, for they are omens of a dire future. This is the world all of us have now been born into. The lack of sleep is making reasoning hard.

I keep on the move as best I can. Quickly avoiding all those that look for me. I manage to maintain some sanctuary devoid of this insanity, but find no comfort in it. I stop only for these few brief moments, just long enough to assess my options. Clearly they are diminishing and I am beginning to lose hope. I cannot penetrate the wall of the secrecy. Still I will keep trying.

If you indeed know the significance of these players, I pray that these documents are in the right hands. If not, I can only say to you behold the Forever Horizon, a dimension of our world that you may never fully comprehend.

Now the terror begins for all of us. We have reached that point in the road. Having gone this far, you may have already learned more than you should have, but I will ask you one last time to leave this alone and walk away. This is my final warning. I may not have chosen you to read these words, but have you have been chosen nonetheless. Go any further and there will be no turning back.

I hope it is not too late for you. I sense the hourglass of my life is nearing the final spiraling of the sands. I must make this attempt at an affidavit while I can. I cannot afford the luxury of improvements to my witness, as I can only deal with that dual predator of time and destiny while I am still able. Time is growing short.

Aristotle once said that fear is pain arising from the anticipation of evil. Dr. Andersen once wrote that sorrow is the only companion of tragedy's lonely child.

From this moment on, only pain and sorrow will follow us.

Part IV

The Lost Diary of Bram Stoker

Act Two

The King of Death

Chapter 13

I'm writing theses notes while traveling with Von Hanes.

My first impressions do not appear to be false now that I've gotten to know him better and we've had several interesting talks.

Dr. Hanes is a very bright man of quiet dignity and underlining compassion. Still, he can carefully hide his personality under a veil of professionalism. He is also a man who harbors deep disappointments and emotional scars from the controversies of his past. It is not that these conflicts have hurt him personally, but because of his disappointment in the snail-like pace of medical progress.

But he is an optimistic man who believes in the future. The best way to prepare for that future, he says, is to learn from the past and not repeat it. When we close our minds to the lessons we have learned, we have wasted the future just as surely as we have already wasted the past. This, then, is Dr. Von Hanes' philosophy.

As I look at Hanes carefully, I can see a bit of myself—at least how I would like to think of myself. He is a detailed and serious man who can still laugh at life's ironies, as easily as life's ironies laughs at us. A clinical man, Dr. Hanes is still soulful in his humor and quick to laugh. We both share an intellect (at least I hope that I do) full of energy and powered by the pursuit of real answers to the questions that we ask.

We both respect and admire the complexities of the human endeavor—mine in the realm of make-believe and Hanes' in the practical science of an uncertain world.

Ironically, and in many ways, he is physically much like an older version of myself. He is a man of medium height, strongly built, with shoulders set back over a broad, deep chest. His head is noble, well sized, broad, and large behind the ears. Big bushy eyebrows streaked with gray dominate this magnificent head. The forehead is broad and fine, rising almost straight, and then sloping back. Such is his forehead that the reddish white hair cannot possibly tumble over it, but falls naturally back and to the sides.

His most striking feature, however, is his eyes: big, dark blue eyes set wide apart, quick and tender or stern upon the calling of that mood. Without his beard (his is a trim white while mine is curly red) and perhaps his liquid and elegant eyes, we are indeed similar in looks. Clearly, our athletic demeanors and personalities are a little less exact. He moves gracefully with small and secure steps and his economically thoughtful manner is that of an austere gentleman. At least until he smiles and he warms you to a grandfatherly presence.

I've always imagined my gait to be heavy and athletic and I know I can be quite boisterous when in that mood. I have never been able to figure myself out entirely, so I cannot imagine what others think of me. But I feel that history will be kind to both of us.

I managed to get Hanes to open up a bit about the controversies that surround him. In his view, any scientist who closes his mind to the expansion of possibilities is showing disrespect for the convention of discovery, the basis for scientific thought.

He acknowledges that this is not true of all of his contemporaries. The root of his frustration is that if one skeptic with political influence rejects the possibilities of anything other than dogma theory, they are doing a disservice to science on a whole. They seek to mute the voices of possibilities, cast away the winds of change, and subdue those theories that conflict with the status quo. They cheer a stagnated methodology that will unravel one day precisely because of its own ignorance.

Witchcraft, Hanes maintains, will not advance the cause of forensic medicine, but the composition of the chemicals used by witches might have medicinal properties. For all the mysticism, it should be explored. The same is true of autopsies. An autopsy is not an evil mutilation of a living body, but a clinical science with a purpose.

Yet, by merely suggesting the study of these fringe sciences creates controversy and subsequent dismissal by pedestrian men clinging to the past. The road to knowledge is not a straight path to the truth, but a fork in the road that must walked in both directions to map the parameters.

Hanes, however, is gratified by the knowledge that there are others seeking the same answers as he. They are moving from long-held beliefs of theological explanations to the cold clear clarity of calculating medicine. They are unlocking thoughts that do not entertain obvious answers. Aggressive scientists who reach past the veneer of limited possibilities reveal an epoch of understanding; those who hide in the shadows doom history to repetition.

We left in good time and came in after nightfall to Klausenburgh. The locals refer to this city as Cluj. We stopped for the night at the Hotel Royal. Our supper was a chicken done up in a red pepper called paprika hendl. Apparently, this is a national dish and is available anywhere along the Carpathians.

In light of an earlier conversation with Dr. Hanes on how he does an autopsy, I let him carve the chicken.

I find my smattering of German very useful here. Of course, Hanes speaks several dialects and we are prepared to meet Brother Jacob.

I still cannot believe that I'm here in Transylvania—such a mystical place! Even the most learned English gentleman would have trouble knowing where this land is located, let alone know that it even existed. I had stumbled upon this place when I researched in the library for *Under the Sunset*. Yet, I'm still unprepared for the journey.

I did once, in fact, visit the British Museum and made a search of the books and maps regarding Transylvania. I made note that one day the place would make a fine setting for an erotic love story of some kind. Now that I am here and it is nothing like I expected.

This is the "land beyond the forest" or the *Uterwald* as it is referred to by the villagers. The region is an S-shaped congregation of mountains called the Carpathians.

We are moving to the extreme eastern part of the country just on the border of three states: Transylvania, Moldavia and Bukovina. This is one of the wildest and least known areas of Europe.

Transylvania might just as well be termed the land of superstition, for nowhere else does delusion flourish in such a bewildering variety. It seems as if there has been a mass migration of demons, witches and werewolves, driven from the rest of Europe by the wand of science, have taken refuge in this land of acceptance.

Among these mountain ranges, deep dark caves and secret mountain chasms those abnormally fabulous beings reside, insinuated into the souls of the local inhabitants, growing fertile in the imagination of poetic minds.

In the population of Transylvania there are four distinct nationalities: the Saxons and the Wallachs, who are descendants of the Dacians, in the south, Magyars to the west, and Szekelys in the east and north. We are heading toward the latter, whom I may mistakenly believe are descendants of Attila the Hun.

I believe that when the Magyars conquered the country in eleventh century, the Huns were already there. I may be wrong, but I do know that the wolves of different nationalities have battled over the bones of this region's existence.

It seems to me that every superstition conceivable is gathered into the horseshoe of the Carpathian Mountains, which has become the center of an imaginative whirlpool. Each nationality brought its various superstitions, intermingling them through the centuries, and embellishing each tale to perfection.

The one thing that strikes me the most is the number of religious symbols that adorn peasant houses; equally impressive are the carvings of the porches surrounding the houses. Hanes tells me that these ingenious carvings are called *pridvor*.

As we walked to the marketplace to gather supplies before leaving in the morning for Bistria, we found that bits of information have started to filter into the city. Most of it is unreliable, and the stories are already steeped in superstitious intensity. Obvious embellishments have been added in the retelling. I was struck by the number of peasants who crossed themselves before telling us of the dark rumors and crossing themselves again when they were finished.

We were told that an unknown number of *murony*, which Hanes said was Romanian for a vampire that can take the shape of almost any creature, attacked the tiny village of Rodna and killed all the inhabitants.

The *murony* drained their victims of all their blood—as any self-respecting *murony* would do, I suppose. This blatant attack was preceded by a series of mutilations of cattle, unexplained disappearances and murders of peasants in the surrounding hills. As should be expected, the Devil is in all the details.

Brother Jacob, in his message to Hanes, stated that the killers will attempt to hide in the Borgo Pass.

My journey promises to be very interesting

I'm having trouble sleeping, but I can't say it is the bed, which is certainly comfortable enough. I am having queer dreams. Possibly, the stories that we heard this day have affected me more than I thought. Then again I have been having these terrible dreams since I began this journey with Irving. What is bothering me now is that they may be prophetic and that thought frightens me.

Meeting Brother Jacob tomorrow.

We have heard all the tales filtering in about the massacre and continue to be surprised at how difficult it is to get accurate information in this region.

Each new description is more sinister and much more fanciful than the last. The stones of embellishment, aided by the fabrication of abject horror, give weight to a disbelief that sinks the reality of understanding far below the waters of truth.

Hanes is concerned about the lack of specific details, and he fears the trail will run cold before we can get there. It is obvious we cannot count on a jury of accurate description to proceed with our journey. We must take it upon ourselves to judge the veracity of what has happened. After centuries of tall tales, how can we expect to get an accurate understanding from a people who believe that werewolves are as common as house pets?

Hanes tells me he is concerned that the sordid details are obscuring the truth. And he is baffled by the reports, because this tragedy has taken place so close to us, less than a day away, we are told. He wishes that Brother Jacob had come to meet us by now. He craves reliable information and seems alarmed by the horrific stories being circulated.

Hanes will be posting messages in the morning. I have nothing to send except a short note to Florence and Noel, and I will direct Irving to go ahead to England when he's finished with the count. I do want to see how all this comes out.

Irish whiskey helps me sleep, but the howling of some manner of dog or beast, perched threateningly outside my room, woke me. Dressed.

All day long, we seemed to dawdle through a country, which is full of beauty of every kind. Sometimes, we see little towns or castles a top of steep hills, and rivers born, no doubt, from great floods. I see beautiful clear water flowing like liquefied glass through breathtaking mountain canyons into rich fertile valleys. As we pass every station, we see groups of people—and sometimes crowds—attired in various native garb. Hanes tells me the fur hats are called caciula.

Some of these people looked just like the peasants I've seen before; others like the ones in Germany or France. Their short jackets, rounded hats and distinctive trousers gave them a flair and made them very picturesque. I especially liked the *cojoc*, a sheepskin-lined vest that was quite attractive.

The women were handsome, except when you get too close to them and discovered they were clumsy about the waist. They all had full white sleeves of some kind or other, and most of them had big belts with a lot of colorful strips fluttering from them—rather like the dresses in a ballet. But, of course, they wore petticoats under them. Their dresses were wide, long and trimmed in black contrasting with a rainbow of other colors.

The strangest figures we saw were the Slovaks, the most barbaric tribe of all, I imagine. With their large hats, baggy white trousers, white linen shirts and foot-wide leather belts studded with brass nails, they presented a fine savage prospect.

They wore their high boots with the trousers tucked inside and sported heavy black moustaches and long black hair. Intimating to say the least! They glared at us grimly, taking our measure as we moved past them.

On the stage, they would be cast at once as an exotic band of brigands.

Bistritz

It was on the dark side of twilight when we finally arrived at Bistitz, the starting point for the Borgo Pass, which leads through the mountains and forest to Bukovina, the third principality in the triad of the new Romania.

Bistritz has had a stormy existence with a history of many great fires and once lost thirteen thousand of its people to famine and disease during a devastating siege. That is what the local historians say of this calamity to outsiders. All references were couched with a shrug of tepid finality. That is the way of this land.

But I'm sure something more sinister happened here. All traces of this tragic event and the true fate of those people have long since disappeared. Only the oral tradition still exists and, when the siege is mentioned, the locals cross themselves and lapse into silence. They will not venture any further. The only thing that remains is an abandoned fortress that gives off flames of various hues that illuminate the night sky. This place is never visited and it is regarded evil.

Hanes has doubts about how much help we can expect from the populace here. Whatever is going on in this region will probably be accepted as fate. The locals are aware that something terrible is happening, but Hanes is not certain they would offer to join us in our investigation. I'm left to wonder why we would need them.

Hanes is hoping his American friends will catch up to us in Bistria. He is almost desperate in his hope that others will join us in our inquiry. He is gleaning something in all these wild tales that alarms him.

When we left Budapest, Hanes telegraphed Mathewson and Gray Shadow about the situation and left further instructions on our itinerary. He also left detailed instructions for them in case they might be willing to accompany us. When we arrived in Bistria, he inquired if they had responded, but they had not as yet.

He is not sure they are fully aware of the circumstances or even what their intentions are. He seems very hopeful that they would come, but he will not explain why that would be so important. They may just have moved eastward directly to join the archduke. I can't imagine that they would come all this way to chase a pack of marauding gypsies.

Dinner with Hanes at the hotel.

I find him more fascinating every time I talk to him. He is very astute and may well be the most intelligent man I have ever met.

In our talks, he shares his views with me—views I really do find insightful. I marvel at this provocative mind at work and at the thoughts presented with an unassuming and kind demeanor.

We checked out of the Golden Krone Hotel and received a message that Brother Jacob would be arriving shortly. While we waited, another messenger arrived with instructions to meet Brother Jacob at the site of the latest attack. Hanes was deeply troubled. He did not share the contents of the letter with me.

Hanes told me of his relationship with Jacob, a German Benedictine monk residing at the Melke Abbey on the Danube River in lower Austria. Jacob's role with the church was as an investigator of the supernatural and he had been assigned by the cardinal to perform exorcisms where necessary. He was always on call whenever evil invaded the conscious world.

Brother Jacob was investigating a plague near the Danube that had all the earmarks of a vampire infestation. High fever, loss of appetite and fatigue were the earliest symptoms. Later, patients tried to avoid sunlight and only seemed comfortable at night. Exposure to bright lights caused a number of the victims to lapse into violent animal-like behavior, attacking people and biting them. Once bitten, the others began to experience the same symptoms as their attackers.

Grotesque facial spasms and an aversion to garlic by the afflicted caused the local church officials to initiate their ancient vampire rites, a course of action that horrified Brother Jacob. He knew that they would soon be removing and burning internal organs and driving ash or hawthorn stakes through the hearts of the infected.

In desperation, Brother Jacob contacted Dr. Hanes. They had known each other by reputation, having been involved in such matters throughout Germany. Learning from Jacob's correspondence that a real life vampire scare was possible, Hanes rushed to the scene as quickly as possible. Upon his arrival, it didn't take long for him to deduce that this was not the work of vampires at all, but an unfortunate outbreak of rabies.

The fact that the church was prepared to accept vampires, as was the populace, was a concern to Hanes. He also discovered that such nonsensical beliefs were deeply troubling to Jacob, who was disgusted that the local church included vampire killing as a ritual. This disturbing doctrine needed to be addressed and it became the cause that united them.

They worked closely for several months, debunking a number of so-called supernatural incidents throughout Europe. Each and every one turned out to have a rational explanation. In some cases, death was the work of desperate animals, and in one particular case, the work of a band of murderous gypsies.

In Romania, this land of ancient folklore, there exists a deep superstition as the divergence of religious beliefs clash with both good and evil. Still further evident is the struggle between the Catholics of this country, bound directly to the Holy Roman Empire and their Orthodox brethren who trace their pedigree to the Eastern church and still mourn the fall of Constantinople to the infidel Muslims.

Romanians of the Orthodox faith, Germanic Catholics and Oriental tribes of Huns and Skelkers, have all lived and fought in this region. The battle of religious and social beliefs has caused an uncertainty of values as deeply rooted and as volatile as the superstitions the people cling to so tenaciously. The dispute goes beyond Muslim and Christian as the very tenet of those beliefs is entwined in ethnic values and religious politics. The war between religions will be waged among humanity long after we are all gone.

And within that struggle is the fact that the Orthodox Church is tearing Christianity into factions as it begins to attain dominance over the Roman Catholic lineage. Theirs is a shifting alliance thinly spread among diverse beliefs.

Political unrest, too, is brewing between the nobility and the gentry, and both are at odds with the peasant movements. A titanic struggle is taking stage as these worlds collide, with an equally complex and growing nationalism searching dominance. This is not just true here, it is happening everywhere in Europe.

Underneath it all is the dark side of human nature. The cornucopia of supernatural beliefs, passed on with blessed reverence as if the truth, is pervasive. All who listen, believe.

Why is the dark side so readily accepted here? Surely the old myths were not absolute inventions; they must have had a basis somewhere in fact. May not the story of Orpheus and Euridyce have been based on some deep lying principle or power of human nature? There is not one of us, for example, who has not wished at some time to bring back the dead. Is that why evil is at the heart of these spoken morality plays? Because much of it is true?

The blood of diverse peoples has spilled into a common cup, making each sip bitter to the taste of a universal theory.

The European sensibilities and the German influences fade as the landscape moves eastward. While still familiar to Europeans, we begin falling under the spell of Asian and Balkan influences as we get away from the larger cities and towns. That influence is more superstitious in nature and less inclined to have the intellectual and cultural basis of the more refined civilization to the west.

Stirred into the Romanian cauldron of beliefs is the certainty that evil forces are allied against the worship of goodness and God. The poetic nature of these people presupposes that the religion of God and the doctrine of evil are two equally believable sides of the same coin.

I've discovered some relevant information in a further conversation with Hanes. There is more to this than I could have initially imagined. I think I have a better understanding of what drives both Jacob and Hanes. I sense that more than just happenstance is driving these coincidental forces together.

I now believe that there is a higher purpose to this journey.

Notes on Brother Jacob:

There has been a prevailing myth among Catholics that the Vatican has long maintained a secret army of most holy warriors versed in the ways of the dark forces and tasked to defeat them. These cadres of warrior monks are not the same as the Knights Templar. These groups of holy warriors fight ethereal battles, not the physical ones. The Templar was chartered to defended pilgrims on their way to the Holy Lands. The spectral warriors of the church fight for the souls of man by knowing the ways of his enemy better then the dark forces aligned against them. From what I am hearing now I suspect it is not a myth at all. Based on what I have learned from Hanes, I now believe Brother Jacob is just such a man.

The Church in Rome supposedly recruits Christian warriors of pristine reputation to represent them—someone versed in the ways of demonology and equal to the daunting task of confronting evil. They are also called Exorcists!

The German Catholic Church in this area, specifically the Benedictine order, is among the cadre of the knights pledged to those Christian orders.

They are waging a holy war against the forces of evil and the superstitions that this land has cultivated.

This holy war has raged for many centuries and has yet to be won. The Benedictines are among the elite of Christianity, feared by all things evil. Only one other order has such a cachet in this land, the tempestuous monks of the Christian Orthodoxy.

Werewolves, vampires, plagues of unknown nature, torment the dreams of these people. Living nightmares haunt the night with deadly designs.

Brother Jacob, as a Benedictine monk, was trained by the Catholic Church to expunge evil from the souls of the afflicted and the unbelieving. He must combat the extinction of Catholic beliefs and the increasing power of the Orthodox religion.

Hanes inadvertently let slip that Jacob was also a member of the venerable Order of the Rose Cross, a shadowy theological group. That confirms in my mind that Brother Jacob is such a soldier. I have long suspected a fraternal conspiracy of orders between the Masons and the church, but this conspiracy of allies may go even deeper. There are forces beyond our understanding in the recesses of the world's most secret places. I have been investigating these conspiracies for years in the hopes of writing a book, but so much has still escaped me. I cannot confirm anything more then the innuendo and have been frustrated by this code of silence that blankets the bed of discovery. Regardless of that, I can see the clues and I feel that there is a level to Hanes that goes beyond the very polished and educated veneer he projects. This may mean that Dr. Hanes is also a Rosicrucian. Somehow that does not surprise me.

Dr. Von Hanes' interest in alchemy and the very stature of his metaphysical being translates well to his enlightened way of thinking. He possesses a bearing that is very potent as if he holds the key to secrets yet to be divulged. Still, I feel a confidence in what he doesn't say; it's as if he holds such truths to a value best left unspoken.

What I have heard is that the Order of the Rose Cross is a secret theological society dedicated to the cause of universal peace. By any means necessary from what I hear. There exists within its temple a subset of knights more fearsome then the Knights Templar themselves. Still, how could something that formidable even exist? One day they hope to engineer a new day of reckoning meant to enforce a New World Order, dedicated to understanding of selfless improvement, which they hope can bring happiness and an understanding of the world around us. I can see both Hanes and Brother Jacob in such a fraternity.

The fraternal order of the Rosicrucian's is rumored to be the custodian of sacred teachings and supposedly hold formidable spiritual power. Then there are their overlords. Those members called enlightened and who gain their power from the forbidden teachings of the Illuminati.

The ancient Illuminati society was so feared that it was thought to have been dismantled and ultimately destroyed by the ruling classes of Europe. But it is well known that the cosmic philosophy of Illuminati still exists in the underworld of human knowledge. The real power of their union survived because they were safe in their nameless unanimity. The mere mention of the Illuminati can bring the most eager tongue to silence and the most powerful of men to deference. No one living takes the call of understanding lightly when it is professed in Illuminati's name.

I have heard these truths expressed by others within those secret orders that admire and fear the Illuminati, but seek comfort in the respectful teachings of the Rosicrucians. Like Dr. Von Hanes, for instance.

Brother Jacob would certainly have shared such information with someone like Hanes. His very being and background must be near the fringes of demonology and its charters. He is wise to the ways of the woods and streams, yet rooted in Catholic theology to its core and wed to the philosophy of real good and real evil. So it is not surprising that he would seek additional enlightenment with the Rose Cross, an order that would arm a Christian soldier emotionally to face the Devil firsthand.

These are the ways of the dark side of mankind in seeking the light. The shadowy secrets of the Illuminati are kept hidden from the common view. In doing so, the Illuminati maintain their power. As we move closer to our destiny and enter this "Uterwald," I can think of no other place on earth where such a convergence of ideals would congregate more readily then this mysterious land of the forest. We are entering the very center of a dark universe.

Malevolence prospers here. Evil in its human form is readily accepted by the populace. Evil in this land is living and breathing in the dress of human cloth; a living and breathing monster capable of taking human form.

This is a historical fact that has hardened in the thick wood of legend. Horrible deeds are passed down by generations of fertile imaginations and compiled like the rings of a terrible tree of history. The forces of an enlightened journey are darkest when the soul is denied the sun of love and understanding. The Devil's influence is initiated in the darkest night of scripted thought. The swords are being unsheathed and good and evil march to confrontation. This resounds in Rosicrucian doctrine. This journey shrouds itself in a determination that I can only feel is preordained, not serendipity. What dangers await us as we move toward this destiny? I fear an epic battle is coming.

Why would they have undertaken such a challenge? Are they somehow forewarned of a coming calamity? There is a sense of expectation in this quest—something Hanes and Brother Jacob have been preparing for all their lives.

I cannot escape this sense of doom as we prepare to leave Bistria. .

The mood of this city is somber and dark, even in the morning light. Rumors are circulating everywhere about the attack and a great concern prevails. But the concern is more related to the inevitability of it all and less toward the possible causes.

I'm struck, however, by the seeming unwillingness of the townspeople to investigate. They seem resigned to some terrible tragedy having befallen the village, but show no inclination to pursue whatever caused it. They are all too willing to accept some dark fate as if it were inevitable.

Hanes attributes this to the centuries of strange cataclysmic events and their own ability to rationalize such tragedies as some evil conation beyond their control.

Tragedies have happened before and they will happen again. This is the way of the land of this life. Strange indeed since Bistria seems more cultivated a city than I expected. How can anyone be so condescending to such news?

We rented horses and embarked on the ten-mile journey to meet Brother Jacob. We were amazed at how quiet the countryside is. Very few villagers come out of their abodes to see us. Only an occasional curtain with a pair of uncertain eyes peeking from behind the embroidery look at us with a glance or frightened stare.

We finally reach our destination. Brother Jacob rushes toward us with as we enter the village. He's a middle aged man with a face of lined integrity, though he is small and of an almost impish size. Behind his kind eyes exudes a wise and steely purpose. His aura is of kindness and strength worn wearily. No doubt he has been worn down by his many battles against evil. Still, he was not what I was expecting.

Brother Jacob seemed almost giddy to see us. Under the circumstances, this seemed odd. I realized that at closer inspection it was not giddiness at all.

What I was seeing in Jacob was an anxiety on the cusp of madness. These terrible events were watering a flower of budding insanity in Jacob. Hanes saw it, too. He commented that Jacob appeared very agitated, a sure sign that something out of the ordinary was at work here.

The seeds of uncertainty and fear were just starting to sprout from the soil of Jacob's fertile soul. I felt some inner struggle was taking place within this once profoundly rational man. The weight of unspeakable horror was straining his mind, the load tipping ever so slightly to the unbalanced. The sight of us seemed to invigorate him emotionally. However, his joy was tempered by the circumstances.

Brother Jacob had a wordless familiarity with Hanes, and after my brief and awkward introduction, Jacob brought us inside into the rectory.

"The magnitude of this massacre is truly frightening," he told us nervously. "The most horrible consequences I could have ever imagined!"

Hanes urged him to tell us more.

"We first became aware of mutilations of livestock. Small instances here and there. Then villagers began to disappear. A few days before the attack on the village, we uncovered the bodies of those missing people. The cruel damage inflicted on them was disturbing. That is when I decided I needed you. This is like nothing we have ever encountered, my friend. I knew I needed you immediately. I thank the Lord that you have come so quickly."

"Why is this so different from anything else we've encountered?" Hanes asked.

"Even in a world as hard and brutal as exists in these mountains, I cannot explain the evil that took place," Jacob answered. "I fear the scope of it is beyond my ability to comprehend. It just cannot be explained.

"We are at the apex of what we both feared. We just had another attack and it was far worse than the last one. Dark clouds are growing into a blackness that will block the sunlight of an enlightened existence. I thank providence for your close proximity."

Brother Jacob then gave Dr. Hanes a summary of what had happened.

"The details are sketchy because no one has lived much past the attack. A marauding band of murderers struck a small village near the hills above us. It is the village of Tinsk, which is a much larger than Rodna. The inhabitants there were attacked at dusk by some unknown force that ripped quickly and bloodily through the village killing all the men, women and children in a most horrible way. Their throats were rent by savage bites and the blood of the victims had been drained from their bodies. In brutal fashion, many of the bodies had been torn apart. Unholy bites, Von. Savage and cruel!"

"Can they be animal bites?" Hanes asked.

"No, wolves don't kill like this, and it is not gypsies, either."

"Is it possible the time is at hand, Brother Jacob?" Hanes asked more or less to himself.

"Yes, but if you ask the villagers they have their own answer: The *strigloi* have arrived and they thirst for human blood."

I asked Dr. Hanes what a *strigloi* was.

"The *strigloi* is a mythical wolf-like species that legend says preys on livestock." Then turning back to Jacob, he said, "No, Brother, and it is not a *nosferatu*, either.

"We are assembling a group to give chase and we will be joined by the great boyar, himself, Advar, and his people," Jacob said.

Hanes looked extremely worried and said, "I sense something unnatural about this and it unnerves me."

Chapter 14

I went outside for a walk and for the first time I understood what I had gotten myself into. My head still reeling from our meeting with Brother Jacob I searched the hills for the evil described just moments ago. Instead I found beauty. Surveying the majestic countryside, I rejoiced in its beauty: rich forests, deep and hilly; the mountains, steep and green and tall. Nestled attractively between the mountains lay lush farm valleys. So peaceful, yet so dark around the edges.

What a tapestry this could be for imagination—this dichotomy of nature's gentleness and its effect upon the locals' primitive fear of the unknown. The fear must be in the darkness of night.

What creatures of their dark imagination howl in the night? What grist for fairytales! One can only imagine the nightmares that haunt their living dreams. Does the silence of their fear shout even in their dreams, echoing louder than the fear itself? Does this silence left unspoken raise its clarion voice to a haunting truth? The realities of those words spoken are knowingly, cryptically and ominously, elusive words meant to hide the true meanings. A nod of understanding, an accepted truth perhaps. This then is the mouth-to-mouth exchange of a superstitious nature. They see it as the unknown but accept it as the truth and that truth is the existence of evil.

The eyes of these people do not stare blankly. They look beyond those simple beliefs, for their eyes are too mature to endure the living evil lurking in these mountains. The peasants nod politely and express no fear of what preceded them, but grasp upon relics of holy protection to ward off evils yet to come. Are they blind to these myths? Not likely. They know they've seen evil and somehow they have survived. The history of the evil in these mountains is too real to be forgotten. At best they know it as the pain of war yet they embellish that pain by giving it a name. Holy wars.

Why has this all happened? Where does such cruelty come from? How can this land of such holy worship bare such a devil's curse—a cruel curse aged like a red wine, aged so much by evil intentions that the blood of history runs cold with each new tragedy? And why are such horrible fates so benignly accepted as simply a way of life?

Endless destruction of humanity in God's name is accepted too easily here. The death of its peasantry is celebrated more as a national rite of passage than as the bane of their society. Why do they not protest?

The ancient and timeworn misery of conquest is acknowledged too readily, despite the fact that it was their blood that flowed in rivers. After each new conquest, the dam of their blood gathered in a whirlpool of God's intentions. Why do they call it a crusade? What virtue do those leaders possess that inspires such blood letting in the name of a selfish vanity? How have they seduced these innocents to accomplish their own ends. Whose cross do these poor souls actually carry? Blood waters overflowing with the Devil's curse, sated with the blood of innocent souls within each new retribution. Purpose long ago lost to the ages

How many of these souls have died in God's name? What true God would accept the souls of such cruel men, covered with the blood of the misled crusaders? It might just be that they were actually being misled and were following the devils lead after all.

One can see why the power of good and evil would be on equal footing here. The Devil has won more victories in defeat than God has in victory. The evil one has never wavered in his intentions. He exists as just another relic living amongst them in these deep forests.

I was finishing my latest entry when a great shadow eclipsed me. I was keenly aware of a large presence coming from behind. When I spun around, I was confronted by the largest and fiercest looking man I had ever seen. His huge shoulders carried a large head with a black flowing mustache and sharp angry eyes. Behind him a group of equally intimidating men, almost as large and just as fierce in their demeanor. My eye also caught a touch of beauty in the woman riding on horseback behind them. She was an attractive dark-haired woman with flashing brown eyes—eyes filled with a determination and purpose. Others quickly joined her. They were also on horseback.

Before I knew it, I was surrounded. They circled around me, curious, I presume, about this stranger among them. I did feel a sense of peril, but I cannot seem to displace their stern comportment with my warmest smile.

I was clearly a stranger to them and, in these times, not the ideal role to be playing. I cannot for the life of me ever think that I could be taken for a murderer, but I seemed to be having trouble making them understand that.

Thankfully, Brother Jacob rushed from the rectory and embraced the large man. The fierce warrior turned out to be Advar, the leader of this group. He is a boyar, a leader of his people, and a member of the gentry class. As such, he and his cast are rivals to the entrenched nobility of Romania.

These boyars come from the land of the free peasants, who are also known as the small property holders. Unlike the serfs and sharecroppers of other times, they are not beholden to the nobility. Boyars and peasants are at the forefront of a building nationalist movement.

They have come here to bring an end to this plague.

With my identity vouched for by Brother Jacob and my friendship announced, a relaxation of tensions was quickly achieved. I was privileged to see the other side of these people as they smile broadly at me. Just as quickly as I felt their suspicions, I suddenly felt at ease. In fact, I felt quite warm and protected in their presence.

With the eyes of a writer, I studied these New Romanians with a heartfelt study. Advar's group was about twenty-five men and four astonishing women. The men were imposing with their many weapons and obvious skill with the horse, not unlike the legendary Huns, I imagine. But it was the women who took my breath away.

Astride their horses, these beautiful creatures made my blood flush with warm attraction. I must admit that my genteel English background had not prepared me for such a sight. My heart raced at the sight of their womanly confidence and intense carriage they displayed, and none too subtlety, their feminine wiles. Their high black boots and brave deportment made them clearly competent, but alluring just the same.

While the cold mist of morning gave way to a brightening sun, we were at once united in the common course of our action. The horsemen have come to end the terror and save their loved ones who are still in the path of some unknown danger.

This formidable group had at once embraced me with their friendship. They were grateful that Hanes and I had come, even though we had yet to prove our mettle. They seemed to know long before I did that we were embarking on this crusade with the help of our God's blessing and under the curse of the Devil.

I realized that I was now a passenger on this journey, sworn by my presence to bring this plague to its conclusion. We are bound by fate to share its dangers and set out upon this dangerous quest.

I am quite taken by the beauty of Antonia. She cannot hide her splendor behind the rough hues of a man's native dress. She only highlights the costume's design fully. I must admit that I'm intrigued by her smile and thrilled when she inspects me with an almost childlike curiosity.

I realize that the attraction only goes one way, but she is unbridled in her attempt to ascertain my value. I am enjoying the blessed fruits of idle imagination and take joy in following her in apt inquisitiveness.

Hers is a distinctive feminine form shaped exquisitely like an hourglass. She flows shapely from behind her masculine wall of leather and cloth. Her bright white smile is a welcome sight. Her long brown hair is flowing from beneath a crown of thick braids. Tiny strands of hair dance seductively in the forefront of blazing brown eyes. Her aquiline nose gently slopes toward her rich full lips that glisten naturally and seductively. Still, there is a pure power and strength to this woman.

Her high black boots shine boldly and serve to draw my eyes upward to her shapely thighs. She flags a mast of colorful scarves worn as bandanas around her forehead with some remnants of the scarves tied into two elaborate pigtails that flap joyfully in the wind. Armored with a thick leather belt wrapped tightly around her waist, she moves with strength and grace upon her horse.

Embroidered on her saddle is a small poem written in German, which I interpret as:

A knight of a woman less dark of day
As the one called woman whose visions slay
The Dragons fire turned away
By the Perils born of her forceful way.

As she rides with her three women companions, I listen brightly as she calls out to Advar in the floral beauty of the Romanian language. Her voice is heavy of native tongue, but joyful to the ear, a whisper so loud that it caresses me gently. Still deaf to its meaning, I am alarmingly attuned to its cadence. I rejoice in a voice of almost perfect pitch, soothing as it excites me.

The other women bear a feminine quality in their manly garb, but do not possess the breath of vision like Antonia. Still, they project able menace in their very feminine continence and should not be trifled with.

The oldest one is named Sonja, and she appears to be a little weathered in face and quiet in her majesty. While she lacks some of the grace of femininity, she styles provocatively upon her horse, cool in measure and stern in quality. She is devoid of jewelry of any kind and swathes her forehead with a blue bandanna. Her beauty is her very presence.

One conjures up the legacy of the young gypsy woman when you encounter Alia, the youngest of the four. Dark of skin and strong of temper, Alia possesses the green flashing eyes of curiosity, hiding an apparent guile with the innocence of understanding. Her feline head and penetrating stare remind me of a beautiful cat.

She is of athletic build, but very beguiling in a shapely way. Watching her on the saddle it appears she's the best horsewoman. She jingles with flashing rings of gold upon her ears, and is plated around the neck with a necklace ringed with tiny gold hearts. She compliments her masculine haberdashery with the flowing eloquence of a bright silk scarf.

Finally, we are left with Radii, who is tall and slim with thick red hair. She is not homely by any measure, but of plain face and blank expression: she lacks the aura of a personality. She remains remote and distant, yet is apparently a capable horsewoman and is the best shooter of the group according to Brother Jacob.

I must say that am amazed by what I see. I never expected to encounter this form of titillation so far away from home.

The gray of the morning has passed and the sun is high over the distant horizon, which seems jagged, whether with trees or hills I do not know. We rode up a mountainous hill and before us lies a green stretch of land, crowned with a cluster of trees and farmhouses, the blank gable end to the road. What we found there still chills my very soul, but I must report on the sickening scene as if I were reliving the awful moment.

A sandy road beckoned us, leading us to a congregation of small huts and a church. The huts are configured on each side of the road. Behind them lies a short path leading up the hill. Atop this hill is a large stone-rimmed well. A bloody red cross is scrawled on the stone cylinder.

Clambering of hoofs announce our entry into the doomed village. Their metrical patter disturbs the unnatural silence that oppresses us. We are ashen faced and mute, brought to this stunned silence by the sheer violence of the attack. All around huts are sprayed with blood. Tracks of human struggle mark the ground. Prints of human hands reaching desperately for some anchor, some last ditch way to brace against an evil pull.

Failing at last to find safety against a violent force, these poor souls have met their maker—an introduction made with the most horrific force imaginable. Those cold remnants of humanity lay contorted in petrified fear, shocked into lasting torment by the cruel hands of death ripping them sharply from the sanctuary they so desperately reached for.

The white of their skin is burning under the morning sun now, unblemished by the purity of their hearts. The wounds inflicted show no signs of bleeding; they appear as if carved in marble, deep white crevices torn into human skin. They rest in awkward peace, left to face an unwanted reality as some terrible force of doom consumed them. How it must have been for them? What are we going to do?

The state of shock is etched deeply into our collective faces, nowhere more evident then with Advar and his men. Grim and silent we spread out, each one of us exploring the evidence of this inferno of despair.

Most of the dead have been buried, but a few still remain, a decomposing frame of human reference. The stench of death lies heavy in our nostrils, the incense hanging like black perfume: the lasting aroma of their last rites. But the heavy sweet smells of the priest's incense cannot mask the overwhelming odor of this senseless fatality.

A burial party of hooded villagers, their faces masked by sweaty scarves draped across their noses, works in unison, slowly and methodically.

A weariness of grim reaping has taken its toll upon the villagers' bodies, slowed to lingering motion by deep despair. They have been digging too many graves. A small pile of religious artifacts and crosses are heaped in an ever-growing mound, amalgamated together like a treasure chest of worthless trinkets. The value of relics fostered little protection for these lost souls.

Upon seeing Advar and his men, the hooded minions of despair bow their heads slightly in recognition and cross themselves at the passing of Brother Jacob.

Hanes points out that demonstration of respect toward Bother Jacob is unusual because they are not villagers, but Orthodox monks, who have traditionally taken a dim view of the Catholic Church and those who serve it. Something extraordinary is happening and Jacob is a little unnerved by it.

Their eyes meet in but a glance of bemused uncertainty, perplexed by a gesture that seems predicated upon a strange occurrence—an occurrence so terrifying it had a coalescing effect upon such rivals. The enemy of my enemy is my friend and in our God we must learn to trust, this look of solidarity seems to be saying.

Advar and his sister are shocked when they see the twisted and torn remains of a loved one. Antonia cries echo heavily throughout the valley, piercing and sharp with pain and anguish.

Advar grimaces and then fixes a steely gaze at the surrounding mountains. He looks determined and transfixed. He and his men dismount and finish the burials, which are then accomplished in quick order. They stand around the graves and quietly mouth their prayers. Advar stares again at the hills above us, his eyes searching for the signs of the enemy.

Dr. Hanes, who must have seen many terrible sights in his life, is trying hard to keep his wits about him. Defiantly, it seems, he maintains a business-like composure as he searches the bloody ground, quietly checking clues and quickly making notes. He looks at the bloodstains with sanguine amazement, then finds something unexpected. He stops every so often to sigh heavily and to shake his head.

A deeply saddened Brother Jacob prays continuously at each grave site. He prays so rapidly that it appears as if he is afraid to stop, as if one single moment without those prayers would bring the world to an end.

I, on the other hand, feel strangely excited and amazed at how much energy flows through me as I confront this overwhelming fear. I am drawn to this as if this is my destiny. Every sinew of my body is pulsating with energy. My heart beats rapidly, my head is bursting in anticipation, even as uncertainty encircles me. This overwhelming tragedy embraces my raw emotions.

I sidle up to Hanes as he tells me what he has seen.

The fierce and violent wounds are unlike any he has ever seen. The creatures responsible, clearly not human, did this damage with uncommon speed and skill, not like any animal he was aware of. He is surprised that there were no bodies of whatever inflicted this slaughter. These villagers did not fight back. He is also surprised at how little blood remained in the mutilated corpses. They were all drained of their blood. He is clearly confused by what has happened. It is apparent that this bothers him a great deal. What in God's name are we facing? What manner of death is this?

Advar wandered beyond the outskirts of the village. Cautiously I followed him, feeling his great size would be of more benefit to my protection than the rosary beads of Brother Jacob or the intelligence of Dr. Hanes. He picks up a trail it seems. He moves quickly into the thick forest of trees. When he reaches a cusp of a small clearing, he stops.

Advar is suddenly startled and momentarily frightened when the bloody remnant of a human hand falls abruptly on his shoulder. A bloodless body slides clumsily on top of him. His fear turns quickly to sorrow as he realizes that this is the body of someone he once knew. The corpse is riddled with deep bite marks. Its throat is ripped wide open.

The boyar's imposing frame wrenches in a shaking anger, his large hands clench in white fury, his powerful cry is filled with the raw language of a man in pain and sorrow. He suddenly and instinctively comes to a stop, for he is now acutely aware of a movement in the woods surrounding us. He prepares his weapons for battle. Without words, Advar hands me a pistol, gesturing at me to point in a specific direction. We stood erect as we wait anxiously to be attacked. But our surprise is complete when, effortlessly, and with the stunning stealth of an American Indian in full battle regalia, a figure slipped in behind us. In front of us a human voice of quiet calm defuses the tension as it calls out: "Peace, we come in peace."

Out from the thick brush comes another startling figure, an imposing American cowboy in fringed buckskin. He has a white flowing beard. His eyes sparkle with a glint of confidence.

His handsome and weathered face unfolds into a sly smile as he senses the tension and wishes to deflate it.

"I'm William Mathewson, a friend of Dr. Hanes. Gray Shadow and I are here to help."

The immense Advar smiles warily. He has obviously never seen an American Indian before. In heavily accented English, the boyar turns toward Gray Shadow and says: "You, darky, you have come a long way, no?"

Gray Shadow smiles quietly and he sheaths his knife

Advar turns to the regally buckskin-clad Mathewson and with dancing eyes and says, "You've come far, too, bison man."

Mathewson laughs and says, "I hope you don't think we are responsible for this."

Advar smiles grimly. "No human could do this. *Strigloi* maybe…werewolf . . .but nothing human."

Mathewson nods solemnly and rips off a chaw of tobacco. He offers some to us. I decline, but Advar swallows a piece whole and turns a yellow green.

'"Only once before have I seen this, but never to this extent," Mathewson says. "Never anything like this."

Gray Shadow looks intently at the body. "No, Mathewson. This is not a Ja-ha-bich. This is the work of Kamiah."

"What does Kamiah mean?" I ask.

"To the Indians, Kamiah is a monster created by the devil," Mathewson says.

"Nothing we speak of can describe this. Not even the Dracul could do this work," Advar says. "We will find our answers later."

We join the rest of the party in the doomed village and we organize our strength to move upward through the Borgo Pass. The sun has set around us. We are heartened by the full moon, gloriously blue hued and bright upon the clear cool night.

The shuffling of equine hooves and jingle of saddle accessories dance around me as we march toward whatever is responsible for this great terror.

Very little is said as move forward. Occasionally, Hanes and Gray Shadow converse in some form of Indian language, while Advar looks on in amazement.

One thing that I am aware of is the fascination the women have for the trim and muscular Gray Shadow. He is awash in beautiful beads and feathers with gay patterns embroidered into his light leather shirt. He rides atop his horse as if floating. His sharp eyes take in the world at a one hundred eighty-degree angle. His smooth dark skin is rich and without blemish and stretched taut to his body as if sewn tightly by nature. The wisdom of his face is etched in experience and with it a kindness marked by a sage understanding of life.

The women cast their eyes upon him and glance at each other with girlish delight, sparkling eyes betraying their intended harsh deportment for what lies ahead. They lapse for fleeting moments into charming little women, precocious in their small flirtations with the Indian warrior. He looks back at them with bemused consideration, hiding a warm smile at the attention, fully knowing that such trivial pursuits are for other less demanding times.

In the scheme of the human adventure such small events are reassuring to us all.

We quickly begin our pursuit of whoever has committed these horrific murders.

Even though they are not familiar with the terrain, the Americans provide us with a sense of relief at their presence. While they do not know what lies ahead of them, they seem to be able to follow any trail by rote of their experience. It is quite clear that we can use their tremendous skills.

Occasionally, I can hear them converse in amazement at the carnage left behind and about whatever we are pursuing. The moonlit sky is making our tracking slow. We move cautiously through the blue darkness. Each deliberate step only slows us to frustration, but not of purpose. We move forward in our sense of urgency.

No one involved can reconcile with what we are actually tracking. Such is the uniqueness of this situation. They do not seem to be able to acquaint the quarry with any known reference. The absence of familiar smells or signifying hairs or furs has not unnerved them, but draws them instinctively to the pursuit of their curious game. We move onward with a fragile conviction.

Clever tricksters, this band of unknown terrors, they have executed an elaborate hoax of amazing proportion. They are making tracks like no other seen before. Mathewson and Gray Shadow are mystified, but are not yet alarmed. While they are confident they are tracking a herd more human than beast, they cannot verify the unusual bearing of the footprints. Equally amazing, is the force exhibited by our prey in the snapping of branches and trees as they move through the thick green landscape. These are signs unfamiliar to any of us and leave us no clue to what it is we are chasing.

We come to an abrupt stop. We have found what we were looking for.

I write from memory. I wish I could forget.

A vast stillness enveloped me as though the whole world had stopped in fear of what awaited us. I felt a warm rasping at my throat, then came a consciousness of the awful truth, which chilled me to the heart and sent the blood surging through my brain. I could not comprehend what was taking place. But I knew full well. I looked among the group to seek comfort in their experience and courage. I was unnerved, for these brave souls seemed to sense something new to their experience and were now afraid.

Some movement among the trees as sleek and powerful shadows move swiftly through the forest, dim messengers of death surrounding us. Only by the light of the full moon exposing briefly their terrible features do we have an inkling of what we are facing.

I feared to stir, for some instinct of prudence bade me to lie still. Through my rapidly flirting eyelashes, I saw the huge eyes of these creatures, not too dissimilar of those of some great wolf, peering menacingly at us. Wickedness poised to strike in great numbers.

I wish to I could remember no more, but what happened next is indelibly seared into my mind: The strange cries, the swift movements, the shadows emerging from everywhere, the flaying flashes of brutal blows from hordes of tearing demons ripping among us.

I watched transfixed as one of these horrible creatures confronts one of the villagers in front of me. The poor villager tried to run, but in an instant this monster had covered the ground between them with astonishing speed.

Forcing the young man down with a powerful blow to his back, the creature strode on top of him. Turning the terrified man around, he began to toy with his prey. He researched the trembling man by inspecting his shaking body from limb to limb. The cruel eyes of this creature seemed to enjoy his terror. The creature looked at his prey with curiosity as the poor unfortunate pleaded for his life. Strangely, this monster understood the man's fear and provoked it further by beginning to tear pieces of flesh from him as he cried in agony. Suddenly a shoot fired from an unidentified location ended the man's torment just as a second shoot tore into the creature, forcing him to run wounded back into the forest.

In the darkness of the forest, great clouds of gunpowder are shrouded up all around us, red bursts of fire exploding loudly from shaking weapons pointed in all directions as these intrepid beasts move savagely into our midst. The unmistakable cries of humanity in fright pierce the night. I stood frozen as a creature began to tear another poor soul apart.

Within the hazy and smoky forest, both man and beast swing madly as they tear and claw with a desperate frenzy. We all fought back hard, such was our desperation.

Then from behind me came a creature. It gnashed its teeth; its claws, if they were claws, stood out stark and full length. They looked eerily like hands, but animal enough to call them claws. The monster's red eyes blazed with lurid fire, and the white sharp teeth seemed almost to shine a purple hue in the moonlight—purple against the splattering red blood, which soaked the creature's mouth.

I somehow managed to aim the pistol that Advar had given me and fired squarely into the center of this howling mass of terror. It suddenly seemed to know it was dead and I will never forget the look, the perfect incarnation of hate, as it slipped downward to the ground.

As quickly as they had come, they were gone. The realization is frightful; my brain is whirling as I write this down.

Relief must come from Heaven's breath, winds blowing this stench of iniquity away forever. No human can bear this suffering, this unnatural plague of certain death.

Am I going mad? A cauldron of bitter tastes gathers in my throat. I wrench a dry cough from my body, still uncertain of my own sanity.

The few creatures we destroyed didn't so much decompose as much as they flaked into a mass of matter, wilting into brown layers of an oozing jelly, then drying quickly to a parched grayish material. Later, we found that this matter turned to a sickly dust, but for now they were beginning a process of melting away in layers. All life had drained away.

"Those are the most savage beasts I've seen since the mountains of Jawbridge," Mathewson said. "But why are there so many?"

Gray Shadow nodded in firm agreement as I make a note to ask what and where Jawbridge is.

In a journey so terrible, I cannot describe with accuracy the depths of raw emotion branded upon my soul. I have already seen more than I ever wished to conjure up. Not these memories again. This very writing pains me and fills me with terror. What sorrow does each morrow bring? I laugh uncontrollably in my twisting plagiary of the Bard: Will flights of angels sing me to my rest? No, angels cannot fly into this nest of evil; good has no common hero in this drama. Our false bravery is just a mask to hide behind.

Oh, this fragile humanity. Death now stalks us in a feast of blood. Bewildered horror cannot hide its face conveniently behind the mask of Mathewson and Gray Shadow. Terror marks their faces when exposed to these raw truths. The look of unrepentant distress is now their makeup, their pallor deep with revulsion; a look that we all now share.

The fascia of shock is the facade of our human mask now; our features dimly colored in shades of gray. Jointly registered with a common fear as we enter the village of the damned.

We are a cavalry in disputed discharge. A frightened army retreating from our most basic instincts, seeking a harbor in our disbelief.

I search for words, reactions, relief, but none will bear witness to this cruel folly when presented to a naked imagination.

I must write alone. No experience ever so grand can prepare a human warrior for these sights of such abnormal acts. Virgin terror births the most beleaguered celebration of tragedy's children. I now know that it is only a beginning.

My words will become more sterile in their emotions as I grow callous to these events. Today, at least for the moment, I am at the apex of these emotions. I feel I'm already hardening to these messages, numbed and then lost in the sheer volume of its horrific nature. Mature understanding will become deaf to the siren call of this dance of death. I rant no more and I feel no better.

Reluctantly, we pitch our camp within an isolated village.

We were on our way to this destination when we fought that terrible battle. We can see in the moonlit darkness that the village has already been visited by the shadows that have befallen us. In our weariness and in our shock we barely notice as we try to regroup. With the sentries posted, we grab at sleep, however fitful it has become.

We do not look forward to the welcoming dawn because we already know what horrible sights daylight has in store for us. We have already seen more than we ever wish to see again.

We encounter small caravans of peasants moving past us toward Bistria. They have heard about the coming evil and are moving to escape its fury. They wish to believe that they will not comprehend the devastation of their neighbors. Even what they have heard is suspended in disbelief, so rare a thought for a superstitious nature. The world is upside down for them. The tale is taller than the telling.

They are the fortunate ones because they were able to avoid the Devil's path. Now, as they inspect the bodies of their brethren, they shake in turmoil and walk in the same fear that blankets us like a shroud. Ashen faced, they pass by us, unable to take more than a fleeting glance at the carnage all around us. They will not look too long.

The women and children cry in terror, their wails heavy around us, swirling like echoes from misplaced hearts. The pain of their sorrow is swept by the winds; we hear those unwelcome sounds coming from everywhere.

The peasants see for the first time the results of what they are fleeing from and are certainly not prepared to meet the cause of such destruction. I know that disbelief is not a part of their makeup, but they were never prepared for this sight. This is the validation of a superstitious disposition.

Others look on stoically as they proceed past us. Every now and then, they stop briefly to cross themselves and then to bless us—bless us that we will have strength for what awaits us. They are cheered somewhat by the presence of the mighty Advar. He is every inch a leader, strong and proud. He sits upright, defiant, atop his brave black mount. He engages in encouraging words with them, vowing retribution on those who have caused this destruction. Pledging by the sword of God Almighty, Advar promises retribution. The deportment of his determination and the evidence of his pure courage seems to give these people hope.

I can only imagine such a scene taking place again and again through history. The knight racing toward the danger as the weak run from it. The hero ready to stop the evil hordes with a line of defiance drawn in the dirt. History always repeats itself in some fashion. This coat of misery is well worn.

Heroes are born at such times; faith raises them to courage in its name. The innocents have no champions like their faith in an avenging God and the validity of true knights. They put their faith and their hope in us to be God's warriors. Thus anointed, Advar and his men are appointed God's vassals. They look expectantly to the higher outcome. Only in this way can they believe in a tomorrow.

The warriors nod silently to Advar, hoping to convey a belief in his strength of purpose.

He nods back assuredly, his brave face showing no fear, but his eyes betraying thoughts of an unknown outcome.

Still, they seem heartened by the specter of Brother Jacob's cross. It is a symbol of comfort in times of suffering. They cling to that image as a lighthouse that shines on a sea of troubles. They seem replenished by the hope that a true redeemer is going forward into the fray to save their homeland.

When we have finished our earthly tasks, we make camp. We do so with prayers for peace and for rest. Neither seems to be imminent.

Chapter 15

After a sleepless night camped near a cluster of hills, we leave the encampment. The black clouds of an impending thunderstorm roll over the looming mountain peaks and quickly engulf us in heavy rain and thunder. We move forward under the thickening rain, slowed by the mud and by the torrential gusts of harsh wind.

We are attacked again as the storm rages. This time we are emboldened by our previous experience, and we are at last firm in our resolve to fight back. Our initial shock has given way to anger and we will not run from our duty.

I can still hear the terrifying screams as before, but they now seem to come at the moment of death and this time with less frequency. We are all a little wiser to the peril. They will not surprise us so easily. We now know what we are facing.

Our deportment in this fight is much more organized and we concentrate our fire in a more disciplined manner. We do not wish to let them get close enough to lay a grip upon us. Still, they do appear suddenly and quickly. The flashes of lighting highlight their terrible features in quick bursts of clarity.

With the thunder clapping all around us, I see powerful beasts appearing everywhere. With rifles, either fired or used as clubs, we struggle frantically, hoping to drive the deadly beasts to violent and splashy deaths.

When one can lay a deadly fire upon them in a rapid order, the powerful weapons inflict an earthly damage. Under such fire, these creatures fall before us in the rain. They begin to wane in their attack, understanding the futility of their aggression. They have stopped coming.

The battle done, we retrench cautiously. We are wet and cold, but warmed by our success.

The rain has stopped. I walk among the remains those brave people once so vibrant and alive just moments before, but now shredded and torn. They are dispersed like bloody scarecrows of flesh, strewn loosely over branches and trees. Body parts slashed and torn, are grim reminders of bodies that were once whole. They seemed juxtaposed by the jellied mass of these fierce predators, melting away before my very eyes. No blood, no soul.

Dr. Von Hanes, for all his knowledge, has no words. He looks on helplessly, unable to comprehend what is happening. His vast knowledge and experience has been rendered insignificant by this pageantry of unrelenting terror. He cannot seem to catalogue his emotions. For a long moment, he stares blankly at this new world of horror. Deep thoughts within him are searching for a way out, but they are bricked tightly behind his expressionless face.

Brother Jacob prays for the souls of the dead—the ones who had souls, anyway. He is not always sure whose soul he's praying for, as the unfortunates are more pieces of a puzzle than the remains of a single human being. Most disconcerting is that he seems even less sure of whom he is praying to.

We have lost twelve from our party and only thirty are left. I cannot account for the number of villagers who continue to join us in the hope of finding safety and who suddenly are not. I fear for the cause of their absence.

As we look forward, we can see that this encounter has left its mark on our adversaries as well. All impressions are of the horde in mass retreat.

Gray Shadow moves quickly through the carnage, stone quiet, his face covered with defiant war paint and, by the arrogance of his walk, shows his contempt for any spirit that would dare to confront him. He has grown accustomed to the menace and his fear is now registered in checked compliance. The mystic warrior is prepared to do battle with whatever faces him. He seems to sense the wind of fate is changing course.

In warfare you press your advantage and the creatures did not comply. They seem to have disappeared over the hills.

Mathewson calmly collects himself and smoothly pulls on top of his mare. He spits tobacco in one large gulp, clicks his teeth together, and takes stock of the situation.

A mounted Mathewson, and Gray Shadow on foot, move quietly among us. They seem confident—confident from years of battle, confident in a belief that the enemy is in retreat. We must give chase. We must follow them while we can and we must annihilate them. They are on the run!

Dr. Hanes has rallied and gives jury to their plan; his advocacy is to pursue. We are aware of a building momentum. We can sense that we have inflicted great damage upon their numbers with this last exchange. We exhibit a growing sense of confidence that the tables have turned in our favor.

Gray Shadow, astride his horse now, motions us to follow him. Impatient, Radii and Gray Shadow ride up into the hills to scout the terrain. No one follows behind them. Mathewson waits for the group with annoyance, feeling strongly no doubt that we now have an advantage. Some of the others seem less sure. They exhibit a reluctance to go on.

Certainly, we are all frightened, but I know none will run. I must say I can understand their reluctance to continue, but what other choice do we have?

The skeptical amongst us convey a deep sense of suspicion at what is happening. They believe they are chasing the Devil's army and seek assurance that theirs is truly a retreat. Brother Jacob is one of them.

"Trickery is the Devil's garden and we are about to be flowering his intentions," he cautions.

Antonia also offers some alternatives to these judgments. "We are frightened," she says. "We are now half the number. They are too many. Maybe we should turn back and get more people. If we are no match for them, we need reinforcements."

Hanes offers up an opinion. "I do not feel we can make it back to get reinforcements," he says. "I believe others agree with me. What if they grow stronger before we finish this. We must hunt them down now. We must pursue them and destroy them or they will destroy us later. There simply is not enough time. Let us finish this now."

My own thoughts are of a like mind to Hanes'. We do not know anything other than we are the first humans they have encountered who fought back. We have survived their fury and we are still standing. We do not know what we are fighting, be it man or beast, but in warfare when the enemy retreats, you give chase.

After careful thought, Antonia nods her head as she pulls back her long hair and jumps upon a horse. Her eyes are burning with determination. She says boldly: "We must go after them."

The others, seeing this remarkable woman preparing to give chase, quickly mount their horses.

Sonja begins to ride forward when Advar motions her to move behind his group. He grabs her bridle and, with a quick look of defiance, she complies. We move out.

The sun is about to set below the white-topped mountains behind us. A blue-hued shadow works its way toward us from a distance. In the gathering darkness, we are aware of Radii is shouting for us in her native tongue for us to hurry. We are right behind our enemies.

Gray Shadow comes over the same hill and signals us to ride quickly. The creatures seem to be on the run. While whipping my horse forward, it suddenly stalls, frozen in fear.

Mathewson comes charging past me with two villagers, slaps my horse, and it charges with the others.

I ride to Hanes, who is in conversation with Gray Shadow. He asks the Indian how close we are. The answer: "The blood is still fresh."

Galloping over the hill and riding swiftly for several miles, we encounter a settlement along the winding road. We enter a conclave of three small dwellings and a hut-like barn. The remains of a small family have been left beside the road, all ripped with sickening fury—at least what was left of them.

The sun has now set behind us. We await what is to come.

The darkness shrouds us from our own sight when we move cautiously up the narrow road before us. The wind has stopped blowing. We are braced in stillness with moonlight now our only guide. We have wasted the daylight in our own confusion and now we face the night.

On our way to this desolate spot, we encountered the usual sites of destruction: small bits of living things torn asunder by a mercurial force. Each new massacre posts us further east and upward through the Borgo Pass. Still we begin to pick up some villagers who managed to escape the terror. Bewildered and frightened, they join our procession in the hopes of achieving some safety in our numbers. Even as we march slowly forward, we are confident of our coming victory.

We are at once aware of our error. The horde has slipped in front of us and behind us. These devils are cunning; they have lured us into a vile predicament. We do not see them, but we can feel them. We gather together as close as possible. We must also be cognizant of the area all around us, considering the difficult terrain. Rustling woods signal their rapid movement. They are maneuvering at breathtaking speed.

Any villager who is at the edge of our lines is making a mistake. They are the first to feel the creatures' anger. Without warning, they are sucked into the darkness. They are shocked by the very grasp of what has taken them. These poor souls, who have been chosen by cruel fate, are pulled violently into the forest before they can even react. The horrible sounds of death are not eased by the agony of their screams. Only when the screams subside, do I feel they are at last at peace.

One villager suddenly bursts upon me from behind a thicket of brush, pure pain etched sharply to his eyes. His face is contorted beyond human recognition. I reach out just as he is jerked back into the darkness. The sickening sounds of tearing flesh pierce my ears with thundering clarity. My horse rears in fright, tosses me off, and flees into the forest. I begin to run. I trip over the body of a villager who was in a death struggle with a deep shadow tearing at his back. Valiantly, Radii arrives and offers me her hand. As I rise, we are both swinging wildly at these shadows. I turn back around and see Radii has been killed. I instantly fire into the creature before he can drag her away for disembowelment.

I am stunned into disbelief when the creature's hand smacks me about the head before he perishes. I begin to float in mind's eye, a voyeur to these dangerous meetings of man and beast in conflict. Desperate death struggles circle around me.

As I move rapidly and with no plan, I seem to have stepped out of my role as a participant and taken on one as an observer. I take heart in the courageous struggle of Gray Shadow, watching as he skillfully maneuvers his weapon upon any that try to harm him. He moves with a grace of purpose, striking swiftly at any creature that attempts to harm him. Mathewson is more violent, swinging his rifle butt and flashing his Bowie knife at whatever creatures approach him. For one brief moment, it appears he is about to be engulfed, but Hanes manages to fire his weapon into the fray and that allows Mathewson to regain his ground.

All of this so difficult to see in the darkness. These are brave souls lashing out at shadows of the night. I cannot tell what the beasts actually look like.

I am brought to tears as I race to help one of the women who is being decapitated. Just as I arrive to her aid, I see the body of Sonja. Her head has disappeared into the forest, ripped off by a powerful claw sharper than an axe.

Antonia is struggling with two shadows in the distance, but she is saved as Brother Jacob plunges his cross directly into the heart of one of the creatures. From a great distance, Mathewson fires a shot with his hunting rifle, killing the other beast at once. He then fights his way to us, smashing his rifle butt with skilled abandon, marching to us with the calm demeanor of a great warrior.

As Advar and his men join us in a group, they congregate to form a line. Gray Shadow and Mathewson lay down rifle fire into the forest with concentrated force. This seems to have the desired effect, as we are able to begin our march up the hill with less and less resistance.

After many long hours, we stop at a small village nestled off the winding mountain road. As before, the horde of evil had been here with a vengeance.

A calling card of grotesque beauty awaited us: no villager left alive to greet us, no animal of any kind remained to warn of our arrival. The silence was an eerie reminder of what had come and left its mark all around us.

An array of torn bodies lay before us, their faces contorted in great agonies of pain and fright. I sense that those who never saw it coming were the lucky ones; those very few who recognized their imminent destruction were blessed with a look of surprise. Why didn't they leave like the others? No one can say. They have paid a terrible price. The pride of these small holders is greater than the specter of an uncommonly gruesome death. Alas, a pitiful final curtain.

Our only hope is that the last battle has depleted them enough to slow them down.

Grim and silent, we begin to spread out looking for any sign of hope. Hanes seems more disturbed than I have seen him yet.

Upon Hanes' urging, we bring one of the bodies into an empty barn. Skillfully, he cuts away at the tattered fabric clinging to the body so he can study it more closely. He is at once within his realm of expertise. All fear has drained from him as he expertly dissects the body.

Satisfied, he then calls for us to bring in the moldering remains of a creature. We comply and place the hideous corpse upon a makeshift examination table next to the body of the villager.

"I don't wish to offend the sensibilities of any member of the Christian Church and with all respect for its traditions, but I need to perform this autopsy. I realize that you may not understand what I'm trying to do, but the reality of an autopsy is an emotional thing to witness. We must search beyond the obvious to find some clue to unlock this mystery or we have no chance," Hanes says.

As he slices the doomed cadaver open, he begins to lecture in a practiced way.

"What we have before us is a very unnatural and violent death," he says. "A normal death, even one caused by unusual trauma, will still share the same basic principles and results, the damage inflicted on these remains, notwithstanding. It is called a molecular death. First, the pallor of the skin is evident because the blood has stopped flowing. A condition known as primary flaccidity causes muscle limberness that lasts for only a short time, the first few hours of the early stages of death. During this period, the body begins to lose water, the skin begins to wrinkle, the eyes lose their luster and the corpse becomes contorted.

"Hypostasis is next as the unoxygenated blood in the capillaries causes bruising of the skin, resulting in dark purple spots developing all over the body. Eventually, rigor mortis sets in and the body stiffens. Finally, decomposing or secondary flaccidity begins and the body eventually turns to dust, so to speak.

"This is not the case with the bodies of these villagers. There are two kinds of deaths taking place here. One is the rapid destruction of a human engaged in battle with a creature. There the wounds are more common, but still extraordinary. The other type of death is very frightening. These are victims who have been attacked by creatures that had time to perform their instinctive ritual. The manifestations are startling. They can only be categorized as a very unnatural death caused by an unnatural act. We are witness to something that is not known to the world of science.

"These bodies are drained of their blood. No bruising took place after death. The wounds are deep and, in many cases, the limbs are ripped and shredded by a violent force. In some cases, deep wounds appear at the throat area and blood loss is apparent. The water content of these corpses is minuscule. Evaporation has accelerated, while some form of fluid exchange has replaced the moisture content, freezing the body into a hard cadaver. Something deadly and alien is at work here. This foreign life force, this terrestrial anomaly, has killed these people for its own nourishment. They are feeding on us and all the warm-blooded inhabitants within our surroundings.

"The victims are drained of almost all blood and around the wound area I have found a residue of some sticky whitish saliva. Deep incisions into vital areas of the body laced with this substance are evident. This saliva-like material is not unlike the sticky material you might find in a carnivorous plant. A part of its digestive system I imagine, eerily similar to the substance produced by a nepenthe plant for lubrication.

"Why, I do not know, but we must also consider that these creatures adopt a psychological approach to their killing. They seem instinctively to produce an element of terror in their attack. They have the ability to inflict death with a lot less effort than they are actually using. It is as if they enjoy the slaughter."

Hanes moves to the body of the creature and pulls off the blanket he covered it with. A sticky mass is apparent, but its terrible features still resonates as if it was a shadow.

"The autopsy investigation of the creatures is telling, These brutes rip apart their victims to create a rapid heartbeat, which, in turn, increases the blood flow from the wounds.

"Now, when we look at the remains of this enemy, we are definitely not seeing a mammal of any known kind. Which brings us to their fast-decaying tissues. After death, the muscle tissue, if you want to call it tissue at all, displays unique properties. When nourished by warm blood, they seem to grow exponentially, like a plant, but certainly not like any plant we know of. Plants exist on a different nourishment system and have basic biological limitations.

"These creatures grow and evolve with the properties of what has nourished them. They absorb the characteristics of their victims and replicate them, not in flesh and blood, but in the sinewy fabric of a plant-like metabolism. The only reference I can think of is the century plant.

"In the world of flora, autotrophs are plants that can survive on simple molecules not processed by others. Conventional plants require only water, oxygen, sunlight and nutrients to survive.

"Heterotrophs are life-forms that require complex organics that need to be processed by other forms of life. Humans and all species of animal are heterotrophic as are bacteria and some plants. This creature here is most likely heterotrophic in nature. It is not an animal in any conventional sense, but it absorbs or sucks blood fluids to achieve sustenance.

"We cannot refer to them as a plants because they do not resemble any plant we could even imagine. Still, these monsters do share some of plant-like characteristics. They are perhaps some order of carnivorous plant as yet to be cataloged. How or why they got here is a mystery.

"However, the creatures seem to be able to survive without chlorophyll and feed somewhat like a parasitic plant. Except these peculiar life forms ingest the nutrients of warm-blooded organisms by penetrating the body of a living thing to suck its lifeblood. Then, the creatures begin a metamorphosis.

"They do not photosynthesize in any known manner and their primal need to evolve appears to be the genesis of their being. They absorb nourishment and evolve, but while plant evolution is limited to the structure that nature has assigned it, these life-forms have no such limitations. Their generic makeup seems to reinvent them as they absorb their nutrients. Then, they selectively acquire traits that are to their advantage, improving the species.

"They have an evolutionary mechanism that allows them to pick and choose their evolution, as if nature had been discarded and they had been told genetically to experiment with themselves, to perfect themselves.

"The only emotion they seem to possess is one of survival and feeding. They seem to be developing as the quality of their food improves. Each new food source arms them to better their quarry. They assimilate the instinctive predatory skills of their conquests and utilize what is beneficial for their development. This, then, is how they grow toward a next level of being.

"So while they probably began in some small measure, they keep evolving further, and their instincts command them to keep adapting internally and externally. That is what they have been bred to do.

"What will become of them in time, I cannot tell you. But I can now say this—they have shrewdness. They are beginning to develop an impressive intelligence. That's because they are some form of organism that drains blood and assumes the shapes and characteristics of the blood donor. Then they evolve. They possess characteristics of a central nervous system and appear to have a growing brain capacity, as each new generation grows larger and stronger.

"Whether they evolve within their own cells or pass on these traits to the next generation is as yet unclear. But if they are indeed plant-like, they may be in essence growing branches from a single entity. We have yet to find any evidence of shedding or fetal discards of any kind.

"Unfortunately, their ability to assume characteristics that will prepare them for their next assault, makes them extremely, no supremely, dangerous. We now face sizable creatures with enormous strength and what I can only describe as a wolf-like cunning. They can walk and run almost upright, and at amazing speeds. They are armed with human-like hands that are sharply clawed and have thick hoof-like feet. These traits, along with sharp and powerful teeth, allow for the tearing of flesh to reach the intended blood source.

"Although their strength seems to grow daily, my guess is that only a small number are stronger than a human being. But each generation will come closer to us with each new cycle. Their appearance is changing, as well. They are becoming more upright and human-like.

"They do not yet have human intelligence, but they are beginning to develop complex predatory skills that make them frightening adversaries. Only when we strike at the heart or nerve center and deprive it of energy, do these creatures wither and die. They are much like a carnivorous plant in that they have a nerve center, but unlike a dying plant that wilts slowly, their deterioration happens quickly. This plant-like creature turns to a jelly, then slowly to dust. As we speak, the cadaver in front of us has already decomposed to its jelly state.

Dr. Hanes paused and wiped his hands on a rag he had secreted in his pocket.

"In conclusion, I lay out the following summary," he said. "This is only a hypothesis, but these creatures were conceived or born with a raw native intelligence that tasks itself to improve.

"They are becoming more advanced and they are developing the survival characteristics of their prey. We don't how much is retained, but one can theorize that they may have evolved to at least the cunning of a wolf because their attacks are much like that of a wolf pack.

"Who knows how much they are taking from man? Certainly, they can hunt us successfully. Their evolution may only be stopped when they have displaced us as the top predator on Earth.

"I fear the next cycle if these hypotheses are true. The creatures will be much more formidable. We will be forced to deal with a human-like intelligence, but one devoid of man's fragility. Human emotions are the gifts of humanity. The capacity to think, to love, and to explore is paramount to the evolution of the human spirit. Mankind's need for family and faith are the quintessential part of being human. Man has the ability to reason and a conscience to remind him of that reason. These traits are not a necessary ingredient to a purely evil mind.

"We do not know what, if any, human qualities these creatures will preserve—perhaps only the characteristics that are important to their life cycle. They are killing machines with no conscience, only instinct. They exhibit no emotions. They have been born with a primal sense of survival, a constant search for sustenance, and this is their being, their role. They do not feel the more tender human emotions, like love, loyalty and uncertainty.

"Compassion is a human weakness and will exist as a rival to their internal intellect. This is the challenge they face in their evolution. How much humanity will they absorb as they develop characteristics of the Homo sapiens? What facets of human emotion will they discard as unnecessary to their task of perfecting survival? What seeds of dominance lie within the makeup of these carnivores? What is the good and evil within them? Do they or will they one day have a soul? How does pain affect them? Do they even feel it?

"Is their final objective to evolve into sublime killing mechanisms or do they have an evolutionary purpose beyond a basic primal need? This is the same challenge faced by man as he evolved within natural order of succession. Over time, nature has weeded out the different varieties of primates until modern man inherited the Earth.

"One human-like characteristic I hope they have acquired is a susceptibility to diseases from their blood source. I propose they may already contracted a form of porphyria that makes them sensitive to the sun. That would explain why we have never encountered them in the bright light. We are, however, in great danger when heavy clouds diminish the ultraviolet rays. We are, indeed, just as vulnerable in heavy cloud cover as we are at night. I expect this trait will eventually be jettisoned as a weakness, not conducive to their evolution. This defect may only be temporary.

"Another possibility, of course, is that they just see advantages to attacking when the sun is down. They may already be that intelligent. Oddly, they do not possess an owl-like ability to see in the dark. This lack of night vision can be postulated because they do not engage in full-scale attacks at the darkest hours of the night because they cannot see in the dark any better then we do. In my opinion they have limited their full-scale approaches to the moon-bright evenings because of that weakness. However, this could be a characteristic they may soon eliminate. How much longer will they be so hampered? I cannot tell. But their evolutionary genesis cannot accept such a deficiency.

"We cannot rule out that they gain some energy from the moon as well. There is no compelling evidence of lunar effects one way or another, but based upon their genetics, they lack chlorophyl and do not rely on sunlight.

"And finally, we know that they are leaderless at present. But at some point, I believe a leader may emerge, making our task that much more difficult. We have so little time.

"What can we do? Our choices are limited. But perhaps the absorption of some deadly human or animal disease will eradicate them. It is either that or we must track them down and annihilate them in their entirety. Those seem to be our best hopes to end this nightmare."

Morning:

We spent the earliest part of dawn sleeping. We draw some comfort as we are aware that we are safest in the sunlight. Then, to our great consternation, the weather turns suddenly and a cold wind from the east brings misty rain and a heavy fog. We do not feel safe in this weather, which I suspect is now more comfortable for our enemies. We have already experienced their ferocity in the pouring rain and know that only sunlight can weaken their resolve to fight.

I take to heart what Hanes says about these creatures. I think that if they had an intelligent leader now would be the perfect time to attack. Soon, I fear, we will be as much the hunted as the hunters. A deep fog has engulfed us. We look anxiously in the mist as a figure moves towards us.

Through the fog came a regal horseman riding straight and true. He arrives upon us with a royal bearing, his head held high. A beacon of hope. Brilliantly attired in the dress of an Ottoman prince, his turban is laced in gold. The man's bright red pantaloons flap like flags against the milky majesty of his Arabian stallion. It is the Whirling Dervish himself.

Arminius Vambery has arrived.

If courage had a face, it would be Vambery's. If knowledge were in need of a scepter, it would be Arminius Vambery. Grandiose and imposing, he arrives tall and brave, like a knight of yore. His dark blue cloak flows behind him. This vision is not unlike seeing a majestic ship of the line coming to the rescue. His curved, emerald-encrusted Turkish sword looks deadly and ready. One can sense he knows how to use it.

Vambery's is a man of handsome face, delicately balanced by a manly beauty. His close-cropped beard is perfection. His forehead is swathed in a turban that is pinned by the golden scorpion of his tiara.

His royal entrance is spectacular and he has lifted our sprits because he has arrived defiant. He steps off his horse like a king descending from his throne and greets each of us in our own language. This display of linguistics is impressive. It is as if he has a sixth sense of which language to use. The Romanians stare in disbelief as he calls out to them in their native tongue. Brother Jacob laughs with joy as Vambery's strong German dialect wraps around him with a loving simplicity and humor. Hanes responds to him in Hungarian and though I do not know what was said, Vambery enjoyed the exchange. His English is perfect as he introduces himself to me. I must admit I'm in awe of him.

Of course, we all wait with bated breath as he cheerfully approaches Gray Shadow. The dervish mystic and the North American shaman look upon each other with a cosmic connection as if words were being exchanged with their minds. Finally, Vambery speaks to him in perfect Spanish and, to our amazement, Gray Shadow responds in the language his people had learned from the Conquistadors.

I cannot believe I am in the presence of this living legend. All of Europe has embraced his marvelous tales of endless caravans marching across the hot desert sands toward untold dangers.

As I look upon him, I can see why he so imposing. He assumes the look of whatever we wish to see. Now we sense a safety in his presence as if the adventure has only just begun.

The man I see before me does not have that disagreeable edge that makes my friend Richard Burton so difficult for people to like. Vambery's smile lights the world around him like the sunlight breaking through a cloudy sky. His intellect has a poetic calmness to it, deep and soft and endless. His voice is at peace with himself, yet sharp to the eager ear, filled with inquisitiveness and understanding. He asks questions as if they need only to be said to be answered.

He questions us from a different perspective than I would have expected. We respond like eager pupils, vying for his favor. We instinctively wish to seek his approval. Oh, what a man he is! He clearly thinks like an educator who seeks knowledge with as much fervor as he dispenses it. Yet he deports himself like a Viking warrior king.

Even in these mountains, the name Vambery is respected. No one would even question how such a man could arrive here alone and unprotected save for a jeweled sword wrapped around his waist. Vambery is that ultimate warrior, knowledgeable, and quick to action. He does seem to know already why he is here. Brother Jacob and Dr. Hanes seem to have expected him. They do not gush with surprise. This is one detail that should warrant some attention, I think

As he sits with Hanes, he seems to know the answers to the questions he asks and the questions to the answers he gives. Vambery, in his professorial way, has a stimulating effect on Hanes. The melding of these two minds, at once different, yet both alike, mesmerizes me.

As the afternoon grows colder, we seek refuge from our weariness. One of Advar's scouts informs us that an abandoned farmhouse lies ahead. We have had our fill of battle for now. We desperately need rest, so it is decided to camp there for the night.

We quickly disembark upon reaching the site and, after carefully imposing an armed perimeter, we move into the structure. Advar and Hanes establish the shifts required for a guard detail to protect us through the night. No one volunteers. Advar admonishes the group. The choice is apparent, he says. It is better to be awake and face the danger than to be asleep and awake to it. With this thought we have our watchmen.

Regardless, we are forced to view sleep as a dangerous luxury, one to be enjoyed only on the edge of exhaustion. Then will sleep come and fitfully at best. We all wonder once our eyes are closed will they ever open again? We still expect to be attacked tonight but if God has any mercy for our souls he will at least let us get some rest before the next battle.

For the moment, however, a sense of well-being is apparent. The tragic tension that has pursued us for so long has united us in our collective fears. At least for now, we feel safe and we will have a roof above our heads. We have become impervious to the fear, but we remain concerned for our safety.

For a few brief hours, we are actually human beings again. Engaging in conversations and preparing our meals, we feel that we have been given a respite, but we do not know why.

Alia is playfully toying with Gray Shadow, while demonstrating the skill of juggling. The Indian shaman then performs a magic trick, making a rock disappear. She responds by demonstrating a gypsy card trick that baffles him.

Mathewson, the old gambler, shouts out encouragement to Alia and it generates great laughter. Enjoying the levity, Alia jingles with gold jewelry and she delightfully performs another card trick.

Gray Shadow reciprocates by tossing powder into the fire and creating colored flames. He then demonstrates how an Indian can feign levitation. Only if you stand behind him can you see that he is really standing on his toes. Still, it has the desired effect and Antonia lets out a shriek of amazement.

I've noticed that Mathewson and Vambery have become close. There seems to be some connection that I cannot place. But it appears to be a common interest. Vambery is also quite taken with Gray Shadow and they have been conversing in Spanish on a wide variety of subjects. Some of the conversations have been very deep in nature and deal with philosophical views one would not expect even the noblest of savages to hold.

Hanes cajoles Vambery to do a rope trick, which Vambery humbly declines. Hanes then good naturally refers to Gray Shadow as doctor and asks for his alma mater. Gray Shadow responds that it was the University of the Little Big Horn and that he was Custer's personal physician. Mathewson jokes that he was his witch doctor and helped the general maintain his golden hair.

Hanes and Gray Shadow laugh together at the irony of this last stand and grasp each other's hand in friendship. The famed alchemist and the Indian medicine man share a holy bond that is mystical. They seem to be able to communicate without words. They come from different backgrounds, but they have attained like stature in their respective worlds.

Advar paces nervously, occasionally stopping to engage those around him in conversation or reacting with humor when he listens to some jest. Yet he seems to be afraid to totally let down his guard.

The camaraderie is building in this moment of temporary relief. There is nothing to account for this relaxation of tension except to believe that maybe we have reached the saturation point. We all seem to feel that on this night we will be at peace, so we are determined to enjoy ourselves.

Even Advar will occasionally lose his frown and fills the room with his booming laughter. Then he catches himself and goes back to the window, carefully looking out again and again. He studies the dark mountains, peaked like fine black cones against the moonlit night, and is satisfied for at least this one moment that danger is not near us. We repose at our ease and light another fire.

Suddenly, we are startled by sounds of the night wind blowing harder than before. More important, we hear something we haven't heard in a long time: The windswept sounds of a howling wolf—a lonely call, so welcome to our ears. We are not alone. It is comforting to know that there is indeed some natural life left and unaffected by this cunning plague of death. How ironic that the howling of a wolf can bring such joy.

Advar smiles slightly and says, "The children of the night, what music they make."

Note to myself: I must use this line one day.

Advar leaves his window perch and stands before us. He begins to speak in the deep rich voice of his ancestors. "We must call for the soul of Dracula to rise from the grave and save us," he intones.

"These creatures must face the wrath of our devil and he will defend this land for our people. In the dark hours of our past, our hearts and our homes were swept away by the scourge of the demon Turks from the east. They would come to rape and to pillage. They would come asking for tribute. They would come to sell our children into slavery.

"Even our belief in God Almighty had to be surrendered to them or we would suffer the terrible consequences. The Turks wanted our very souls!

"Then one day the Turks came and the Vlad the Impaler appeared among us to drive them away. Those who would not leave his land would face his terrible wrath. This country is the land of the Dracul—the Devil. To some the word Dracul means dragon, but to most of us it means Devil, as well.

"That was his name—Dracula, the son of the Dracul. The Devil's son. Dracula, who would impale the Turks upon a stake and drink their blood. Dracula, who would boil their children as he sipped his wine. He would stand atop his tower looking down at his victims as they received terrible retribution for invading his land. We tolerated him because he kept us free from the Turks. Yet we feared him no less than the Turks, whom he drove away. Such was the power of the Devil's son.

"When the sultan tried to make peace with Dracula, he cruelly nailed the turbans of the sultan's emissaries to their heads. With that, he warned the world that one does not disrespect the customs of a prince. He then cut off their limbs and sent them back to the sultan in pieces.

"The infidel Turks were his most ardent enemy. They feared Dracula like no other man before or since. The *voidoid* Dracula would defeat all the great armies they sent against him.

"Then the Dark Prince would inflict horrendous carnage on the retreating Turks. Soon they would run in fear from the very mention of his name. They could not defeat what they feared so much. The Devil's son would devour their souls. The Impaler would cast them upon the bloody stake and count their screams as they slithered down the evil pole.

"He would appear from nowhere with his army. He would come down upon them from the mountains and smash them in battle. In the darkest night, they would hear his voice—the howling winds would have been welcome in its place, such was the terror of Dracula's commands. His enemies would shiver in repulsion when his battle cries were heard. They knew what fate awaited them if they did not defeat him.

"With his black cape flowing and his horse breathing fire, Dracula would slash at their souls. He would carry the vanquished back to his castle to spill their blood upon the fires of his burning passions. He played them in ugly torture as if they were puppets for his amusement. He was the Prince of Darkness! They say that Dracula was the only man in the world whom the sultan feared. The Turk quaked at the mere mention of his name. Such was the legend of Dracula.

"Only through the betrayal of his friends and his own brother did his enemies destroy him. They set a trap that took thousands of soldiers to bring him and his army of ten down. They fought like demons and sent many Turks to hell before a stake was driven deep into Dracula's heart.

"When they finally killed him in battle, they killed him ten times before he died. No death of an ordinary man would do, such was the desperate fighting.

"Was the battle for his soul or for theirs? No one would win that day. To insure that he was really dead, they beheaded him. They buried his body in Snagov. Then the Turks took his head back to the sultan. Triumphantly, they displayed the Impaler's head on a stake, but still the sultan shivered in terror because of Dracula's stare. His eyes could not be closed. His evil death stare followed wherever the sultan moved, gazing with hatred and lusting for revenge.

"In desperation, the sultan ordered that the Dracula's head be buried in the sand and had the grave covered with a thousand stones. But come the night, evil howls and strange screams filled the air and Dracula's head would rise from his grave again and again.

"Dracula's would haunt the sultan in his sleep, tormenting him, mocking him. Those eyes of death would flash with hatred; his cruel voice warning all those who came to take his land that they would face the wrath of the Devil's son.

"They dug up Dracula's head and burned it in a high fire. Still, the ghost of the Impaler would appear, time and again. Finally, they took his head and sent it to be joined with his body in his homeland. They hoped that the earth of his native soil might bring peace to his soul.

"But the nights would bring terror as the living death of the Dark Prince would haunt the land of his ancestors. He would prey upon the blood of his rivals. He took vengeance on all who crossed his path.

"One day the monks came to move the prince to a secret place, but when they tried to dig up Dracula's body, they found that it was gone. Only the head remained. Then they saw that the head was no longer burned, but opened its eyes to them. They threw it from a mountaintop, but still the head would not die. Dracula ordered the monks to do his bidding. In terror, they threw the head into the lake, but in the darkness they never heard a splash. And to this day, neither the head nor the body of Dracula has ever been found.

"But the spirit of Dracula still haunts the land. Now these evil creatures we chase have invaded his land and once more we must call upon the Impaler to drive his stake through the hearts of our enemies."

Gray Shadow rises from his crouch and addresses Advar.

"These are not the spirits of our world," he says. "They are not spirits of our good or our evil. They are beyond understanding, beyond the Holy Spirit. They are but shadows and even beyond the reach of your evil prince.

"I have tried to speak to them, but they do not answer. I cannot talk to them and they do not listen to me. It is only in their deeds that I can see what they want. And I can see all too clearly our own destiny.

"This is a story that has been foretold by the Great Spirit. We have been warned that the black spirit would strike the Earth one day and only those prepared for this attack can save the world from destruction.

"The spirits have also told such a story and said that only by the courage of the warrior and by the knowledge of divine powers will peace be granted. There is no escape from the evil spirits from the sky. Only destruction.

"Our ancient history tells us that until the battle is joined by the chosen ones and won by those deemed worthy of the challenge, dire is the human birth. Many innocents will die.

"I, Gray Shadow, a chief among my people, call upon the Great Spirit for guidance. I call upon Coyote with his wisdom and his courage to join us in this destiny."

Vambery, who had been listening intently, joins in. There is something deep and foreboding about this complex man when he appears so serious. He knows more about what he won't tell us than what we already know. While he is a man of infinite kindness, I still fear something about him. There is a mysterious side to this man's equation that I just cannot place. With the authority of a worldly presence, he speaks in that strong and confident voice.

"I have seen what they have done and I know what they will do," he says. "Nothing in our experience can train us for this. What we must do, we must do alone.

"We are not facing an evil that was created by the Devil nor have these monsters been placed upon the Earth by any god we know. This is the challenge that we have feared from time immemorial. Many faiths and many religions have dreaded this possibility.

"I cannot say more other than to repeat that we have been forewarned and we have all been chosen. We are indeed the knights of light against this darkness."

"My friend Dr. Hanes has discovered this already, but he won't tell you. We must stop running in fear and facilitate a means of their destruction. Just as Gray Shadow has said, the time is at hand. But we may not be able to defeat them until we find their lair. We must march forward to the beast and cut him apart from the underbelly of its cruel existence.

"If we are under siege like this, we are nothing more than the hunted. We must use what knowledge God has given us to destroy this evil while we still can. But we cannot defeat them until we face them head on. We must move with a purpose and a plan. We must look for a ground of our choosing.

"Von, it's time that science and the occult join forces, don't you think? We have the best trackers in the world among us. We have the brightest minds and the greatest courage necessary to defeat them. We have been chosen for this, all of us."

Now Brother Jacob rises and he continues in this same vein.

"It is God's will that we are here. We are his knights. This has been foretold in the ancient scriptures. The evil is not of Satan's making and only those pure of heart and mind can light the darkness from within, and strike down these beasts born not of His image. One day the earthly angels of enlightenment will face this devil's curse and only through our own devices can the children of man be saved. "

Brother Jacob pulls out his Bible.

"I swear upon the oath of my Lord that we must use the resources that God has provided us to find the lair and destroy them before they destroy us," he says.

With this, Brother Jacob sits down and we look at each other with a determined silence.

I finally break the silence by nervously asking if we have enough guards outside.

We managed to finish a quick dinner before Gray Shadow speaks again. He looks directly at Vambery.

"This man of many mysteries is right," he says. "No spirit will come to save us. Still, take heart. In our own ways and in our own histories we have all faced such evil before and we have prevailed. So too have my people preformed this task before. I speak of Jamaich, the monster."

Gray Shadow lights up a hand-carved pipe and tells us of Jamaich.

"Before man there was the Titwa-titya-ya, the animal people. They were powerful, at once animal and human and spirit. Through them all things began to take shape and form, guided by the wayakin, the guardian of spirit of life in the midst of savage darkness. It was the animal people who set the ways to live upon the land and prepared the world for the human people.

"The Titwa-titya-ya traveled the land encountering the many dangerous demons that preyed on the animal people. The most dangerous of all was Jamaich. Even brave and powerful creatures like the grizzly bear and eagle feared Jamaich, who was called the swallowing monster.

"The greatest of the Titwa-titya-ya was Iceyeeye, the coyote, who tricked the Jamaich into swallowing him; then he carved his way out of the belly of the beast with his knife and thus created the Indian people who rose against the monster and tamed it and the great tribes were born.

"This is what is happening here," Gray Shadow says. "These spirits are like Jamaich. And we must cut our way out of the monster or he will rule this world and devour all humans and a new animal people created in evil will walk the Earth.

"Like the coyote, we must go to the monsters' cave, destroy them and save our people. We are coyote, we are the earthly spirits, we are the chosen."

Mathewson counters swiftly and with a glint of humor. "I'm not sure we're coyote, my old friend, but I am real sure we are in deep shit."

The nervous laughter is interrupted. Suddenly, we are alert. We are aware of movement outside, the sound of a gathering. All in the room tense as we reach nervously for our weapons.

Brother Jacob moves quickly to the window, looks out and says with surprise: "Horses coming."

We rush outside as a splendidly uniformed cavalry troop surrounds us. They are the Carosi Regiment of the Romanian Army, recently formed in Turience to patrol in the Carpathian Mountain region.

The horse soldiers clear a path just as Advar comes to our front. The boyar is face to face with an impressive cavalry officer of obvious high rank. The deportment of this white-haired man is one of arrogance as he strides toward us. He is dressed in an immaculate blue uniform; his high black riding boots are polished with precision. Advar's face immediately flashes annoyance and it is obvious that the feeling is mutual. He curses in native tongue when the officer haughtily marches past him and into the cabin.

Brother Jacob greets the man and introduces us to General Anton Crititan, the highest-ranking cavalry officer in the region. Crititan is of the exalted boyar class, one constantly at odds with lesser boyars like Advar. With apparent disdain, Advar asks if Crititan should be called general or if he still is to be called count. With stiff formality, Crititan insists that he be called general.

Crititan announces that he is trailing the horde and expects to annihilate them all by daybreak. He is confident that he will track down these worthless gypsies and will hang each and every one of them without the blessing of a trial. The sickening carnage he has seen calls for immediate justice, the general says.

Mathewson tries to tell the officer what he is really chasing, but the general pays little attention to him. He looks at the buckskin-clad American as if he were a peasant and dismisses him without inquiring why he would even be here. He does present some interest in Gray Shadow, who has turned his back on him and quietly smokes from a pipe with condescension. The general mocks these *doinas* [fairytales] of wolves traveling in packs at night doing their worst to both man and beast. What evidence is there for such a story? He asks, obviously unaware of Hanes' autopsy.

He expresses surprise that such learned men could believe that such unnatural creatures existed. He mocks the assembled group as a costume party of wayward tourists who have traveled far from home for no reason. He remains certain that these so-called creatures are nothing more the marauding gypsies on a rampage of terror. He expresses confidence that he has them tracked and that they will be dealt with by morning. He stiffly bids us goodbye and his large cavalry unit rides ceremoniously into the dark night.

An ominous farewell, I think.

Morning:

We awaken early and begin to load up for our trek into the higher mountains. We are going to find the lair of these creatures, some center of their community, the place where they sleep. Our only hope is to reach the source of this evil and root it from its very existence.

As with any living creature, there must exist a structure or a society. We are racing against time. Can we destroy them before they become so powerful that they become invulnerable?

We know we must keep moving northeast through the twisting and winding roads of the Carpathian Mountains. Mathewson and Vambery believe that this is the place of their origin. Based on Dr. Hanes' theory, the creatures probably inhabit some remote location that has allowed them time to breed. They would seek safe shelter to allow them protection from the interference of a hostile world. This, at least, is our theory.

We must search out evidence that will give us clues to their presence. Hanes feels that we might find some vestige of their origin, but their domicile would be well hidden. They are too smart now to be found easily.

We have ridden through a narrow pass into a valley of thick trees on a rising rock face plateau to the right of us. The valley of these trees is wedged among the three peaks of this particular mountain range. We round the bend of the first peak.

There before us are the carcasses of several horses. We can tell immediately by the military saddles that something grievous has befallen General Crititan and his men.

Moving into the trees, we encounter the telltale signs of an attack: strips of clothing and broken branches leading us to the center of great butchery. There, among the trees lie the mutilated remains of the general's men.

Something even more alarming has caught our eye. Several of the bodies have been strung upside down from the tree branches. Hanes says the victims' feet have been tied in some form of crude twine; then the men were strung upside down so the blood would flow from their wounds more swiftly.

Hanes inspects one particular corpse twisting in the wind. He is startled to see that it's General Crititan, whose bloodless face is staring at him wide-eyed in terror. The general's white beard is caked red from a wound ripped cleanly across his throat. A river of blood has cascaded down his body, ending in a dark red pool by his head once-noble head.

Other trees are adorned with the grisly remains of the general's men. We start cutting them down. This is a new development and it has demoralized us.

We are all shocked to learn from Hanes that he believes these poor souls were not ripped apart like the others, but were captured first and strung upside down. The victims then had their throats slashed open like flasks of red wine and died painfully and slowly while the life of their bodies drained away through the gaping wounds. The creatures fed upon them as from a spigot. They are no longer just sucking, ripping and gnawing for sustenance.

This is most peculiar and frightening to us. The victims were alive as their blood was consumed. What vile notion is this?

They seem to be experimenting in some way, Hanes says. Their intelligence is starting to evolve more quickly. He believes that they are learning to effectively feed their young. Ironically, they are becoming a nurturing society by sucking the living blood of humans in an organized way. Are these creatures any different from the legends of vampires and werewolves that haunt these forests?

The answer is definitely yes. Those monsters were just flights of fancy told by a superstitious people to explain away the shadows of the night. These new creatures are different because they are real and they are truly frightening. For all our knowledge, for all the knowledge present among us, not one of these learned men can explain these shadows in the dark. This is man's worst nightmare.

Vambery is most concerned by this situation. He seems to be working under the illusion that there is an even more to all of this. How do you deal with a secret that should never be told? How will civilization react?

Still, what is happening around us is whispering so loudly that the world will soon hear about it. Should we simply say that it never happened? Not likely! But that seems to be Vambery's position: to keep everything we have heard and seen and smelled a secret.

We know we can't explain it. We have yet to even defeat it. How can we pretend that it never happened?

One thing is perfectly clear to me. It is up to us to find these creatures and destroy them completely. They have grown in strength, in numbers and in intelligence. Mankind's destruction is the final answer to their evolution. Our future is the key to their future. If we cannot survive, we will be devoured from the face of the Earth.

Vambery has an even more sinister view. They will eventually become our masters and enslave humanity as a food source, he says. They are, he adds, only short weeks away from being as smart as we are.

We have at least coined a name for them now: Dominus—the uncaring creature with superior intelligence.

The massacre of the general's men has been by all appearances an organized attack. The troopers had fallen in clusters as if a concentration of specific areas of attack had been engineered. This is troubling. Is it possible that they are now being led? Has their intelligence developed enough to devise and implement such a plan? What form of communication are they using to organize themselves?

The hourglass of time is flowing against us.

Chapter 16

As I inspected the carnage that was once a fully equipped cavalry regiment I heard voices coming from behind some bushes in the distance. Moving quietly closer I could hear Brother Jacob and Vambery having a somewhat bizarre exchange. The strain is etched deeply in their voices, their face grim.

"We have arrived at the genesis of our destruction." Brother Jacob begins to pray. He quotes from the Bible. It is from Revelation 14:10. "And the smoke of their torment ascendeth up forever and ever and they have no rest day nor night, who worship the beast and his image, and whoever receiveth the mark of his name."

Vambery crossing himself and offers, "I can certainly understand the need for prayers Brother Jacob. This is the start of Armageddon. No single point in history will be of significance if this beginning leads down the path to a dismal end. No single Dominus can be left alive or we will have turned our world over to them."

"Yes, I agree, Professor, no single Dominuis can be allowed to survive. This is, indeed, the fulfillment of the prophecies foretold by the elders and protected by the Knights Templar," Vambery interrupts. "No sacrosanct secret order is unaware of the testament. The blood covenant warned that this day would come. The Book of Knowledge, more sacred than the Holy Grail itself, has predicted this awful day. You give the Templars too much credit for what has happened in the past. You know as well as I do that we will need to answer to the concordant and the concordant only. "

"You cannot hide behind the veil any longer, Professor Vambery, you are among those who know the secrets. The time is now at hand. We need to bring in more force, Professor, and you know this cannot be done alone. This situation is far too dangerous "

Vambery rises and offers his words in a stern, but soothing manner. "When we wear the coat of responsibility to our vows, Brother Jacob, the coat of our armor must survive the arrows of this destiny. Such is the burden of those touched by this abomination. Such is the burden of enlightenment. We fight our demons in silence. It is the way of our orders. Once again, we must face a cadre of supernatural creatures who have come to obliterate us. We will once again unite as one and implement their eradication from human history, or we will be subjected to an evil purpose beyond human comprehension. Some among us will not be subject to this responsibility. We cannot have strangers amongst us when we have this final fight"

"That is not an answer, Professor, those are only confusing words," Jacob says. "Don't you think the others should understand what this is about"?

"Brother Jacob, we are sworn to our vows, the others are just fighting for their lives and I'm glad they are here, but we must let them leave," Vambery says curtly.

"Only the knights of mankind, chosen by our maker, have been aware of this possibility," Brother Jacob says. "We at the Vatican have been expecting this day. The Rose has feared this day as well. We who are the soldiers of these ordained orders are now called to our post. God knows why we are here, Professor. We all know why we are but what about those who may die in this struggle. We need them all, Professor, and we must tell them what this is really all about. We cannot send them home"

"If anyone still doesn't know why we are here," Vambery says to Brother Jacob, now aware of my proximity and concerned about what I may have overheard, "I'm afraid that you are about to tell them."

With that Brother Jacob calls out to Mathewson, Gray Shadow and Hanes and asks for their attention.

"Generations have been in waiting, priming and searching for the coming dusk that now confronts us," Jacob says. "Those cruel warnings, written in the blood of sacred knights, have now come upon us. Darkness has arrived. The prophecy of the inner mysteries is upon us now. The time is at hand to meet our destiny. I ask for your vote gentleman.

"Should we speak as one order or exclude the unenlightened of the real dangers, regardless of the outcome. I will remain one to this cause. All of us blessed with divine courage to conclude this struggle. Let us pray anointed warriors that with His divine help, we will defeat the scourge and prepare mankind for His glory. Together or alone we should prepare the others for this ordeal. Is it right to leave it all unsaid, or do we owe them a full explanation? What do you say to this?"

Mathewson interjects, "If there is one thing that Gray Shadow and I agree on, it's that you Europeans sure do talk a lot." Mathewson looks directly at me and can sense that I may have heard more then I should have. "Better to leave the reasons behind you, Stoker. You and Advar's people should just worry about killing as many of these things as you can," Mathewson drawls warmly, "and face this menace with the single purpose of your own survival." Mathewson then turns to Vambery. "Gray Shadow and I are also students of the way of knowledge. and in our travels we have come across evil in many forms. While we have never seen anything like this before, we also know that we are experienced in the ways of survival in dangerous times. So, if you gentlemen will excuse us, we are going to go find these creatures and we are going to kill them. So much for our destiny."

With this, Mathewson and Gray Shadow move back toward the clearing.

I am surprised by the emotion in Jacob's words. I have no idea what he was even talking about. All through this journey Brother Jacob would suddenly break into emotional speeches and parables. The manner of these outbursts lends itself to the theory held by others that Jacob's is coming undone. I can see that all of us are taking an oath, but I do not know to whom. Brother Jacob wants to tell me why, but the others seemed to have just voted against it. This is a confusing time for me. Why do I not understand this code within a code? I strongly believe that the bloom of Rosicrucian methodology is on display here, but what of Vambery? Why is he so inclined to dictate these events?

Vambery is growing increasingly concerned with Brother Jacob's growing instability. I must also surmise that based on some cryptic statements made by Mathewson, he is more than a mere hunter from the American plains. The telling sounds of Masonic belief have crept into his equations and now they are starting to add up. All that seems to be missing are the secret handshakes and passwords. They whisper words like inner secrets.

They all knew that they were going to be here. They have been preparing for this event their whole lives, it seems. Now they seem to fear the truth as much as they fear the Dominus.

Why did I not know I was to be here, too? Why do I think that somehow Irving, with his wide array of friends and interest in the vagaries of the human condition, is behind this?

Vambery and Hanes have been talking to each other in secret. I can tell that something is being discussed at my exclusion. I feel that way because they look at me as they do it—small quick glances, sly looks in my direction. I've been around the theater long enough to know that these conversations are about me. Hanes will shake his head in compliance then turn away.

Mathewson and Jacob have also joined in the dialogue in the last few hours and I feel that is a bit uncharitable. I wonder why they do not include me. I'm a little frightened by it. Well, maybe not that frightened compared to what is happening here.

Dr. Hanes has approached me. It seems that Professor Vambery believes that we should destroy our notes—provided we happen to survive this ordeal. I can't think that he was serious. This is the story of a lifetime. Why would I suppress it?

His reason seems vague and lacking in logic. This is surprising for such an erudite man. He mentions that the others feel the same way. I joke that it's because I didn't know the secret handshake. Hanes, uncharacteristically, looks blankly at me. I was sure that he would have laughed at my assumption. Strange doings and I find myself at a loss. They have not convinced me with their arguments.

Hanes apparently feels that we should conceal these events because the truth is too atrocious for the world to comprehend. Comprehend? The facts are staring us in the face. We have been burying a lot of dead people lately. I think that fact would be hard to explain away so easily. When I point out that many people are already aware of what has happened, Hanes says that they have not actually seen the creatures. No one has actually survived contact except for what's left of our party. The few of us who have dealt with them will be no problem. We will all be sworn to secrecy. He mentions that the local people will accept what has happened in their own superstitious way and not prove to be a vexation.

Hanes also notes that he has already seen the dire consequences when science and religion cannot recognize the truth. "This episode would be a cataclysmic occurrence beyond the notion of biblical proportions. Here, the evil lacks a face that civilization can recognize. No soothing words from any science or any religion can explain what we confront.

"How does a world that universally believes in one true God accept evidence that there may not be a God at all? Just look at the struggle that exists when science disputes the Bible. While it's inconceivable to some that God created man, there are a thousand more believers who find it inconceivable that man—and all things on Earth—was not.

"Just imagine what they would think about this situation. Our world would crumble. The disruption and the panic would affect all walks of life and all forms of belief. Life would be altered forever. This situation is destructive on all accounts."

I find his arguments difficult to believe. I will talk to the professor myself when I get the chance. Still, I anoint myself to this cause as I choose to be one of its warriors. While I fly under the banner of my own design. I will stand united with their danger.

The crusade begins its ultimate quest: The death of pure evil.

We are his knights and providence has provided us with the sword—the sword of understanding about what must be done. God bless the holy knights among us. To paraphrase the Bard: "Once more dear friends into the breach."

The group is riding upward to the more mountainous region of the Borgo Pass. We are drawn to a clearing that shows devastating damage. The center of a steep incline reveals a furrow dug into the earth. It measures about a hundred-feet deep and thirty-feet wide. One is first struck by the violent impact of whatever smashed through here. Trees and earth were pulled down on impact into the dark crater. Brown earth. Barren and absent of any texture.

The most curious thing about this gaping trench is the absence of any life. The area around the crater is devoid of any living thing. It is as if a plague had usurped life and consumed whatever lay in its path. The desolation is uncanny and unreal.

Brother Jacob is fired to a fever pitch. He calls it the awakening of the beast. The road to Armageddon has been laid before us. He extorts us to face the challenge. He is starting to get on my nerves.

The once-green vegetation is blanketed in a dry brown and dusty cover. No grass or flowers remain in the immediate area. The rotting carcasses of small animals lie withering away. In this state they are unattractive even to the scavengers. As we widen our search into the devastated forest around us, we find varying species of animals in various stages of decomposition. There are no insects anywhere; the plant life has been sucked dry. The remains of all living things have been devoured in an ever-widening circle.

This is where it all began, I think. The evolution started from this point.

Dr. Hanes lays out the genesis as best he can ascertain from the dire clues before us. I write a summary as he speaks.

We can chronicle the development of the species by analyzing the killing fields, he says. The unknown life-forms appeared to have been transmitted to this location by means of a foreign object, most likely the fragments of a comet, which was no more than ten to twenty centimeters in size. Released upon impact, these microscopic creatures immediately began to adapt to this hostile environment. They were doing what they were designed to do—survive, thrive and evolve to dominance. Somehow, the seed of man's destruction found their way here and are flowering all around us. We are in the Devil's garden.

These lifeforms were able to survive this journey by means that we cannot explain at this time. We do know that they began to endure by adapting to the resources readily available to them when they reached this destination. It must be why they survived their journey here.

The first of their breed subsisted on small earthly life-forms not much more elaborate than themselves. Wherever they came from, this survival and evolution mechanism was not necessary to them. They probably matured in a totally different way and dominated their world of simple organisms.

We can follow the evolutionary chain of their growth as we move deeper into the surrounding areas. As they found larger prey, they too grew larger. The clues related to an ever-increasing growth of the Dominus are apparent.

At some point in their evolution they grew into real predators and began to hunt in the hordes we are now all too familiar with. Hanes can tell this by the corpses of the dead animals. An evolution of killing that has grown in capability and intensity. While in the earliest stages of growth, they began to incorporate the characteristics of the prey they fed upon. They have also established a new location for their lair.

A very primitive lair was first established here. But, with their continuing evolution and growing numbers, they needed more space and a more sheltered environment with each new generation.

The signs all point to a migration eastward to the protection of higher grounds. You'll note the small pod-like cocoons discarded and decaying along the path of destruction. They have also begun to carry their young with them as any pods or other vessels were not evident along the trails where we have confronted them before.

This also means that they will be even more difficult to eradicate. They have developed a cunning that will provide a requirement that they protect their lair from predators. This migration to higher ground will make them harder to find.

Some form of organization is taking place, one that is difficult to explain at this point. It may be possible that there are now one or more packs in the area.

Could it be they are amassing a collective strength or establishing a society of some kind? We must seek out those answers as quickly as possible.

We are now aware that we are being watched. In the distant hills, red eyes flicker as darkness descends. We look at a mountain ledge high above us and we are able to see something quite extraordinary. High atop a protruding cliff, a most magnificently frightening sight appears above us. The most advanced specimen we have laid our eyes upon yet.

Standing majestically as any king surveying his domain, he looks out at us across the valley. He is studying us as intently as we are studying him. He appears to have a deadly purpose.

Slightly taller than an average man when he stands erect, this creature looks down upon us. He surveys the landscape with a face savage and hateful. His eyes are red and he has a sharp wolfish nose that is perched menacingly on his large head. He growls and shows a sardonic smile of sharp teeth. We hear in his growl a voice that is seemingly intelligent, but his roar bears the consonants that betray attempts at language. A singular voice of authority!

His hands are almost claws, with long sharp nails. His dark skin is made of cropped fur, and reminds me of the sleek hide of a panther glistening in the moonlight. His thick legs are powerful and shorter than an ordinary man's and they lead downward to almost finger-like thick hoofs. He is the Anti-Christ of anyone's imagination, twisted and evil. I cannot see a tail.

This well-toned creature, powerful and wide muscled shoulders, is now standing almost fully upright and staring intently at us. He begins to goad us as if he is mocking us to the legion of followers set before him in some unknown place. The Dominus must be all around us.

He is taunting us with his glare. His eyes are as evil and as intelligent as any description of Satan himself could ever have described. We have met the Daemon and he is set upon our destruction.

He looks as if he is investigating our possible escape routes. The frightening thought that he has planned a coordinated attack against is too horrible to contemplate.

Mathewson has seen enough. "If that thing is their leader," he cries, "then he is going to die."

The buffalo hunter quickly unfurls his hunting rifle and loads. In one fluid motion, the barrel is up and pointed. He fires.

Daemon immediately responds to the loud explosion as if he has a heightened sense of hearing. His reaction is swift and graceful. Daemon avoids the bullet and with a terrible series of bloodcurdling howls echoing high above us, he unleashes an order to attack. The language is primitive and rudimentary, but it is a call to action.

The horde descends upon us. The sheer numbers are unbelievable. They move in groups and with a purpose. They run as if they had been directed to take up certain areas. This is having a terrible effect on us and we frantically try to reach higher ground to fend them off.

Advar and Vambery jump onto their horses and lead us the way we came.

They are shouting that we must backtrack to the clearing. We hope to fight them there. For once, I imagine we will see them coming.

We assemble like a frightened flock of cackling birds searching madly for our nemesis. To our right a group of them charges at Advar. With axe in hand, he plunges his horse at them, pounds powerful blows, and rips them to pieces. Vambery, astride his Arabian, quickly unfurls his bejeweled blade and slashes away. Many of us swing wildly at the creatures.

Suddenly, Advar seems to recognize something in the distance and begins to exhort us to follow his lead. He pushes his horse up what appears to be remnants of a stone road snaking up through a break in the hills, its destination hidden by the overgrowth.

Our horses seem to realize their fate and are driven with power and speed. We plunge forward desperately, frantically following Advar's lead.

Vambery and Gray Shadow are at our backs twisting and firing to slow the horde of Dominus hard upon our heels. Looming above us in the overhanging trees, the creatures overtake our rapid lead. Without warning, a creature will leap upon our desperate trail. They arrive suddenly, flying into our midst. The havoc of their arrival cannot be diminished by an explanation. While we continue to destroy them in great numbers, more and more seem to appear.

Oh, the souls of the intended victims! The sounds of bloody battle are serenading us in the key of horror. The deadly and terrifying screams of victims alerting that many more had joined the long list of fatalities. The creatures are swarming all around us now, pouring over the steep mountain walls and thick trees like ants upon a discarded apple.

Advar has reached a rock-built gate structure. He calls us to him and forces his horse up the trail that leads to a ledge overlooking the ancient gate. He calls us to arms and we continue to ride toward him.

We are at the gate of a long slim road flanked on either side by a precipitous drop—a road that leads upward toward a mountain peak.

Mathewson joins Advar atop the ledge and begins to lay down a devastating fire upon the mass of creatures all around us.

Antonia rides recklessly up the hill just as Hanes falls off his horse. Two creatures rush forward to confront Hanes. Vambery rides into the fray swinging his sword and he beheads one creature. Jacob rushes up on foot. His horse is nowhere to be seen. As the beheaded beast rolls to the ground, Jacob steps his foot upon the body of another fallen creature and drives a stake through its slimy heart. In apparent agony the creature suddenly stops and expires.

Hanes is pulled atop Antonia's mount and the two of them ride up through the gates.

All those who could have been saved have been. We crouch around the arch of the stone gate. We are protected on either side by steep hills; the road behind us disappears around a winding curve. We see on the upper level of the mountain the dark outline of a structure. Sanctuary!

We have been able to stop the attack for the moment. But our situation is tenuous because we fear we will be outflanked and then surrounded. Advar admonishes us to fight our way up the road and into the fortress. We move in small groups up the winding road in an almost military fashion.

"Where does this road lead, Advar?" I inquire.

"To Castle Dracula, my friend," he says. "We must find refuge within the ruins."

Von Hanes, who was listening intently, nods expectantly. We turn our horses upward and onto the spiraling road that is almost as steep and treacherous as the mountain itself. Our progress upward is slow.

Heavily we advance, aware that one misstep will have us hurtling down the mountain. For all their newfound skills, the creatures cannot navigate this unruly landscape. They have not been able to follow us directly with our rifle fire picking them off. They desperately seek to find other directions to approach us. Though they try with a great deal of speed to navigate the steep hills and sneak up silently behind us, they cannot. Many fail and skid off the sharp inclines and plunge to their deaths.

We can hear them sliding down the tree-lined crevices as they lose their balance attempting to flank us on either side. We hear their desperate scratching claws reaching hard into stone to achieve a balance that is foreign to them; then they lose their grip and disappear. Still, we keep looking backward, certain of their eventual approach.

I notice that great thick clouds are drifting rapidly across the sky from north to south and at great height. There are signs of a coming storm in some lofty stratum of the air.

Although chilled to the bone, I yearned for the stormy weather as a possible respite from the evil hordes pressing from behind us. We knew we had to reach some form of safety or we would be doomed.

As we reach toward the structure, I marvel for one quick moment at the mountain valley below. The mountains all-powerful in God's glory. They rise to the heavens as a reminder of our once peaceful existence.

We may be safe at last on this ground so pure. Sanctuary found among the ruins of a castle belonging a man so evil. The paradox is not all together lost on me.

Each turn in the road elevates us higher into the mountains and the thickening clouds now kiss us with snow. Would the heavenly blanket provide us with sanctuary? We know we cannot see our coming death and hope the coming death cannot see us.

As I look all around me, I feel a cold shiver in the air, more so in thought of what we have been through than the air itself. I sense a moment of hope as snow began to fall. I think of the miles and miles of bleakness and terror soon to be lying under the pure and virgin snow. What will the footprints look like in the red blood calendar of these terrible days?

I cannot imagine I could have possibly conceived this horror in any prose or fiction. Nothing that we can humanly relate to would ever compare to the reality we face now.

The sky grew darker and darker, and the snow fell faster and heavier until the earth before us became a white and glistening carpet of snow. Then the snow stopped.

As we reached the snowy plateau, we came upon it—the ruins of Castle Dracula. Towers of evil, pointed and sharp, pierce the sky. The winds exposing conical towers spiraling in bursts of rising stone. We get quick glimpses among the hard cloud fury.

A gate of rotting wood fragments dims the joy of a happy welcome. The hinges creak like buzzing bees as the gates swing listlessly in the wind, clapping their wooden hands against the wall of our desperation.

Ironic is my feeling that we are looking for well being in this abode of such unimaginable pain and suffering. But here we are and hope to safely remain until a way out of this nightmare appears.

We are entering Dracula's fortress.

Chapter 17

Castle Dracula

Now and again, through the black mass of drifting clouds came a straggling ray of rising sunlight. At last the night has ended and we have not been attacked in any great numbers yet.

We breathe in the crisp air with certainty, relishing the pull of each breath. Our exhausted party quickly assembles in the choppy courtyard surrounded by crumbling walls. Two stiff towers loomed over us, their circular walls pocked by holes and decayed by time and nature.

Expertly, Mathewson and Advar set up defensive perimeters, taking advantage of the castle's intricate defenses—stone ramparts whose designs were woven by centuries of war and sieges. A partly roofed main building stands before us.

The castle is small and pedestrian, not romantic or imposing like others we have seen in Europe. Remote and easy to defend, its design is such that does not allow easy entrance. This is a strictly a functional structure.

Although no more than two stories tall, the towers dominate the skyline above us. They are imposing for such thin cylinders and render the main building an afterthought of construction. The grandeur comes alive when we enter the great hall. We move through it exploring the ravages of time upon its existence. Wood, once richly carved in intricate design, hangs morosely from the once delicate walls.

Moving past the hall toward a circular stone staircase, we march slowly up the winding steps to the top of one of the towers—the same one that they say Dracula used to observe his impaled victims in the courtyard. We look out onto a commanding view of the countryside. I stare at the trees below us and see a strange silhouette of death. Sitting patiently among the limbs of the trees are the black gray shadows of our nightmares.

Cold and calculating they seem, probing instinctively for a weakness in our position. Their red eyes, almost humanly aware of out insecurity, measure our resolve. We are nervously riddled with anticipation. Our bodies are soaked with perspiration and cloaked in fear. The air is filled with an expectant finality.

They are night creatures no more. They look comfortable in the coming daylight.

There is stillness. The storms have long passed and, perhaps in sympathy with nature's silence, my heart also stops beating. But only momentarily. It begins racing, its pounding drumbeat punctuates the awe I feel for the ever-increasing numbers of gray shadows filling the skyline.

My eye catches something below me in the ancient graveyard where the tombstones are scattered in disrepair—all except a lonely granite monolith. I grab a pair of binoculars to read the inscription on it. Engraved in German was not a name at all, but a forecast: *The dead travel fast.*

I could feel the blood rush from my brain. There was something weird and uncanny about that moment and it made me feel quite faint. That's when the thought struck me that the maitre d' had been right. It was Walpurgis Night. The truth of that realization filled me with terror, for this is the time for witches and other evil creatures to descend upon the Earth.

They have arrived. These creatures are the children of an evil not of Satan. Survival of the fittest, which man has used to explain away his lust for domination, has a new name: Dominus.

If God created man in his own image, then these creatures must be the personification of an evil that has been spawned among us in that image of detestation. Evil that champions us to bend them into a frightful compliance or be subjugated to their destiny. Our perceptions of good and evil are only human. No manmade god could have made this evil. Higher powers we will never understand are now at work here.

The universe of all that surrounds our tiny planet has brought us this wicked visitation. Only man can eradicate it from our lives. It took all of my courage not to collapse in a paroxysm of fright.

As the sunlight broke into the coming dawn, I thought about the hellishness of our battle for the night. Mathewson and Gray Shadow had prudently armed themselves in preparation for the assault. They were not disappointed.

All through the night, small groups of creatures would venture forth and Mathewson would pick them off with his rifle. Still, no large rush was forthcoming. This was surprising because we had hoped to profit from the seeming advantage of the castle walls to lay down a heavy fire upon them as they tried to rush us. We knew that the curving mountain to our backs would be a difficult climb and we felt that we had a natural perimeter of protection on our flank. At least for a while.

We also hope to find some way out of this. Mathewson and Gray Shadow propose to scout around for the lair. Von Hanes was not happy about this request, not so much because he knew the danger, but because he seems to recognize the futility. That's what the creatures are waiting for, he reasons, our own impatience. What chance do Mathewson and Gray Shadow have alone?

Hanes, more so than anyone else, has respected the awesome power of this enemy and has despaired of our very survival. Is it now the time to deplete our numbers further? he asks. Still, without destroying them in their liar, what chance do we have?

Throughout this ordeal, Hanes has stoically maintained a quiet calm borne of a great and courageous intellect. In this case, however, I sense the fear in him as he cautions his two friends not to go outside the perimeter. But his words fall on deaf ears. The Americans are determined to find alternatives.

Hanes' affection for his friends overcomes him when Brother Jacob prays for their souls and wishes them well, knowing full well that they would not change their minds.

They had already loaded up the necessary gear, including, to our great surprise, several sticks of dynamite that had pilfered from General Crititan's wagons. They scale down a side wall and disappear, quickly engulfed by the thick green forest below us. With astonishing speed the two great warriors are gone.

Advar decided to lead his men out to find an escape route. He also knows we are running out of ammunition and food and we must make some kind of move before it is too late. He proposes that a party be organized to bring back the general's supply wagons.

Advar was irritated by the actions of Mathewson and Gray Shadow. In his view, what he is proposing was a better use of the manpower, but he agreed to wait until they return.

Mathewson and Gray Shadow had left amidst many debates. They wanted to scout the area looking for the lair. They sensed that we were close to it by the discomfort they pick up from the beasts. The creatures do not want to come closer to the castle. Mathewson believes that they are now afraid that they might drive us to their lair. They seem to know that is their weakness. They also seem to know that they are only vulnerable when they sleep—an

Achilles heel, if you will. That's why he believes they haven't come into the ruins yet. Attacking us has never been a problem for them before, so why have they stopped? Advar would probably believe that it's because of Castle Dracula. I tend to think that Mathewson may be on to something.

We have not seen or heard from Mathewson or Gray Shadow for hours. Advar and his companions are growing impatient. They finally decide to move out anyway. We know that if we wait much longer we will be in the darkness of night.

Advar and his people mount without delay and start down the slopped road from the ruins of the castle. He has laid out two basic goals. First, he hopes to find the enemy sleeping and destroy them. Then, he will bring back the general's supplies.

Vambery and I decide that we must ride with Advar. We leave Hanes and Brother Jacob behind with the others. We expect to be attacked upon venturing out of the gate and we are surprised when nothing happens. Vambery deduces that they want us to leave the castle and are waiting for another time. He offers that Mathewson was right. We are close to the lair.

Now we look for the wagons. As we search the forest for clues to their existence, evidence abounded everywhere. The trail to the general's final resting place is also an easy one to find. We simply follow the trail of torn limbs strewn everywhere. We could also see that we inflicted some damage upon them during yesterday's battle. The road to Dracula's castle is littered with the melting corpses of the creatures that had been killed.

The night is fast approaching when we finally came upon the wagons from General Crititan's doomed cavalry. One wagon is filled with ammunition, dynamite, and weapons. Another contains food.

We start a slow return weighted down by the heavy wagons. We didn't really envision how difficult the trip would be and we grow increasingly nervous. The coming dark brings the eerie stillness again.

Advar decides to stand firm with half his men to fight a possible holding action, while he sends ten men to escort the wagons. Several men offer up their horses to help pull the wagons, but that leaves those brave men almost defenseless. The wagons, however, could be our last, best hope for survival.

I tried to engage Vambery to my view that we should leave the wagon until tomorrow. He argues that the creatures might figure out why the wagons are important to us and destroy them. Advar is also of that thinking. His sense of urgency is growing by the minute.

As the wagon train moves from our view, the extra horses doing their job, and we who are left are increasingly susceptible to attack. Our breathing heavily explodes from our bodies, spewing out the nighttime air like smoke signals. Then the horses grow restless and sniff the air in fearful anticipation. They stir in anxious short steps. We are being watched.

At this Advar grows very grim. He checks his weapons and pulls off his horse to reach for his axe. To my right, Alia grows pale and, while looking around in a frightened way, her horse suddenly jumps forward, racing into the forest with Alia clasping the bridle tightly in an attempt to rein it in. Vainly, Advar, who is on foot, tries to stop the horse, but it is too late. She disappears into the dense forest.

We do know where she went, but her screams are continuous and horrifying. We race up the winding road in pursuit. Everywhere, horses and men are screeching and shouting, their cries permeating the air. Small pockets of creatures lash out at its prey and pull their victims into the forest. In total fear, some horses break ranks and begin to race into the forest.

With our horses screeching and jumping in fright, we finally force them forward. We ride up the sloping hill toward the stone road. We try to double up on the frightened horses, but they will have none of it.

Advar is now back on a horse and is attempting to regain order. As I turn around, I can see he has turned back down the hill, trying to rescue one of the men who had given up his horse for the wagons. He is resisting a small group of creatures pulling him into the forest,

Advar charges forward and reaches for his compatriot, but he misses and the unfortunate warrior is swept into the forest. Only a tepid cry for help and the rustling of the bushes signify his fate.

Advar is then surrounded and the creatures engulf him. They had managed to slip above him by crawling among the overhanging tree branches. Even as the powerful Advar swings an axe at them, they swarm over him. He kills more than a score of the grotesque monsters before he meets his death from a creature swinging down upon him from behind and catching him by surprise. He falls heavily from his horse. The sickening sound of gnashing teeth ripping into the sinew of his wide strong back coincides with a painful roar from the injured boyar. Eyes burning with hatred, Advar rips the nuisance from his back and, with bare hands fueled by anger, rips the creature's head off.

Daemon himself strides smoothly toward Advar, and with razor-sharp teeth bites Advar violently in the neck. He inhales the blood of Advar into his system as if the infusion will bring him great power. This wound is swift and fatal and Advar slips away from this life. To whatever Valhalla warriors really go to, I'm sure Advar is there.

All discipline escapes us now as we break ranks in a rapid and clumsy retreat. We race back up the hill fighting feverishly to reach the gate. As we cross over to the winding road, welcome fire from the castle above has slowed the creatures' advance and we manage to pull the wagons up the winding road.

We now have ammunition, food and more dynamite. We have also lost more than two thirds of our men. There are only twelve of us left.

Antonia is inconsolable when she realizes that Advar is dead. She swears to avenge his death. So many debts of vengeance are owed now. Dreams of vengeance have left most of us bankrupt of original thought. We register our insults and injury to a deeper meaning and move on. All through this we have sworn their death, each and every one of us. I can only hope that one among us will finally succeed.

I fear for humanity if we fail.

I walk out to the courtyard and I can see that the valley below us is clear for the moment. We once had unrealistic thoughts of sleep, but we now know that is impossible because time is an adversary that we cannot surrender to. Time is better served awake to their possible approach. There will be no rest for the weary—except a final rest.

Professor Vambery is growing impatient. He refuses to submit to the fear that we can be defeated in this drama. He racks his brain for answers. "Destiny is our friend and our guide," he exhorts us with robust determination. "Let us find the way to our salvation by the courage of an indomitable mind. We must use the intelligence that God has given us and the Devil is trying to take away. There must be a way out. The evil nobility that once lived here must have faced similar perils. How did they escape? A hidden passageway or secret doors? They always had some escape plan. This is a possibility we must explore."

We search for a secret passage and hope to find the lair. We now have an incentive to hold on, but so far we have been unsuccessful in our quest. We still have not heard from or seen Mathewson or Gray Shadow since they left in the morning. We fear the worst has befallen them. Now we must concentrate on finding a way out of here. We will die here if we stay.

Advar's death has had a devastating effect on the men he left behind. They do not seem to know what to do without him. Nervous and confused, they jump at any noise. They have lost their swagger as much as they have lost their souls. Heavy of heart, they are growing all too weary of this battle. They are almost done.

They wander around the compound looking for a secret passageway, but do so without a real plan. They are agitated and melancholy and seem preoccupied with the certainty of their own deaths.

Antonia invokes Advar's name in elocution, but that seems to have little effect. The remaining men have become somnolent to the task and vulnerable to the fury. Time has disillusioned them into a rapid decline. They will not respond to her encouragement or her cajoling.

We still do not understand why we have not been attacked en masse, but we seem to know that the time is coming. I can almost sense that a final plan is in the making. Something extraordinary is happening beyond us in those hills. I can feel it.

They have evolved so quickly that we do not even know what they look like anymore. Or how they might look an hour from now. For all we know, they may look like us—actually be one of us. Or perhaps one of us may be one of them.

How can that be? Have I lost my mind? God help me when I'm like this.

I see Vambery finally taking charge of Advar's men. His presence seems to buck them up and he begins to issue orders to which they respond. His overpowering presence is most evident at this time. He leads them up into the second tower and they begin to search within its walls.

I am alone now. I look for Dr. Hanes, who is inside searching for an escape route.

Antonia has joined Dr. Hanes and myself in our search. She is bitter at being ignored by her countrymen. She is angry at the plight that has befallen us and is determined to get her revenge. Nothing will stop her.

After much digging and pounding, we come across a small opening in the great hall. The tiny fissure in the stone to the left of the staircase seems to have a hollow backing. Hanes points out that this wall actually looks different from the others. It appears to have been bricked over at one time.

We peer through the tiny crack and can feel the slight current of air blowing gently through the opening. We may have found what we were looking for. With great energy, we pound at the wall with rocks. After many hours, we finally hear an echo—something reverberating behind that wall. It is a dark chamber leading into a black abyss.

With trepidation, we pull away the debris and see that the opening once concealed a passageway leading down a flight of steps. Cautiously, Antonia,

Hanes and I move down the constricted steps. The air is heavy and musty and the flames of our torches illuminate the stairs only well enough to see one step ahead of us. At the bottom of the darkened stairwell we come into an area carved out of mountain rock that leads directly to a rectangular opening and another tunnel.

We enter into the pitch-black tunnel. Hanes surmises that this must have been an escape passage for Dracula, and it probably leads some great distance down the mountainside. As we slide perilously down the slim tunnel, we move cautiously so as not to extinguish the flames from our torches.

After what seems many miles and even more hours, we see a light at the end of the tunnel. We debate about how much farther we should go. We deliberate with almost every step we take. Maybe we should alert the others to our find. Antonia seems to want to push farther and farther with a single-minded purpose. We must see this through, she reasons. Dr. Hanes is simply getting tired. I, on the other hand, am afraid of what we may find ahead of us. I certainly do not wish to die here in this cavern. We decide we should keep going until we have something further to report.

We finally reach the light ahead. To our astonishment it is not daylight, but the opening to a chamber spilling into a vast cavern and lit by small air holes bored into the ceiling. Most certainly this was designed to bring in sunlight and fresh air. Despite this, the vast cave is still shadowy and dark.

The vast cavern before us has several chambers behind it, one after the other. They move in a downward direction, making it difficult to see the end of the cavern in the distance. In all probability, this must have been an ancient hiding place or staging area used to assemble armies or hide large groups of people from the Ottomans.

Then we hear murmured whooshing sounds emanating from far down in the cavern. We go silently forward, moving as stealthily as we can. We are drawn closer by the rhythmic sounds of heavy breathing. We can hear them clearly now, but we are not sure in which chamber they reside.

Laid out before us is a series of large chambers. Along either side are ledges that serve as pathways over them. We move closer to the first compartment and closer to the breathing.

We are shocked by what we see!

Hundreds of the creatures are sleeping in the first room. They are so peaceful in slumber, so different when awake. They appear harmless to us now, but that defies their very nature.

They are lined together and are suspended upside down. Sticky vines, which snake down from the ceiling of the cavern, cradle them in brownish cocoons. Others sleep peacefully in greenish pods laid against the walls like grotesque coffins. These pods are the maturing ones, Hanes says. The cocoons are for the young. Other males are curled atop each other without a cocoon or pod casket. They are large and very human-like in an ugly, very ugly, way. We can see they are multiplying in great numbers. The young are on the way. The rustling movement of the cocoons is sickening.

As Hanes points out, the mature Dominus are breeding very much like bats. Their arms are furled over their bodies in a repose of flying rodent simplicity. We have found the creatures' lair. Now what?

On the other side of the cave, we become aware of movement. We brace for discovery, but are relieved at what we find. Mathewson and Gray Shadow slip out of a hiding place to alert us to their presence. We are happy to see them. We had feared they were dead. Hanes speculates that they must have been trapped by the sheer number of creatures, and were probably waiting for an opportunity to escape.

We motion for them to come toward us. They point back at us that they are going to split up. Mathewson holds up some matches and a stick of dynamite. We have found an escape route for them so we immediately understand what he means. We are going to blow them to eternity with the first chance we get.

In the darkness, Gray Shadow finds a winding ledge against the cave wall and begins to scale it toward us. In mid-climb, he stops suddenly and freezes. Suddenly, we are aware of a loud rustling. A group of Daemon-like beasts have awakened from their slumber. They are an imposing group and look more like Daemon himself than the other creatures in the chamber.

A class structure seems to have developed because they appear to intimidate the smaller creatures. They point toward an area at the back of the cavern and the weaker ones comply with some type of order. With grunted instructions and crude hand gestures, the weaker ones, possibly females, prepare something just beyond our sight. They start stacking wood.

The rhythmic sound of rock tapping hard upon rock echoes through the chambers. The tapping continues until suddenly a flicker of light is followed by a red glow. The many chambers outlined before us become illuminated. With a disturbing clarity, the developing flames of a small fire light each chamber. They have learned to make fire!

We watch in disgust as the creatures prepare their garish breakfast. They seem to be experimenting more than we could have possibly imagined. They are now eating pieces of human flesh. They have moved past simple blood sucking. They also try to burn the flesh by roasting human appendages on the open fire. In a nauseating way, they are becoming civilized.

The now fully illuminated chamber has left Gray Shadow in a precarious position. He is in danger of being exposed while stranded like a fly against the wall. He slowly climbs toward a group of rocks for concealment.

As we watch, a group of very large creatures files into the chamber. Following into the main chamber behind them is a herd of lesser beasts. We can see that there have been several levels of development going on since we last saw them. There is now a community of sorts, a pecking order. They have begun to break into peer groups as the strongest creatures intimidate the weaker ones into compliance. Several versions of Daemon seem to be the most dominant of all. The smaller and more humans-like creatures are defiantly treated as a lesser breed.

There also appear aberrant creatures that seem to be cruel accidents of nature. They are a bizarre mixture of animal types, merging parts of a pig or wolf and, in one grotesque instance, a creature that looked partly like a cow. These pathetic creatures are abnormalities in this society and follow the other creature as if they know they are inferior.

Suddenly, the Dominus part in awe as Daemon makes an appearance. Even the strongest and most formidable of his ilk bow in rapt compliance to this majestically evil presence.

He has come to survey the awakening. He moves among the diverse groups of varying creatures and we notice that an entourage of thug-like beasts follows him. Hail to the king and his retinue of scoundrels! Daemon's attendants are thick, ugly and appear to be following his every grunted command. Like their leader, they are tall creatures with a sinewy muscle structure, heavy and strong. Still, one can see that there is a difference between these impressive creatures and their master. They lack Daemon's keenness of eye and may in fact not have his level of intelligence. Something very imposing has blessed Daemon, it seems. He alone possesses the qualities of true leadership. Everything in his behavior suggests that he is not only aware of this, but is determined never to give it up.

We watch with horrid fascination as Gray Shadow, slowly working his way toward us, finds an indentation in the rock wall. Surprisingly, a crude straw curtain that is meant to conceal something is covering the opening. Gray Shadow slowly parts the primitive curtain and an appalling sight confronts him. Hanging upside down in a semiconscious state is the comatose body of Alia. The creatures have gagged her by stuffing mud and grass into her mouth to silence her screams. She is probably in a stupor due to her difficulty of breathing. She is lucky in that respect.

It took all of Gray Shadow's immense courage not to react and betray his position. He slides back in stunned silence. This sight sickens us, but Hanes cautions us to lie still. He places his hand over Antonia's mouth.

Before Gray Shadow can conceal himself, he is aware of a group of creatures moving up along one of the ledges and heading toward him. Reluctantly, but swiftly, he moves to hide. Undetected, he is only a few feet away from them as the creatures prepare to bring Alia down.

They unfurl the semiconscious woman from the spidery vine-like web that encased her and bring her down into the chamber. They place her limp body against the wall. A wooden post-like gallows rack is then brought into the chambers. They take Alia and hang her upside down so that her head is suspended several feet above the ground. They do this by twisting vines around her ankles until they hold her weight. They then leave her to take care of other matters.

Daemon strides toward the wall, which is lined with pods and cocoons and inspects them. Then he orders several creatures to rip the sleeping beings from their pods and throw them into the fire. We are staggered by this development. Daemon is indulging in his own judgment day.

Daemon is perhaps more human now than we could have possibly imagined. Is he trying to consciously control the evolution of the Dominus by selective breeding? Is it possible that he is afraid that he will lose power if certain types of maturing species evolve beyond his own capacities? Is he feeling threatened by the genesis of beings that are becoming too human?

Daemon is displaying ambition. He is demonstrating a human trait in one of its most evil forms: domination of others. Like any human tyrant, he is destroying his enemies. Most troubling to us is the type of creature he is killing. Apparently, any being with a strong resemblance to a human being is being consigned to the flames. What Daemon fears most is man.

As he pulls the evolving creatures from their cocoons, we are horrified to see that several of them are uncannily human looking. He rips their heads off or he slashes his clawed hand directly into their heart cavities and pulls out their bloody organs. Even more disturbing are the almost human shrieks that the victims make before they die. Daemon then discards their remains unceremoniously into the fire.

He leaves the pods of the Daemon-like beasts alone, allowing them to flourish. He is all too human in everything but looks, it seems. Daemon has developed ruthlessness and selfishness and cruelty. Would ego not be too far behind? His personal evolution has reached the point where he is very concerned about his own survival. He alone will control his society and he alone has chosen to make them in his own image.

Vambery has found the way in. He has also brought along the dynamite. We are more than glad to see him. He says that Brother Jacob is holding the remainder of the group together to find and then protect the entrance. They will try to buy us as much time as possible before they will attack the front and they have already sealed the tunnel behind him. If we are ever to get out of here, we will have to go through the front of the cave. The die is cast; the battle is to be decided this very day.

Only about twenty feet below us, Gray Shadow is hiding in a small opening. He peers out, waiting for an opportunity to get back to us undetected.

We are then alerted to the sounds of movement throughout the cavern. Daemon is assembling something it appears. He orders Alia to be strung up before him. With a large group of creatures looking on, Daemon attempts a crude examination. He pokes and prods at her as if he is looking for an explanation. As a Christian, I will not divulge the cruelty of this episode, but only pass on the demise of Alia and of the death of Gray Shadow ensued because of it. Although my memory revolts at recalling such a sickening episode, I must somehow unburden myself.

Enraged at the loathsome cruelty being done to Alia, Gray Shadow reveals himself, leaps down upon Daemon and a desperate struggle begins. Mathewson jumps up and fires upon the creature, attempting to help Gray Shadow. His attention is diverted as several creatures rush him. Gray Shadow is now in the grip of Daemon and despite his desperate attempts to escape his grasp he has lost any semblance of an upper hand. Vambery lights sticks of dynamite and starts tossing them at the hordes of the Dominus. Exploding chaos erupts into full battle. Creatures are flying everywhere.

They move toward us en mass. In desperation, we began firing our weapons. Almost on cue, an explosion was heard from the far end of the cavern. Brother Jacob and his men have found the opening of the cave from the other side and are attempting to force their way in.

Jacob has managed to fight his way into the center of the chamber and he drives a stake through a creature's body. He shouts out exhortations proclaiming the imminent arrival of God Almighty.

Just at that moment, Daemon kills Gray Shadow. Holding the weary Gray Shadow high above him, Daemon's claw firmly on his throat, Gray Shadow still manages to give this monster one last look of defiance. He then composes himself and as Daemon rips powerfully into Grey Shadows chest and pulls out his still beating heart, The majestic Indian seems to transform into a beautiful spirit of acceptance as he closes his eyes forever.

Satisfied, the beast Daemon then thrusts his claws into Alia's heart and brutally rips it out as well. He lets out a primal roar with this act that echoes loudly through the cavern.

For one brief moment all motion seems to stop at the sound of Daemon's cry. Then this magnificently hateful creature turns his attention to Brother Jacob. Jacob tries frantically to light the fuse on a stick of dynamite as the wretched creature moves towards him. He cannot get it lit. The frightful Daemon steps closer and closer to Brother Jacob staring at him hatefully. With a look of determination, Brother Jacob stares back and shouts: "In the name of God, I condemn thee to damnation!"

The creature is unmoved.

With his crucifix held before him like a shield, Brother Jacob shouts prayers and curses at the advancing Daemon, beseeching God to strike this scourge from the Earth. But not being a creature of God, the leader of the Dominus is impervious to the threats of eternal damnation. He is already in hell—a hell of his own making—a hell he rules without satanic advice, but by the scriptures of his own evolution.

Still, Brother Jacob stands before the beast, empowered by the courage of a humanity that does not fear such lesser gods. Another beast moves swiftly to confront Brother Jacob by stepping in front of Daemon as I lose sight of them for a moment.

Suddenly, sharp red claws rent the thick air of the cave and I see one of Daemon's own, a human-looking creature, die on the points of his master's rapier-sharp hands. Daemon is killing his followers to get to Brother Jacob.

The beast strikes at Jacob with stunning accuracy, ripping his claws across the center of the monk's chest, lifting the cleric high into the air. From the very heavens from which he is suspended, he cries out, "Vengeance is mine!" It is a final judgment, for Brother Jacob is already dead, impaled upon the claws of the monster. His valiant death seems to call down the wrath of God, though, and the entire cave explodes with shaking fury.

Suddenly, the earth beneath our feet begins to shake. A horrific rolling sways the entire cavern and the walls crumble around us. We are in the middle of a terrible earthquake and we are aware that the danger of being crushed is even more perilous to us than these fierce creatures. I run through the shaking cavern, dodging falling debris and race toward the opening. I thought I had almost gained my goal when the earth suddenly opened up and swallowed most of us, man and beast alike.

I watch in horror as Hanes disappears into the bowels of the earth, along with a number of creatures. When I reach the opening, I can see that only Vambery and Mathewson are left. Antonia is trapped on the other side of a large crater and it appears unlikely she can reach us. Mathewson is about to turn back to rescue her, but she is grabbed by a creature and is killed. Mathewson fires a rifle shot and dispatches the creature.

Vambery decides that we will dynamite the opening and entomb whatever creatures have survived this earthquake. Most seem to have been sucked into the void of the crater or have been crushed by falling walls. The chance we have been waiting for has been given to us. We must finish this battle once and for all.

As Vambery sets up the dynamite in strategic places. Mathewson and I can see that Daemon is attempting to escape by climbing up toward us as quietly as he can. Mathewson waits patiently for him to reach the top. Then he pulls his Bowie knife and slashes Daemon's head off with a swift and angry blow. The leader of the creatures tumbles backwards and falls into the abyss. The few remaining creatures seem to become confused as they watch the decapitated leader of their pack fall deep into the black abyss. The do not know what to do as they try and process what is happening to them.

Vambery announces that we are ready. We yell out for any survivors and then light up the cave. The explosions bring down more rock, which pours deep into the opening and thus the cave, sealing it for eternity.

We can see that the earthquake has caused severe damage. The mountain has fallen into itself. Castle Dracula is no longer there, swallowed whole by God's fury. No one has survived this ordeal but the three of us. We are just beginning to understand the truth; we are just beginning to mourn the passing of such brilliant and brave men. We are lucky to be alive. Surely, there must be a reason for our survival. Some higher purpose.

I have written all that I have described from memory. We managed to walk all the way down the mountain and found a wagon and a horse. The three of us trudge back to Bistria, relieved to be alive. We are also overcome by the deaths of our companions.

I know that Vambery is curious about this diary. The fact that it is in shorthand makes it impossible for him to read over my shoulder. That disturbs him greatly. He reiterates that we should not allow this information to reach the public.

When we stopped to rest, Mathewson warned me that Vambery did not want this diary to be published. He mentioned that he felt the same way, but said he would not interfere. That is not his way. He asked me one last time if I would destroy the diary voluntarily. I refuse.

He wishes me luck.

I am aware now that Vambery must be some form of Bishop to the higher powers. That would explain the deference accorded to him by the others. I will lay out my case to him as logically as I can but I definitely intend to publish this story. It is too important not to.

Vambery asks me point blank to destroy the diary and when I demur he insists we discuss the matter one more time. He offers to make Turkish coffee for us, coffee he has been saving since he arrived. He suggests that we share a drink and have a friendly talk.

When I finish this entry, I will sit down with him, but I will not bend to his will.

The truth will out.

Part V

The Dragon's Order

Chapter 18

Journal: L.O. Wynn

Time is running out for me now. I can see the shadows from my window. I hope they have not found me. The visitation of an evil matrix with designs upon my existence lurks threateningly, omnipresent. It is an evil trolling for my soul. I will not have much time left to complete this journal, but I will try. I must try.

Friedrich Nietzsche said that he who fights monsters should beware that he himself does not become one. When you gaze into the abyss, the abyss also gazes into you.

I know now that the abyss is staring back at me. The monster will soon to be at my door. Still, I struggle to make sense of this for you—what is known and what is not known. I search for words rapidly, racing to complete this chronicle. But I fear I will never be able to explain the effect the diary has had on all of us.

This is the paradox faced by a logical mind attempting to rationalize a world not of our making and out of our control. As humans, we wish to understand our world and bend the facts to assure ourselves that we alone are the makers of our universe. We are hard pressed to give credence to the anomaly laid before us in detail by Stoker. That mankind may have triumphed over this anomaly, only makes believing in such a concept that much harder. Yet, are we sure we are safer for it?

We all grasped at such meanings while we reviewed the reasons for the diary's suppression, fully prepared for a judgment based on logical assumptions. Those assumptions were never forthcoming. Decisions were made far beyond our reach and far removed from our understanding.

All of us were unprepared to accept the rationale, even as evidence of an earthquake in that area that took place on October 5, 1880 helped confirm it. [See attached report.]

Edith Toro
National Institute for Earth Sciences
4 Beethoven St.
Timisoara, Romania

The investigation into the historical seismicity of Romania evidences the occurrence of a strong earthquake in Transylvania [central part of Romania] near the locality of Tarnaveni in 1880. Historical information on the 1880 earthquake allows a detailed study. The investigation concentrated on time, epicentral location and intensity distribution confirms possible severe damage criteria in and around the Borgo Pass area.

The macrosiesmic map details a large area of I=VII (r7=20.7km) the center of which complies with targeted area.

The pieces of the puzzle began to come together. The earthquake confirmed the struggle. I was about to receive the missing piece—a validation far more ominous than I was prepared to meet. A danger lurked undetected. No explanation from this point on will make sense to you. They never really made sense to us, either. But I was even guiltier than anyone for not trying. I must admit that even with the evidence laid out before me, I did not choose to believe it was true. It would be the others who would pay the price for my failure to protect them from the unknown. Vambery made his reasoning apparent to me, but to what effect? I ignored the signs that there was no happy ending to this saga. He unwittingly opened a Pandora's box by not destroying the diary, but he never expected that it would still serve as a warning.

In doing so, Vambery sealed our fate so many years later. What he did not realize was that other forces would never want that diary exposed. He thought that the story was over, but it was only beginning.

I understood that better than anyone, but I failed the test. None of the others could have accepted such a notion. Would you?

[See attached copy of papers hidden by Professor Vambery.]

UNIVERSITY OF BUDAPEST

By order of the Illuminati and as a humble servant of the Cabala, I bear witness to the following proceedings and have acted accordingly.

I lay my actions out before the jury of the elders.

Judgment has been passed upon these events. My conclusions have been validated and I have performed my duty to the Concordant Dominion. I present witness to the sacred sources.

We of the order pledge our honor to the Concordant and to all its commands. No higher authority exists and we subjugate ourselves to the wisdom of the eternal books of understanding. We record this to the Book of Knowledge.

I was not alone in this decision. Our brothers joined us in the suppression of Stoker's diary. They seek such union with us and are pledged to the oath. Each one of us seeks the guidance of grace and wisdom from the Illuminati, the sacred keepers of the Concordant.

They have pledged their allegiance as our brothers and swear by the powers of the Temple and of the Rose to bow down before the enlightenment of Illuminati.

Whose judgment supports our work? We stand relieved of the burden of decision and rejoice in the sacrament of fulfillment. The dark time professed by the ancient scriptures has been dealt with. For now...

I submit this brief fully aware that my actions are to be decided by the power of the jury before me. I alone will let history judge me as I place the events before the providence of discovery.

The occurrence that has transpired was not unexpected. Not by the Church in Rome, the sacred mosques of true knowledge nor the temple horizons of Tibet. The works of our divine spirits are at one with a universe that humanity, as we know it, could never understand. This then is our vow of protection. Graced by the authority vested in our institute, I remain humble to its existence and seek comfort in the wisdom of our order. Knighted by the blood of our eternal saviors, we concede to the tasks at hand and are sworn to the secrecy of its instruments. We have fulfilled our duty. Only God himself dictates the end to this aberration.

The sacred scrolls that have given us warning forced us to draw our swords to meet the challenge. Blessed by his grace we performed our duties bravely.

The gifts of our maker to bless our existence are the drink of knowledge from the grail itself. This has now been done. Time will decide the outcome…

I have been witness to, and a survivor of a most extraordinary event—an event much too horrible to contemplate and even more shocking to comprehend. I have dedicated my life to understanding the differences between cultures. I have witnessed why some cultures may never be fused, but torn apart by divergent beliefs and mutual distrust. In God's name, acceptance is never equal and God himself is never just.

An historic clash of cultural sensibilities has always made tolerance impossible. Mankind struggles to accept the unknown, to accept the differences. Civilizations must endure the pains of understanding to educate themselves to a respect for their own teachings and the teachings of others. Still, these differences may never be accepted. Regardless, we must try.

Life exists in its many forms, but now for the first time I have seen evil in its most extravagant form. This realization has unnerved me and motivated me to repress its announcement in all ways possible. Except I will not destroy this diary.

No rational mind can accept the findings that lie before us. We are forever perplexed by the mysteries we should better understand. What is to become of this world of ours if that understanding comes at such a price. A price we alone have agreed to pay. What would become of human society if they realized that we were not alone? Within our universe exists a realm of living forces not remotely interested in the concept of a single God. What would the fabric of human existence be if it were possible that God does not exist at all?

So inhumane are these life-forms that they must be kept dormant, locked away from us until history unmasks this reality on a better prepared world. The Dominus and it brethren offer a possible prove that the concept of any God is not universal.

No human mind can comprehend the awesome danger that brought us so close to a true Armageddon. No monument can pay tribute to the souls of the brave men and women who fought this evil to its demise. Yet, this whole truth will burden our psyches with a trepidation that has no answers.

The mysterious forces of the occult, the folk tales, the myths, the legends that arise as visions of imagination from which reality is endorsed is a very human concept. But they remain nothing more than fantasy. What if the dangers are no longer fantasy, but true terror? On those steep hills of the Romanian mountains we found such terror. How will mankind ever feel safe again if Pandora's box has been opened?

Ignorance of the truth is humanity's only real protection from such panic. The keepers of the ancient secrets knew this. The orders of the enlightened know it now. We have acted upon it with an ever-present fear that this is nothing more than cosmetic prudery, but we really have no other choice.

The Illuminati are the arbiters of the unknown truths and in their name I have so decided. This confrontation must be accepted as myth and be forgotten. Mankind will be better for it. History itself will tell us when we can speak. Only when mankind can face such evil with confidence should this information be made available. Until that time, we must protect the innocent from these dangers. We must pray that those dangers never return. We must be prepared for their return. Evil comes to us in many forms…

The centuries of werewolves and vampires can be explained away as a theory of an occult force. Instinctively, man rationalizes the irrational by seeking comfort in the unreal. By giving the occult a name, we give it an understanding. Only the Elders can ever give this unwanted reality a name. Assured in the knowledge that real terror is at least manageable, we are safe in our belief that ultimately our horror is nothing more than fiction to those who are not enlightened.

This is the perplexing reality we face. The concept of horror has placed itself in our domain. The horror is real and yet to lionize its dangers any further will only play havoc on our believing minds and impossible to explain to a populace that is of a mind still undeveloped to the ways of scientific explanation, a mind already too prone to superstition. The effect of these truths would be cataclysmic. I must hope that this danger, which is now dormant, will be a unique event. I feel compelled to eradicate it from memory.

That is why I rendered Bram Stoker forgetful of these proceedings. We have thus spirited away all evidence of what has happened. As stated before, the brothers of the enlightenment have already sworn an oath to the Concordant and all its secrets. Bram Stoker is not of such responsibility and is not anchored to such reasoning.

I induced Bram Stoker to swallow the drink of oblivion, which causes the imbiber to suffer the loss of memory of recent events. While this potion of the ancient druids is quite powerful, I lessened its potency by using tincture of absinthe. With the potion, I have removed Stoker from this equation. The other survivor, Mathewson, is the ghost warrior of the blessed Masonic temple. He accepts his duty to its domain. He will protect the secret of the Illuminati he is sworn to defend.

The written record must be expunged. That is why I gave Bram Stoker the gift of not remembering. His memory will be clouded, but not destroyed.

I have explained his predicament as one of illness and defined his condition to him, which had caused him to be left behind. He was, of course, disappointed to hear of the results. Never having met him before, it was only my past association with Henry Irving and Von Hanes that he trusted in what I was saying to him. Henry Irving is one of us and is prepared to follow the decree of Illuminati.

I must say I was quite flattered by the attention Stoker provided to me and felt extremely guilty at what I had engineered. He was a brave and valiant warrior and shared our dangers with distinction. I only wish that I could have told him that. Instead, I resorted to subterfuge.

I shared with him the tragic events leading to Dr. Hanes' unfortunate death—death caused by an encounter with a wild animal. I assured him that I had made arrangements to ship Dr. Hanes' body home for burial.

I sent him on his way quite willingly, as he needed to get back to England to help Irving start the winter season. William Mathewson arranged and traveled with Bram Stoker to insure his safe passage back to London…

One day this testament of our agony will be of importance. This is my disagreement with the sacred sources. We just cannot assume that the world will never know of the Dominus. We need some record of this, despite the decision to destroy it. They will come again one day. Of that I am sure. As you read this, they may be here now. Trust no one with this.

This has been a difficult decision, one I am not yet ready to make. Some record needs to be maintained. As per my own position within this structure, I reserve such right to make that choice.

So I feel I will not destroy his diary at this time, but will place it in indeterminate state. Destiny is to decide if it will one day resurface. I put the matter into God's hands.

Signed: Arminius Vambery

Journal: L.O. Wynne

Professor Andersen had a different, less mystic view of the Stoker diary, but one I found compelling at the time. [See Andersen Conclusion attached.]

Columbia University: Private Data
INTERNAL MEMO

Andrew Andersen

There is no truer saying than that of Grim to the effect that "superstition in all manifold varieties constitutes a sort of religion, applicable to the common household necessities of daily life."

What do you do when superstition is no longer a guide, but is prevalent in ways that go beyond human understanding, when legend is no longer a viable alternative, when the truth goes beyond such simple explanations and challenges the very essence of all things human? This is the same crossroads that Professor Vambery faced then and we face now.

Can we explain today the reality of some alien invasion, which if not for the courageous stand of a few select men and women, may have rewritten history? The mere suggestion is ludicrous, but compelling nonetheless. We cannot totally dismiss this story as mere fantasy. Or can we? That would certainly be a safer road to travel.

This whole concept is similar to prevailing arguments about contact with extraterrestrial beings. While existing science hasn't proven that intelligent lifeforms exist anywhere in the universe, scientific research has begun to discover possibilities that some very minuscule life may have once existed on neighboring planets. Or is there now, hiding under the ice of Jupiter's moon. Only by our own arrogance can we state that life, as we know it, does not exist at all anywhere else in this vast Universe. Who can prove that life never existed and even as we speak may actually be sharing the universe with others?

Years ago such an hypothesis would have been considered quackery. Has the world changed that much from Dr. Von Hanes time? Science fiction is still inching closer to a possible validation of a once outlandish thought. How long before such a possibility will be accepted?

For all our knowledge of the universe, the underworld of possibilities much like the Land of the Forest in Stoker's time may never fully reveal its secrets. We cannot do full justice by explaining everything away.

The most compelling argument concerning alien life follows Vambery's rationale.

What if mankind was finally able to make contact with alien lifeforms? What would be the consequences if we attempt to do so? In facilitating such contact, will mankind actually be alerting a threatening form of life to our presence? What if that very contact was a recipe for our own destruction? We routinely make the assumption that any intelligent life is friendly. But perhaps Vambery's reasoning was correct—what we do not know may never hurt us.

Maybe we should remain ignorant of anything that would threaten our way of life. We may actually be safe in our isolation, benignly unaware of the real danger awaiting us in the vast universe. In our search for understanding, do we invite such a calamity by introducing ourselves to it?

Conjecture, yes, but it has some value. Perhaps we are better off thinking we are alone.

In its simplest form, we can argue that a meteor of some unknown origin struck Earth and a living microorganism of an unearthly nature fashioned itself upon the landscape of its new environment in order to survive. It was a cunning and evil life force charted with an unemotional desire to evolve. Tasked to survive, these creatures sought nourishment by enriching themselves instinctually upon the sustenance of living things. Then these heroes emerged, these mythical knights stepped forth and destroyed them. The blissful knowledge of the true dark forces threatening humanity and its perception of that true had been preserved. As an educated man, I cannot accept this. As a believer of science in fiction, I can.

So why did Vambery do it then? Why did he keep everything sub rosa, as it were? We are forced to accept his belief that what happened was very real to him. For that reason, we can hypothesize the scenario regarding the Illuminati to be a clever twist.

The rationale of an isolated philosophy, suppressed by an enigmatic organization with access to secrets beyond existing knowledge, is as old as civilization itself. Does such a world order exist today?

While I find the Illuminati decree to be an interesting concept. I think, overall, the concept is a bit farfetched. We would have to buy into a world filled with dark secrets and conspiracies to accept such a rationale. As a serious scholar, I cannot contemplate or endorse such a scenario.

So, what exactly happened? I believe that this is an example of overactive imaginations at work and, for whatever reason, the promise of this story was never fulfilled. The secret died with Vambery and Bram Stoker.

My conclusion is that the lost diary of Bram Stoker is real, but the story itself is not. In the interest of not besmirching the reputation of Professor Vambery, we will conclude that the suppression of this journal is unexplainable and his motivations are lost to history.

I shall assemble these findings and pass them on to Budapest. I expect we will discuss the matter further with them.

Signed: Andrew Andersen

But Budapest was suddenly gripped by fear. Whether the university really believed the diary was a forgery is moot now, but they took immediate action to quash the inquiry. [See attached telegram and news story.]

TELEGRAM

To: Dr. Andrew Andersen
From: Yton Oton, University of Budapest

It is with deep regret that I must inform you that despite evidence to the contrary, the University of Budapest is prepared to announce that the diary of Bram Stoker is a fake.

Upon receipt of this telegram, we request you immediately return to us all materials in your possession. As per our confidentiality agreement, any and all discussion of this matter is strictly forbidden and a breach will have far-reaching consequences.

This is binding on every person involved in the research. I cannot emphasize this enough. Please refrain from any deviation of the confidentiality agreement. A violation will have the dire consequences.

Reuters News Service
BUDAPEST, Hungary (January 29)

> The University of Budapest has announced that the so-called Bram Stoker diary was a fake and has been destroyed. No further information is forthcoming, other than to say that the world was saved from the spectacle of another celebrated forgery along the lines of *The Hitler Diaries*.

All of us were shocked by this announcement. It ran so contrary to what we had found. Andersen immediately ordered the destruction of all material by the research team. He did so without comment, which was very unusual for him. He was never able to communicate to us the sense of urgency that he had gleaned from Budapest. Then tragedy began to strike all of us. Anyone involved with the documents was suddenly in great danger. I did not see the signs in time. I could only save myself.

Andersen destroyed his documents in our presence and asked us to do the same. McManus joked that he wished he had made a copy. The irony is, I did just that. It was a choice I now regret. I did not regret the action, but wish I had said something at the time. I had other reasons to keep the file. I knew that I could never suppress the findings, so I went incommunicado for the next several days, searching for additional information. I only wish I had received what I was looking for a few days earlier. If only it had come sooner.

Suddenly, and without warning, Professor Andersen was brutally murdered. We were devastated by this news. But things would get worse, much worse, over the coming days.

[See newspaper clippings attached.]

New York *Daily News*

Columbia Professor Murdered in Ransacked Office

> Professor Andrew Andersen of Columbia University was murdered in his office on Friday night, after an apparent botched robbery attempt. He was found face down on his

desk with his throat cut. The office was ransacked. In an equally disturbing twist, the perpetrators took the professor's keys to his townhouse on Riverside Drive and burglarized his home immediately after the murder. The investigation is ongoing.
Police say they have no motive and have no clear suspects, but are awaiting the results of forensic tests done at the scenes.

New York *Newsday*

A former New York FBI agent died yesterday after he fell from a ladder while doing yard work at his home on Long Island. Retired special agent Steve Garret, fifty-seven, was pruning a tree in his Port Washington backyard when he fell and suffered fatal head and neck injuries, authorities said. Last night, his former FBI counterparts mourned their well-regarded former colleague, who had recently set up his own investigative agency specializing in document analysis. He is survived by his wife Florence and daughter Chloe.

New York *Post*

Page Six

Was it Murder, Sherlock?
The recent untimely death of renowned philologist Allen Clay from food poisoning has made several of his close friends suspicious. The leading autograph collector and handwriting expert, who was a disciple of the late Charles Hamilton, died last week at his home. What is most troubling to those around him was the fact that he was supposedly died from consuming bad beef. That he was a strict vegetarian makes this whole case very odd. Friends are quietly pressing the NYPD to look into this because they suspect murder.

Within a few hours of each other, I was being asked to attend funerals of all those who had participated in our study. One after another, they would die, quickly, violently and without warning. I had already started my own research. I had my suspicions from the first reading. I alone was among this group who knew of the significance of the participants. I did not need proof that this was all real. But until those tragic last days, I did not realize that time had already run out. I failed to see the true danger until it was too late. The danger escaped my comprehension.

Each death was more mysterious than the last. A cruel fate had befallen us. All who had touched the Stoker documents were being eliminated. Only by the grace of God did I avoid the slaughter. And only by my attempts to reach certain sacred sources did I avoid calamity. I had already initiated contact with the secret world to find the truth and I was hidden from their view. To search for confirmation, I could not leave a trail because such a journey requires invisibility.

No one except me could see the connection. First, Andersen's office and then his townhouse were ransacked. My understanding is that Garret's files disappeared shortly after his death. That was three hours after I had learned of Andersen's murder, so I began to have other ideas.

One of our interns who did research for us never returned from a fishing trip, while my assistant died falling down an elevator shaft in her building. I decided I must stay underground. Then Allen Clay died and I knew I needed help.

Three days later, when I inquired at the gallery about Clay's file, they said that he had no information concerning this project in any of his papers. The very next day another researcher was killed in a car crash while driving a rented car. That person, I know for sure, did not have a license and didn't know how to drive.

I was becoming acutely aware of being followed. I could not seem to place who it was, but the unmistakable sense of being stalked permeated my entire being. Then, a few days ago, angry animals, of such odd description that I cannot to this day place their pedigree, set me upon. What struck me was that they did so at the command of a strange and dark presence whose very presence plunged my soul into mortal terror. Ironically, I had my knapsack filled with the Stoker material and used it as a weapon to beat off the beasts and escape.

At first, I held out hope that my attempts to communicate with the Illuminati were more than just a fantasy. I knew I did not have the reach, but

I kept trying and hoping that somehow this shadowy group was aware of me. But all I received back were whispers and rumors that shocked me to the core. I was no closer to the center of power than when I began. I may have no other choice then to trust in you at a time when I can trust no one.

I sent out signals in all the ways that I knew, but I have been betrayed. It was only after that terrible encounter with the dark presence that I began to suspect a more sinister possibility.

The letter I received confirmed it.

I remember that it came just hours before Dr. Andersen was murdered. A letter, due to these horrible events, I wish I had received before it was too late. Then I would have understood fully. When I finally did read it, I knew immediately that my fate and the fate of all the others had already been sealed. I realized that what had befallen us was the direct result of that letter.

Here is a dark saga even more dangerous than the diary—a danger that lives in the shadows! Somehow, I was able to escape it until now.

Still, I realize that it is only a matter of time. Even as I document this story, you will choose not to believe me. I promise you that decision will be a mistake.

I was able spirit away these documents, but to what end I do not know. I do so in the pathetic attempt to tell the world of these truths. I will not disclose my location even as you read this, for I would then have made a fatal decision to introduce these documents to you. In many ways, I hope that as I write these pages, no human being is actually reading them.

If only Yton Oton had left that diary in its hole. If only Vambery had destroyed it. With the resurfacing of that diary powerful forces knew that their secret would be compromised. The forces of enlightenment would be aware of their survival.

I sense that they have found me. I must remain composed.

I hear footsteps outside my door.

Sunimod has been unleashed.

Chapter 19

It took Walters only five minutes to arrive at Grand Central Station, but in his anxious state it seemed like hours. The meeting with Arsine was important because there were still so many unanswered questions.

The station was quiet at that time of the night. It was long past the evening rush hour and the number of commuters in transit could be counted in the hundreds, not the thousands. The usual roar was muted, now just a melody of footsteps on the marble floors. Distant conversations could be heard like whispered echoes.

If Arsine had been planning on a meeting in a public place, this was an excellent location, Walters thought. The west balcony bar overlooked the vast station. It had no roof over it except that of the station itself. Arsine could hide anywhere within the vast canyon and yet go completely unnoticed.

The bar area was quiet. Only a few people remained. With only half an hour left before closing time, the staff was preparing to shut down for the night. Walters moved to the back of the bar, picking a corner table with a direct view of the entrance. He waited more than ten minutes, but no one had come in. He was getting impatient.

Then a slim man of about fifty arrived. He was wearing a tan overcoat and a hat pulled down over his eyes. He scanned the open atrium, clearly aware of Walters sitting at an isolated corner table, but he made no acknowledgment. He looked around as if he were expecting others to be watching. Finally satisfied, he walked into the bar and made his way toward Walters. Without hesitation, he looked directly at the detective, confirming Walters's thought that a man like Arsine would know a cop when he saw one.

"I'm Rufus Arsine," the man said, removing his raincoat and hat. "I understand you wanted to talk to me."

"Sit down," Walters said, noting Arsine's expensively tailored dark gray suit and red silk tie. The illusive Arsine had sleepy, olive green eyes set deeply into a face that was long and narrow. His skin was pale and smooth as if it had been cosmetically altered. Arsine smiled, but Walters could tell he didn't mean it. By all appearances, Rufus Arsine was a very confident man and Walters knew that he had better be on top of his own game.

"I imagine you would like to talk about Laura Olsen Wynne," Arsine said, his voice was as hard and raspy as a shot of whiskey.

Walters nodded.

Arsine patted his salt-and-pepper hair, making sure every strand was in place.

"What makes you think I have anything to tell you?" Arsine said.

"Have you found her yet?" Walters asked.

Arsine laughed. "No, and I don't think I need to. Laura has found us."

"What?" Walters was clearly surprised.

"She's somewhere in the station right now, watching us. I'm certain of that," Arsine said.

Walters reacted quickly. He began searching the vast station, trying to confirm Arsine's information.

"Don't bother," Arsine said. "You won't find her. Laura Wynne does not want to be found at this time."

"I don't understand," Walters said.

"I wouldn't expect you to. You're already in over your head."

"What does that mean?" Walters asked incredulously.

"I don't really know for sure what this is all about," Arsine said with a sigh. "I have no further interest in the matter. If I get involved any deeper, there will be no turning back. So I'll be leaving the rest to you."

"The rest of what to me?" Walters asked.

"If you know anything about my reputation, you know that I don't play games. All I can tell you is that this situation you are in is a serious one and I want nothing more to do with it. All I ask is that you keep an open mind. If you don't, you'll be making a grave mistake. Laura is aware of the risks. Are you?"

"What the hell are you talking about, Arsine?" Walters asked. This interview was not going according to any plan he could conceive of.

"A few weeks ago, I was contacted by one of my clients who had an assignment for me. He is a very dangerous and powerful man, so when he talks, I listen—hard. He wanted me to meet someone and warned me not to be alarmed by this man's appearance. More important, under no circumstance was I to refuse whatever this man asked me to do."

"Can you give me names?"

"Come on," Arsine said. "If I gave you my client's name, I doubt I would be safe—even in the next life."

"Arsine, can we move past the riddles?" Walters interrupted impatiently.

"I know you will be skeptical, but I implore you to listen carefully," Arsine said urgently. "I arranged a midnight meeting at the piers near the Bronx terminal. The waterfront is dark and desolate at that time, not exactly the venue I like, but the request was clear—it had to be outdoors and as secret as possible."

"Go on," Walters said.

Arsine took a long breath before continuing.

"I waited for a few minutes wondering if my contact would even show up. Then before I knew it, I was surrounded by a pack of snarling black dogs. At least I thought they were dogs."

"Yeah?" Walters said, intrigued despite the feeling he was being fed a load of lies.

Arsine shrugged and moved closer to Walters, cutting the distance between them in half. "From the shadows, a thick mist appeared. Then a voice commanded the dogs to back away from me. I saw a tall angular man dressed in a black frock overcoat with the brim of his black hat pulled down over his eyes. He moved toward me. When he got into the dim light of the pier, I saw that his eyes were coal black. The look he gave me was malicious and frightening. Frankly, his eyes scared me and I've dealt with many dangerous characters in my time. He came so close to me that I could smell his breath—hot and ugly. His presence seemed to enter my being like a fiery sword. I felt completely helpless before him." Arsine shivered.

Walters kept quiet, wondering if this man was really scared or simply a consummate actor. If Arsine were lying, he was doing a masterful job.

"What else can you tell me about this man?" Walters asked.

"His skin appeared to be translucent, white and veined," Arsine said. "His mouth looked vicious. His thin lips were reddish blue. I only caught a glimpse, but I could see that his teeth were sharp like tiny daggers. Walters, let me tell you, this man was truly ugly. But it was his voice that I remember—the cruel and merciless timbre of his voice. He said his name was Tepes."

'What was the job this Tepes asked you to do?' ' Walters asked.

"He asked me to find Laura."

"Did he say why?"

"No. All he said was that I was to confirm that the Andersen project had been destroyed and I was to bring Laura to him."

"The Andersen project," Walters said. "What do you know about it?"

"I knew nothing about it at the time. When I asked Tepes about it, he refused to tell me. He didn't think the file still existed. The most important part of my job was to bring him L.O. Wynne,"Arsine said.

"Why did he choose you?" Walters asked.

"I usually find what I look for. And I am not a stranger to the darkest corners of the world—a world that is stranger than anything you could possibly imagine. I have witnessed things that humanity cannot—and should not—comprehend. I have seen ancient evils that have infected mankind since the dawn of time. I am just a mercenary who has never divulged their secrets. "

"But not in this case?"

Arsine smiled his wry smile before answering.

"There are some things that should not be kept secret. I'm no warrior, but whatever Laura has found needs to be dealt with before it is too late. She is trying to tell me what it is, but I value my life too much to get involved. Now I'm hoping she will tell you."

"I'm not sure how I'm supposed to react to that," Walters said.

"I suggest you act and react carefully," Arsine said.

"How am I supposed to help her?" Walters asked.

"Keep her alive," Arsine answered. "Her allies may not be able to help her now. Whatever this Tepes represents is very powerful. He is the extension of a dark force which I heard may exist, but whatever was in that file confirms it is real. The master will be forced to confront her allies if they discover that he has survived. He must stop her before that. We are facing pure evil."

"What do you mean by her allies?" Walters asked

"There are things about Laura that you may not know. It's the Andersen project that she's trying to expose to those who understand its significance. What she found in the file itself—"

"You mean the Stoker file, don't you?" Walters said interrupting.

"Very impressive. The Stoker file is a major part of this, I'm sure."

"How so?"

"I went to Columbia and asked to see the Andersen project. Dr. Lawson told me no record of what was in that file remained. Now, Laura took flight almost immediately after Andersen was killed. So I have my suspicions. She was one of the people who had access to it. But what alarmed me most was that other members of that team were dying at an incredible rate. I told Allen Clay about all this and he died the next day. You see the connection?"

Walters nodded.

"I'm convinced that Laura took the file for a reason," Arsine said firmly.

"So the Stoker file is the key," Walters said. He was gambling that Arsine wouldn't realize that he has no clue what the Stoker file was.

"Yes, it is the key," Arsine said "I was able to confirm that all of the recently deceased were working on the Stoker file. A diary written by Bram Stoker."

"I had a hard time making the connection with Stoker," Walters said, bluffing again. "How did you figure it out?"

"I don't require court orders to obtain information like you do. So I backtracked a great deal of information using my connections. The Andersen project concerned a previously unknown diary written by Bram Stoker that had inexplicably surfaced in Budapest. Andersen had been engaged to authenticate it, but the main reason I was interested was that Arminius Vambery had hid it. Anything involving Vambery gets my attention."

"Who's Arminius Vambery?"

"Let's just say he is well known in some circles. I'm not sure the others would have known him, but Laura would have clearly seen the connection. Whatever information Vambery hid and Laura saw, Tepes wants destroyed."

"So where is the Stoker diary now…can I read it?"

"Apparently, no one can read it. Budapest quietly announced that it was a forgery and supposedly destroyed it. Just as well, perhaps. It hasn't been a very good read for anyone."

"It wasn't a forgery, was it?"

"No, and that's why this situation is so frightening. Andersen, I understand, proved that it was not a fraud."

"Then why was the diary declared a hoax?"

"Someone in a very high place scared them off," Arsine said, his face tightening "Someone who wielded the type of power that you don't want to know about."

"Then how did you find out that the diary was real?"

"Shortly before his death, Andersen sent Yton Oton at the University of Budapest a telegram stating that the diary was authentic. I'm sure Andersen was shocked when Oton replied that the diary was being declared a hoax. Budapest informed Andersen and his team that they were to destroy all copies of the findings and to totally disavow any knowledge of the project. We can only assume that Andersen complied, but apparently there was some doubt that all the copies of the file where shredded. A great deal of doubt, I suppose, because even as Budapest issued a press release claiming the diary was a hoax, the bodies starting falling."

Walters nodded. He didn't want to press the man. "So you think this Oton was being intimidated?"

"That man has always lacked courage, but if my guess is correct, he is also not long for this world."

"Is Tepes going to kill him?" Walters asked unable to hide the alarm in his voice.

"Tepes is only a messenger. If the secret is revealed, if some manifestation of this evil is exposed, the powers of enlightenment will attempt to destroy it. This is what Tepes and his organization are trying to prevent."

"How did Laura get so deeply involved with all of this?" Walters asked. "What is she trying to do here?"

"Laura is trying to reach her allies, but the path is blocked. She's just trying to stay alive long enough to alert them about what she has uncovered. How much do you know about her?"

"Not all that much," Walters said truthfully.

"You know that her parents were killed in an automobile accident?"

"Yes?"

"Well, Laura's father was a multifaceted man with quite a past. While he was extremely rich, there was always a dark aura about him. He was very mysterious about the source of his wealth. He was, by the way, a member of the Bilderberg Group."

"Bilderberg. Yes, I've heard of it," Walters said, lying through his teeth.

"But the real power goes beyond such groups as the Bilderberg. I always believed, but could never prove that he was what is known as an Elder "

"So, her father was a player?"

"A player in more ways than one. I knew him, and nothing about him would have surprised me," Arsine said.

"You knew her father?" Walters asked, mystified.

"Yes. He once tried to hire me to help him find the Amber Room."

"I saw something on TV about it," Walters said. "Russia's lost art treasure stolen by the Nazis."

"When a man like Lane Wynne is interested, it makes me think that the Amber Room contains mysteries that go beyond the obvious."

Arsine paused. Then, in a serious tone, said, "The wealth of a nation can be increased overnight if the Amber Room and its riches were to be recovered. The communists knew this better than anyone. So did the Stasi, the East German secret police. They were all actively involved in trying to find the room, even after the collapse of the Berlin Wall.

"But there are some who believe that the wealth of the Amber Room has always been intended for the funding of the Fourth Reich and they will do anything to protect that wealth. Sinister groups well versed in the art of protecting what is theirs. They may also have been protecting something that Wynne suspected was related to the artwork. An answer that could lead him to the very heart of their power and unlock its puzzle. He had defining interest in those types of secrets. I, for one, did not want to find out where that money trail would lead if I found it. Just by his asking me, I knew this would not be some treasure hunt. In my line of work you do not want to get too close to either side or you become dangerous to both of them. I declined the job, but Lane kept going. They must have learned that Lane Wynne was close to finding it. So they killed him."

"You think that Laura's father was murdered because of the Amber Room?" Walters asked "Do you have any proof of this?"

"No, but I do have some suspicions," Arsine said. "His car accident happened only a few hours before he was to meet a man named Georg Stein. Stein had actually found the location of the room and he was on his way to meet Wynne. Neither man made the meeting. They found Stein's body in a field with his own knife stuck six inches inside his throat. Suicide?"

"Possibly," Walters said. "But what makes you think that Laura's father was murdered?"

"When Laura's parents left their estate that morning, it was a bright, clear day. They were being driven by a professional chauffeur. The brakes on the car were new and the roads were dry. Still, the Rolls skidded off the road while traveling only twenty miles per hour. That makes me suspicious."

"But it doesn't necessarily make it murder," Walters said.

"True, but when the car went over the side of that mountain, they found her father behind the wheel. No chauffeur." Arsine smiled ironically. "And the chauffeur has never been seen or heard from since. I suspect that Wynne had no idea of the real danger he was in."

"What does all of this have to do with Laura?" Walters asked.

"She inherited more than her family's fortune. She inherited her family's place in the hierarchy of the Wall of Knowledge. Like her father, she entered the humanity beyond the wisdom.

"The what? Are you saying that Laura Olsen Wynne is part of some...some cult?"

"I wouldn't say a cult, but she is definitely spiritual in a most unconventional way. She took that first step when she was at Yale. Aided by her father's formidable connections, she became one of the first women to join Skull and Bones."

"I've listened patiently to your weird tale, Arsine, but just how does a frat house like the Skull and Bones fit into all this?"

Arsine smiled knowingly.

"That's what they want you to think," he said. "That Skull and Bones is some kind of animal house fraternity and, in some ways, that's true. But if you are one of the chosen, you could be invited to take the first steps into the world of the sacred sources. At least two of its alumni made such a journey and were allowed to be among the keepers of Book of Knowledge."

"What the hell is that?" Walters asked. *Was Arsine a lunatic or just seriously brain damaged?* He wondered.

"The Book of Knowledge discloses the mysteries that the Book of the Dead does not. It contains the secret writings of the ancients, a book that was spirited away by the Knights Templar during the crusades. Behold the inner mysteries of paganism and the gospels of the witness, it's all part of it. This remarkable compendium is said to predict a coming evil—an evil more powerful than any made by the God of the Bible. The Book of Knowledge includes the matrix for the Bible Code…the parts of the code that computers haven't found yet."

Walters shook his head in disbelief. "I don't believe one damn word of this nonsense."

"I can't blame you, "Arsine said with a shrug and a half smile. "They will be counting on that from you and that might just keep you alive.

"Suspend your skepticism for a moment and trust me. All the clues are there. Think about it for a moment. Look at Laura's background, the languages she learned, the degrees in medieval and religious studies—even the type of research she was doing on her own and the type of articles she was writing. She was an apprentice of the Way to the Forever Horizon. She was preparing the path for her illumination. This woman is acutely aware of things that I'm sure even Andersen didn't know."

"If her knowledge is so great, why can't she just get help from the people you say she's in league with?" Walters asked.

"She does not know how to get the kind of help she needs. She can't just pick a phone. She was placed in the lower echelon of the pecking order and that is why she is having so much trouble going higher. It's a very complicated process if you don't have the right contacts. Contacts she would have to trust. She is not very close yet to finding the Elders of the Concordant

Dominion, and I'm sure she is confused about whom she can trust. I'm a perfect example of that."

"How?" Walters was surprised—again. *Whether conducting an interview or questioning a witness, it was never good to be surprised*, he thought.

"Laura has no idea that I am looking for her," Arsine said. "While you've been out there actively seeking her, she's been desperately trying to contact me. I could have delivered her to Tepes a week ago, but I just can't. I fear what would happen."

"Why would she want to contact you?" Walters asked.

"Because she knows that I'm one of the few people in the world who is capable of reaching the people who could help her."

"Why haven't you then?"

"I'd be putting a target on my back. That's why I'm talking to you...maybe you can help her...I'm staying out of this for now."

"Then maybe I should be staying out of this as well." Walters huffed. "I'm sorry, but I cannot believe a word you are saying."

"To be expected, Walters, but you do not know it yet, but you may be more involved then you could have ever imagined"

"How so, Arsine?"

"On a much lower level, these were the same evil forces your mother was pursuing, Walters. I hear she had a nervous breakdown? That's what they said anyway. She paid a terrible price, regardless. At best she only touched the surface of what she was looking for, but that was enough to either drive her mad, or somehow made to seem that way."

"Would you like me to shoot you right now, Arsine. It's only because of your reputation that I haven't reached across the table and snapped your neck like a twig bringing my mother into this nonsense."

"It has nothing to do with my reputation, Walters. You always knew there was something more to her death, didn't you? I could sense that in you just by watching your reaction. On that terrible day you came face to face with evil in a most horrific way, and you better start getting prepared, Walters, because it's nothing like what is coming next. Or you can just get up and walk away."

Walters paused for a moment. His years of experience taught him not to show any emotion in times like these. He must quickly decide whether he was being played by Arsine, or Arsine was trying to make a point. He knew he had always had these doubts about what happened to his mother. He remembered the strange look in her eyes seconds before she died. He knew he had seen something evil, and it was not his mother. He saw some indescribable evil force. He also knew Arsine would not have brought this up unless there was some purpose. Arsine was just too smart to play this kind of game with him. Oddly, he actually felt in some strange way that he could trust him. Ludicrous as the entire concept seemed to him

"I won't do that, Arsine."

"Regardless, Walters, just remember they will know your background and you now have a target on your back. Trust no one. I hope Laura knows that as well."

Arsine relaxed for a second. *He is looking drained*, Walters thought. *This might be the right time to spring the last question on him.*

"Why can't she trust Sunimod," Walters asked forcefully, looking carefully for Arsine's reaction.

"Sunimod is not just a name," Arsine said, clearly shocked at Walters's knowledge. "It's a code word used to describe secret documents that were never meant to seen by mainstream historians. It is also meant as a warning of the impending evil. A code word invoked if that evil has arrived. In the past it had a different name, but when it is needed, it is the clarion call to action. Sunimod is a relatively new term dating from the late nineteenth century."

"And?"

Arsine sighed heavily. Walters could tell the man was very uncomfortable, but he hoped to get an answer anyway.

"Although there is some debate about this, the Illuminati probably created the word Sunimod," Arsine said. "In its documentary form, it identifies religious artifacts from antiquity that do not conform to the secular view of the history of mankind. Understand this, Walters. If you're having trouble getting your arms around what I have just told you, there is no way you could accept what I am about to tell you now. In the infancy of early man there existed an advanced civilization far superior to our civilization. In the history of this society they were forced to confront invasions from dark forces that came to destroy them. In doing so, their own civilization began to crumble and die out due in part to the ensuing carnage of those battles. In the archives left behind they warned that one day these dark forces would return. A few of these ancients survived beyond the destruction of their civilization. They became what were known as the Elders and, in order to survive, these Elders assimilated themselves into our societies. They became the teachers of this hidden knowledge. Over time, as the true Elders died out, the mantle of this protection was passed on to the Human Elders, who, as keepers of the knowledge, formed the Concordant Dominion to hide and protect those secrets. The Concordant quickly became the real power on earth, and twice in its history they found and eradicated alien forces that tried to come here. The issue of their existence was compromised when the Knights Templar found the Holy Grail. It was actually the proof of the Concordant's existence and why it was formed. This forced an uneasy alliance of the Concordant and the Templar. Later, an arrangement was made to destroy the Templar and only a chosen few were allowed to become Elders in return for their compliance. Over time, other societies were formed, and only when they reached what is called true enlightenment was a very select group of people allowed to share in its secrets. By taking the oath to protect the Concordant, they became part of a Jihad designed to keep the veracity of the true history of the earth secret by any means necessary. Over thousands of years this small group of Elders had built a structure of immense power and influence. They further protected themselves by being fronted by secret societies like the Masons, Bilderberg, and several others. Eventually the most powerful became the Illuminati. The leaders of the Illuminati had direct contact with the Elders and they had immense influence over all the other secular and non-secular powers, including the Church. The earliest Popes where made aware of the fact that the very tenet of Christian beliefs were threatened by the knowledge held by Concordant. They also became active participants in providing warriors who joined with the elite Knights of the Concordant to destroy what is called evil when it has been found. Over centuries smaller events happened, but for the most part only two major confrontations took place where all the knights were needed. I do find it interesting, however, that people like myself and the other mercenaries who came before me have never met an Elder or a Knight of the Concordant. Despite the fact, we are paid tremendous amounts of money to find and destroy artifacts that protect them. You know what's also funny, Walters? I don't even know why the Illuminati chose sunimod as its code name. Go figure, eh?"

"Help me out here," Walters asked. "Can you at least get me in contact with the Illuminati? Providing that all this nonsense is true, however."

"I can say nothing further on this topic. Just by my telling you all this I may have signed both our death warrants," Arsine replied. "But let me ask you a question: How did you find out about Sunimod?"

"In Laura's apartment."

"So those thugs who took her computer never figured out the hidden shelves?" Arsine said. "They are the ones who have been doing all the killing, Detective. They work for Tepes."

"Why didn't they just rip the place apart?"

"They're not that stupid. After what happened to Andersen, tearing up Laura's apartment would have very hard to cover up."

"But—"

"Our meeting is over," Arsine said suddenly. "I've already told more than I should. Here, take this."

He pushed an envelope under the table.

"What's in it?" Walters asked.

"The key to a post office box that Laura sent me. I will not open it. But I'm sure the answers to all your questions are there. Don't let them see you take this from me."

"Why not?"

"Just remember, while Laura may be watching us now, so are the eyes of Tepes. Don't try to contact her unless she gets in touch with you first. If you do, you'll just lead them right to her and you will both be dead." Arsine rose and offered his hand. "Take heart...you'll need it."

Walters watched as Rufus Arsine grabbed his hat and coat and departed as silently as he had arrived.

"Last call," a young blonde waitress said to him.

"Yeah," Walters said. "My last call. Depending on whom you talk to."

"Well, do you want a drink or not?" the waitress asked, an edge in her voice.

Walters shook his head. He had to think about the wild story Arsine had told him. *Could it possibly be true—any of it? Or was he being played the fool by an expert?* He looked at the envelope with the key. At least that was real. He could feel it. But whether the locker contained anything valuable to his investigation was debatable.

Walters plunged the envelope into his pocket and, as he did so, the paper with the word Sunimod written on it fell on the table. He looked at it sitting on the glass-mirrored table and saw at once that sunimod spelled backward was Dominus.

"Dominus?" he said out loud. "That really tells me a lot, doesn't it?"

Chapter 20

Walters decided to check out the post office first. Heeding Arsine's warning, he continually checked to see if he was being followed. But, all the way to Lexington Avenue, he couldn't spot anyone. *Either Arsine was full of it, or professionals were tailing him*, he thought, making a conscious decision to not sweat it. If Arsine was right about Laura also watching him, then he wanted to make sure that she saw him retrieving the file. She needed to know he was involved now.

After the massive Foley facility on Eighth Avenue, the post office at Grand Central was the most famous in New York City. And although the lobby was closed to the public at night, the back office was still operating. Walters could get inside just by flashing his badge.

But, before entering the freight entrance, he paused to look around one last time, hoping to catch a glimpse of whoever might be following him. Except for some homeless people in the distance, he couldn't see anyone on the dark street. A group of vagrants was the perfect blind for undercover work, but he was too anxious to see what was in the damn box to bother to hassling them on a hunch. He could always deal with them later.

After knocking on the back door, Walters was allowed inside and was directed by a postal employee to the boxes. He inserted the key into number 2695, and then he hesitated for a moment, wondering just what he would find. He turned the key and discovered a large manila envelope. Walters placed his business card in the box and closed it. Then he headed back to the station house as quickly as possible, fearing he might be ambushed anywhere along the way. But, with a stroke of good fortune, he flagged down a patrol car and got a ride to the precinct.

Once behind his desk, Walters opened the thick envelope and pulled out assorted documents. What immediately caught his eye was Laura's journal.

The first line read: *If you are reading this, your life is in great danger.*

According to Arsine, it was a bit late for that now, he thought, but he had no intention of heeding her warning. He had to help her no matter what the cost.

Reading the pages of her journal, he could tell that Laura was under great stress, yet he was impressed by the way she had compiled the dossier. She had carefully chronicled the progression of events in a way that even he could understand. The one difficulty was a letter written in a foreign language. He would need to get it translated. But overall, he marveled at her ingenuity.

All the players were in her journal—Andersen, Allen Clay, Yton Oton and the others. The newspaper clippings and the telegrams were intriguing evidence. So were the obituaries. Laura had complied quite a database on the project. He looked with fascination at the diary. Captivated, he glanced through the pages. With Laura's guidance and Arsine's input, a very compelling story was outlined before him. Now, if he only believed it. The skeptic in him still had doubts. Why all the deception and the theatrics? What did any of them have to gain?

The one true thing he knew was that Laura Olsen Wynne was in grave danger—a danger so unimaginable that no one would be able to protect her. He knew this in his heart, if not his mind. Her only advantage was that she had foreseen the peril and had taken flight. Her pain was very apparent in the pages of her journal. How she had wished she had done more to protect the others and to warn them. Her angst was so evident to Walters that it broke his heart.

It was equally obvious to him that Laura had not been exactly sure who would read her journal. It seemed to him that much of it was written on the fly with Laura always looking behind her. Walters was struck by her continued effort to apologize for the danger she had placed the reader in. It was as if she expected the reader to not survive—either.

Walters closed his eyes, suddenly realizing how exhausted he was. He has been up all night, and in only a few more hours it would be dawn. He needed to go home and get some rest before he could truly comprehend the material he had read. Right now, it was not making much sense to him.

Maybe tomorrow would be the day he found Laura after all, he thought, collecting the papers and hiding the pile behind his file cabinet. For one brief moment, he had thought about placing the report in the evidence room, but it would be vulnerable there. Real power, he knew, had the reach to find the evidence and have it expunged. Walters could not, and would not, underestimate the people Arsine had told him about.

Satisfied, he began the three-block walk to his favorite parking spot on a side street next to the UN Plaza Park. The streets there were extremely quiet this night. For a city that never slept, he would have sworn that tonight New York was taking a nap. There was absolutely no one in sight when he got to First Avenue and crossed to his parked car. Except for the regulated flashing of the traffic lights, everything was quiet. The moon had dipped to the horizon and a strange winter fog had enveloped the empty park. It was a sight Walters never remembered seeing before. Something was moving in the shadows of the fog. Curious, he disappeared into the clinging gray mist.

From inside the park, he could make out slight movements all around him. Figures began to take shape in the shadows, fascinating him, but making him uneasy. Peering into the mist, he could now see several unusually large black dogs staring at him. Their furious red eyes pierced him like daggers through the fog as they moved slowly toward him. They were indeed as horrific as Arsine had described them. He had learned a long time ago how to hide his fear, but this was a challenge so alien and frightening that it was completely beyond his experience.

Walters stared firmly into the eyes of the absurd creatures and smiled. That seemed to enrage them further. They glared at him fiercely, daring him to take them on. There was no barking, just hideous shrieks that rattled Walters to the bone. Terror pulsated through his body, and he instinctively reached for his gun. The feel of cold metal comforted him, but he suspected that Tepes would make an appearance at any moment and braced himself. He was not disappointed. What he wasn't prepared for was to find Tepes standing right behind him. He knew it was Tepes by the heavy breathing hard upon his neck. Outflanked, Walters turned around to face him.

Tepes's coal black eyes were as Arsine had described them. They were set deep within hollow sockets and seemed to stare right through him. He was too stunned to speak. Then Tepes placed a long angular hand on his shoulder, digging in with long, sharp and pasty white fingernails. Walters shuddered in pain until Tepes loosened his grip.

"Your time is short, Walters. You will bring the file and Laura to me tomorrow night. This is your only warning," Tepes said in a raspy voice that was sinister and menacing. "Because of her, the master is coming. There will be retribution."

Walters tried to regain his composure. With an attempt at sarcasm, he said: "What's in it for me?"

"All I can promise you is a painless death. Do not take such an offer lightly."

Just as he finished speaking, the largest of the black dogs moved alongside of Tepes. The creature snarled viciously at Walters and seemed poised to attack at any time.

"Well, guess what?" Walters said with false bravado. "You and Lassie over there have just threatened a New York City police officer."

Walters reached for his gun and pulled out his handcuffs. "You are under arrest. You have the right to remain silent and anything you say might—"

"Silence!" Tepes was enraged. His black eyes turned blood red.

Walters felt as if he were suddenly engulfed by a hot fetid wind and was paralyzed by Tepes's blazing eyes.

Then Tepes reached a bony clawlike hand into Walters's chest. Sharp nails dug deep into his ribs with a penetrating thrust. Pain shot through his body. Tepes grimaced with effort as he twisted hard inside Walters's chest, reaching for something. Walters lost his breath and almost his mind when he saw Tepes pull a bloody, pulsing mass of bleeding tissue from his chest. Tepes held the still-beating heart in front of Walters and said: "You have been warned. Do not fail me." Then he forcefully plunged the thumping heart back into Walters's chest.

In agony, Walters almost lost consciousness and dropped to the ground. Watching with dimming eyes, he thought he saw Tepes change into a swirling, twisting mist and with his dogs faded away with the retreating fog. Before he blacked out, he heard a voice echoing in his head, "Tomorrow."

The sun was beginning to rise when Walters regained his senses. The memory of his pain was still vivid, but the wounds of his encounter with Tepes were not. Only the throbbing of his shoulder hurt him in a physical sense. The rest of him was throbbing in an emotional way. He felt as if he were coming out of a trance, making him wonder if he had just been hypnotized. Walters was covered with sweat and exhausted, but he was able to get up and trudge back to the precinct. *Neither he nor Laura had any defense against Tepes*, he thought. *How was he ever going to protect her?*

Reaching the sanctuary of his desk, he sank wearily into his chair. But as he closed his eyes, Gabowski's rough voice startled him from behind.

"Hey, Mounty, you're one hell of a detective. You know that girl? That pretty one? The one in the picture that you keep staring at like it was a *Playboy* centerfold?"

"Laura?"

"Well, she just dropped by to give you this envelope," Gabowski said, flipping an envelope on Walters's desk. "She was wearing a black wig, but it was her. Great job. Only you could arrange to have a missing person find you before you could find her. You're a friggin' legend." When Gabowski started to walk away, Walters shot straight up in his chair, adrenalin coursing through his veins.

"How long ago?" he asked.

"What?"

"How long ago was she here?"

"Five minutes, tops," Gabowski said. "Is it important?"

Without answering, Walters jumped from his chair, raced out of the precinct and onto the street. He saw people everywhere, but he couldn't see Laura. He had to make a decision, right or left, which way had she gone? He took a chance and jogged around the corner of Third Avenue. Two blocks away, he could see a dark-haired woman moving east. She was walking briskly, but not running, obviously not wanting to draw attention to herself.

The woman stopped and turned around. Even with the black wig and the distance between them, Walters could see that it was Laura Olsen Wynne. She looked back at Walters, and she knew who he was because she smiled at him. It was the same enigmatic smile he had been looking at in her photograph all this time. Finally, Laura's smile was just for him. At last he had found her. Laura nodded her head, turned the corner and just like that she was gone. Remembering Arsine's warning, Walters didn't follow her.

Back at his desk, Walters opened the envelope from Laura. It contained two letters. The first was addressed to him. In it, Laura had written she was aware that Arsine was unwilling to help her and that she was grateful Walters wanted to try. She said she had seen him with Arsine, but unfortunately she could tell they were being watched by others and had left the scene before she was discovered.

She warned him that Tepes had observed his meeting in Grand Central and to be prepared for a visit from that strange being who could induce a hypnotic state in his victims—one that could conjure up horrifying hallucinations. But, she said, Tepes wasn't the real problem. His mind was controlled by an even more terrifying power that was still far away.

Walters remembered Arsine saying that Tepes was only a messenger. *If that were true*, he thought, *just how dangerous was his master?* Tepes had been quite enough for him, but it was obvious that they were not just running from Tepes and his minions. A far greater evil was coming to confront them. The battle was yet to be waged. Laura wrote that she was desperately trying to elicit help, but that she needed more time.

The second letter was a translation of the one in Laura's original file—the one written in a mysterious language. Walters read it and then put it carefully on his desk. His mind reeled at what he had just seen. A child's worst nightmares could not have created the monster that was coming for them. According to the diary, the manifestation of this ancient evil was thought to have been defeated more than a hundred years ago. *The evolution of the Dominus must have been extraordinary*, he thought.

It was no wonder Arsine refused to confront these beings. To boost his flagging spirits, Walters tried to ready himself for the coming ordeal. *They are about to enter my world*, he thought, *and they will get more than they bargained for. He had just found Laura Olsen Wynne and he swore no one would harm her on his watch. But how could he defend her?* For a moment, he thought maybe he should buy some silver bullets or a crucifix. But he dismissed the notion because he realized he had absolutely no idea how to fight the evil that had suddenly descended upon him and Laura, and apparently the whole world.

Walters closed his eyes and wished he could sleep for a week, but he reached for the second letter again. When he had finished it, his hands began to shake, his breath came in short gasps, and he felt his heart beating wildly.

He finally understood. The master was coming for them.

The sheet of paper dropped from his cold fingers and fluttered to the dirty wooden floor.

Letter from a villager to his family.

Record archive 1880, Transylvania.
Discovered 2004/Sunimod file research
L.O. Wynne Copy

My Dearest Ilya,

I've found a small child crying in a cave. After many hours of digging through the rubble, I managed to free him from his potential tomb. This poor and frightened baby seems to have been one of the few survivors of the terrible earthquake that had recently befallen us. I could not find any way to identify the poor baby, so I took him home. I must admit I am baffled by his ability to have survived on his own at all.

The baby is pale and, just like a puppy dog, seems to want to suck and gnaw on anything within his grasp. I found it amazing that he devours insects when they fly into his room. My wife finds this comical. This little boy is alert, very intelligent and eager to learn. But he seems to have trouble with his voice. Its timbre is very hoarse and he is slow to speak any language.

We have debated for days about what to call him, but I think I have decided. Because this boy was born to us from the depths of a fiery cave, much like a dragon, we look to call him the Son of the Dragon.

Our new child will be named Dracula.

Lightning Source UK Ltd.
Milton Keynes UK
UKOW04f1714250913

217910UK00001B/73/P

9 781424 166527